Mortgaged Goods

Lorraine Cobcroft

© Lorraine Cobcroft

Pottsville, NSW Australia, 2015

Cover design by Peter Cobcroft

ISBN 978-0-9805714-9-3
Published by Rainbow Works Pty Ltd, Pottsville, NSW

DEDICATION

For Suzie, who is indeed a woman of value...

ACKNOWLEDGEMENTS

Suzie and Danie, for inspiration, and understanding of what truly defines a woman's value.

My husband, Peter, for his companionship, endless patience and support of all my endeavours.

Helga, Carol, Findlay, Maggie, Maxine, and all the other members of Fairfield Writers Group, and Marj, Sharon, Kevin and Alex, Patrick and Allison, Christine, Sue, Diana, Cherrye, Barry, and too many others to name, for their generous encouragement and valued friendship.

"The only disability in life is a bad attitude."

Scott Hamilton

DISCLAIMER

This is a work of pure fiction. The characters in this story exist—and have always existed—only in the author's imagination. They are not based on, nor intended to bear any resemblance to, any specific person, living or dead. Any resemblance to actual persons is purely coincidental. Readers may judge for themselves how likely it is that some events described in this story might have actually happened.

Please note that this work contains implications that certain professionals may be involved in sex crime, physical abuse of women and children, and corruption. The author cautions persons who are easily offended by implications that some persons in certain professions and offices—persons we are taught to respect and honour—may be depraved, self-serving and dishonest, that this story may confront and shatter illusions. The author accepts no responsibility for any discomfort caused by her exposure of reality. There is no intention to imply that depravity, cupidity, selfishness or dishonesty is either a characteristic of, or limited to, individuals in particular professions.

ONE

They buried a woman this morning–and with her, a thousand fears and nightmares. Lies no longer haunt them. Burdens have been lifted, ambitions lost and souls found. Trauma, a birth and a revelation have transformed them all

#

"I'm pregnant," Natalie said.

It should have sent Hetty floating in the clouds, but her daughter's eyes were cold, and there was a harshness in her tone that sent a little snake of fear to wrap about Hetty's ribs.

"I have to abort, Mum. Unlike you, I'm not cut out to be a mother."

Hetty stared at her in silence. An old wound had opened deep inside her, and a thousand memories, like playing cards, were shuffling in her head. She felt heat rising in her neck, and ice forming in her belly. She studied her daughter and saw the coldness give way to nervousness. Nata was waiting, now, for the shout of horror—for the chiding and recriminations.

"It's a new world, Mum," Nata protested weakly. Her forehead creased and her eyes misted, but she kept up her pretence. "Liberation. Women have choices now."

"Man-made changes, Nata," Hetty sniffed. "Physics and nature… they don't change. We're still all made the same."

Hetty knew her coolness frustrated her daughter, but Nata should have been grateful for her response; for the calmness did not come easily, but that Hetty knew was required of her. She arranged cups and a platter of fresh-baked muffins. "Fancy… my little girl a mama," she exclaimed. Her tone told Nata she was not taking the second part of the announcement seriously. Not for an instant.

Joe would focus on that last declaration. He would talk about morality and God's will… about right and wrong. He would lecture Nata about a woman's place… the role God intended for women… being grateful for God's wonderful gift. Hetty always tried to be more understanding, more open-minded, a confidante for her. She needed that from her mother, Hetty believed. But she couldn't hide her thoughts. Nata knew her mother considered abortion a wrong that could never be forgiven.

Nata frowned deeply, and Hetty could tell the guilt demon was biting. She'd seen that look often enough.

"Mum, please," Nata whispered. "Don't make this harder for me. I need for you to understand. I can't have this baby. Our careers… everything's right at a critical point. We're working on a huge case… one that will make Karl's name in the profession. Success will secure his partnership and secure our future, but an interruption now would ruin things for us."

Hetty forced a smile. "What you're thinking… it's not so unusual for a woman who finds herself in the family way unexpectedly, 'specially given all the plans you and Karl made. But you'll adjust. Maternal instincts kick in and—"

"I have to abort, Mum," Nata whispered. Her tears flowed freely now as her hand crept down to caress her belly. "Karl insists I must. He—"

"It's not Karl's decision, love," Hetty told her. "This life…

it's living in your body, and—" She halted in response to her daughter's weeping. She rose to walk around the table and pat her shoulder.

"I shouldn't have expected you to understand," Nata sobbed. "It was selfish to tell you even, knowing how much you wanted children... knowing you never... How could you know how—"

"Ah, but I do know, love. I've been where you are now."

The protest died on Nata's lips. Her disbelieving eyes challenged Hetty.

"When I was quite young, long before I met Joe. Lost it at five months. Should have been a relief. My circumstances... they were far, far worse than you can even imagine. But the pain of loss... I never forgot. A woman doesn't. It's in our make-up: maternal love. We can't fight it. No matter what our situation, once that tiny life starts to grow inside us—"

Nata shook her head and raised pitying eyes to meet Hetty's. "Oh God, Mum! I never knew. I just always thought... Why have you never told me? If I'd known, I never would have—" She broke off in a shuddering sob, then waited, crying silently, while Hetty dusted off the sad old memories and replayed them, then put them aside.

"I feel for you, suffering such pain," Nata said, putting her brave face on again momentarily, "But career women are different, Mum. Modern women, we're not like your generation."

Hetty refilled their teacups. "Modern women? Yes, they're different, all right. Smarter. Better educated. Higher expectations. Regarded differently by menfolk and society. The rules have changed, Nata, some for the better. But young women still bear babies and push prams and play in parks with toddlers. They still talk on and on, at gatherings, about their offspring. And those that can't conceive... well, they spend a fortune on IBM don't they?"

"IVF, Mum." Nata laughed softly, but her fragility showed through.

"Whatever," Hetty continued, "Making babies artificially. And that's after they tried all the natural treatments and fertility clinics and such like. Modern women want to be mothers just as much as I did."

"Some modern women. Some of us are quite content to pursue careers and live as childless couples. And some don't even want a man."

"Lesbians were about in my day, too, though they didn't make such a noise about it back then. And spinsters, back then, generally admitted openly to being unhappy about being left on the shelf. Barren women? Well, they just had to live with the pain, unless fate stepped in. Like it did for me.

"Do you remember the day you came to us?" Hetty's eyes misted now as she reached into a store of favourite memories and selected, again, that so-often replayed recording of the joyous June day, in 1985, when Lidiya Popovich brought her little Natalya—now known as Natalie—for Hetty and Joe to love.

#

"She swear she luff her, Hetty. She say she come back for her… soon." Joe's voice was low and pleading. His Dutch accent came through strongly, as it always did when emotions ran strongly. It had been 22 years since Gottfried Johannes Dreyer migrated from the Netherlands, settled in the Melbourne suburb of Footscray, and changed his name to be more Australian. Aged 34 when he migrated, he had married Hetty two years later. Hetty had come as an infant and grown up an Australian in a Dutch household. Joe was still Gottfried, and he was still Dutch.

"She's a child, Joe, not a chattel," Hetty shouted.

He stared at her, disbelieving. In twenty years of marriage, Hetty had never raised her voice at him before.

"So long as she never know," he said mournfully. "Pray she stay long time and never learn why."

Hetty dabbed at her eyes and swallowed hard. Her anger

wasn't with Joe.

"We want child, Het," Joe protested. "What it matter how she comes to us? Can't we just be grateful, and luff her?"

"For how long?" Hetty sniffed into her handkerchief. "I'll love her, for sure," she mumbled. "But that's the problem, isn't it? What do we do when they come for her?"

"Maybe never will. Meantime, at least child haff proper care. If we refuse, where dey take her?"

Hetty sniffed again, then retreated to the bathroom to repair her face. *The child mustn't see a woman distressed.*

Returning to the kitchen, Hetty set to making sandwiches ready for toasting. She arranged fresh-baked pastries on a silver tray. She set the table with her best lace cloth and the good china, and placed a dozen prize pink roses in a glass vase in the centre. Then she dressed in her Sunday best. Her long black hair was pulled into a tight bun near the nape of her neck, and she fastened it with a thin ribbon instead of the usual plain band. She even pushed two jewelled combs into the hair above her ears. Returning to the tiny, cluttered parlour, she plumped and rearranged the cushions, adjusted the blinds and straightened the ties that held the curtains back. Then she set to pacing nervously about, eagle eyes searching for any little thing that might be slightly out of place.

Joe perched on the edge of an armchair, pulling at his goatee beard. Outside, the sky was muddy. The few trees that lined the streets were naked. Dead leaves skittered in an irritable wind, dancing with empty cigarette packets, chocolate wrappers and soiled Kleenex.

"Sergei's old rattletrap got no heating," Joe said. "They get here chilled to the bone." He stoked the fire and placed a little stool by it for little Natalya to toast her freezing toes. It crackled and popped as the flames licked blackened logs. Orange lumps of glowing charcoal fell by the hearth. The walls were smoke-stained and there were little burn holes in the carpet near the fireplace, but the room was cosy and inviting.

Moments later, a dented brown station wagon clattered to a halt at the front gate. A thickset man emerged from the driver side. He was a hard, ruddy-faced fellow, shabby and unshaven. His belly flopped over the top of his trousers, bouncing as he walked. A grubby, shrunken jumper stopped just short of his waist. The sleeves were too short. He rounded the car and stepped onto the creaking boards of the veranda without stopping to open doors for his wife or daughter.

The woman unfolded herself from the passenger seat and tugged at the rear door, beckoning to the frightened child huddled against the far side door. The mother tottered perilously on thin, heavily-veined legs, liberally littered with bruises and scars. There was a ragged cut across her top lip and she sported a prince of a shiner. Hetty could guess who gave her that. Sergei looked every bit the beast Joe had described.

Natalya followed her mother with downcast eyes, shoulders hunched, dragging reluctant feet. Joe opened the front door without waiting for a knock and urged them to hasten in to the warmth. Sergei helped himself to the best chair, his bulbous nose snorting disdain. The woman nodded silently as she passed and perched on the edge of the chair farthest from the hearth. The girl, though, spoke precisely and politely.

"Hello, Mr. Dreyer. How are you?"

"Call me Joe," he replied with a smile, but the father glared at him and barked that she must never be so disrespectful.

Natalya was not a pretty child, though she had the look of a girl who might grow to be beautiful. Her ginger hair, in a blunt bowl cut, was too short for a girl. A gappy fringe sloped awkwardly across a high forehead above dull green eyes, shadowed with dark circles. An angry pink welt travelled from left ear to chin, and a bright red nose seemed to run incessantly. She sniffled and snorted and made little coughing noises.

Lidiya Popovich looked mournful. Worry lines creased her

brow, and her nicotine-stained fingers danced nervously in her lap. Hetty could find no words to say to the woman. *How could a mother do this?* It defied comprehension. *What could one say in such a strange and tragic situation?*

Hetty went to the kitchen to toast the sandwiches and reheat the water in the kettle. Lidiya and Natalya followed, watching her in silence. When she was done, she fetched the pastries and cakes from the larder and called the men to the table. She caught the appreciative glances as they eyed the feast she'd prepared, but the girl and woman nibbled with polite reserve. Sergei gorged without restraint—not even a pretence of manners.

When the meal was done, Lidiya rose and reached out a work-hardened hand to stroke the child's head gently. "Mama will come back for you soon. I promise," she whispered. The child gave no reply, but just stared, expressionless, at a photo-covered wall.

"Min' your manners, girl. See you behave proper, y' hear?" Sergei's voice was harsh. There was no affection in it. He turned to Joe. "Teach her right, von't y'. Like her Papa do. Gotta train her be a good girl. Beat her good if she disobey. No spoiling. She gotta learn respect."

Joe glared at him. "I'll not be raisin' hant to child. Never struck woman or child in my life, an' won't be startin' now."

Sergei glanced at Hetty. "Must 'ave got lucky in the vife stakes, eh? Got one already trained proper. Not like Lidiya here. She need lots a' teachin'. An' de girl too. Inherited 'er moder's stroppiness. Y'll be needin' to beat that outa her."

"I'll not be raisin' hant to child," Joe repeated firmly.

"Achh! Never been Papa before. You learn quick. Kids need discipline. Sparing stick spoils child."

"Dere's other ways," Joe said, with a sympathetic glance at the girl.

"Sure. Belt instead of stick. Vorks as vell. An' I make sure not spare it. You follow my example. Train her up know her place… respect men… vork hard… make some man a good vife. I don't stand for any cheek… not from 'er or 'er mozer."

Hetty nursed a gratifying thought that, after today, Sergei wouldn't be deciding what he would or wouldn't stand for from the child, but she kept the thought to herself. She felt for the poor mother, but then, the mother chose the man. The mother brought the child into this dreadful man's world. There was no help for those that chose such a fate.

"Just go," Joe spat. "We take goot care of child."

"Better care than she's had these past eight years," Hetty muttered under her breath, turning so they couldn't read her lips. She turned back to ask the woman had she brought the child's favourite toys. She had no interest in the faded, tatty clothing she expected would fill a battered suitcase—were there one—but a cherished doll or teddy? Something familiar to give the child comfort. They had brought nothing at all. The girl had only what she stood in.

Hetty left Joe to show the couple out. Taking the child by the hand, she guided her through a door at the rear of the kitchen to the little room they had prepared, so many years ago, for the child that never came. Joe had papered the walls and Hetty made pretty blue and yellow floral curtains. A patchwork quilt covered the bed and a huge black and white panda with a yellow ribbon around its neck perched on a pillow. Joe had painted an old desk and fitted the drawers with new plastic knobs. A patterned rug covered most of the polished linoleum floor. There was a wardrobe in the far corner that would now be filled with dresses. Beside it, a tall chest of drawers waited to be loaded with pyjamas, underwear and play clothes. A porcelain doll sat on top, in the corner, presiding regally over a neat arrangement of combs, brushes and hair ribbons—a few meagre treasures kept from Hetty's own long-forgotten childhood.

There was no reaction from the child as Hetty led her into the room. She just stared blankly. *Of course she must be quite overcome with fear and confusion. Strange people. Strange place. Her Mama and Papa gone, with doubtless little explanation. She won't go to her old school and she won't see her friends again, if, indeed, she'd been permitted to make any.* Somehow, Hetty suspected life in the Popovich household was rather lonely and dull.

She will surely settle here soon enough and enjoy the warmth and love we'll surround her with.

Ah, such plans they'd had for a child. But year after year had passed with Hetty cursing the monthly period that always came right on time, until, finally, they had accepted the awful reality of her barrenness. But now? Perhaps only for a fleeting moment, they were parents. And however brief the interlude, they would cherish every minute and dote on the child as if she were their own.

#

"They never came back for you," Hetty whispered, returning to the present. "I often thought perhaps we did wrong, just keeping you. Maybe we should have gone to the authorities. But we loved you so much. We wanted you. You were the perfect daughter… the child every mother dreams of raising."

"Until now," Nata said softly. "What I'm planning to do… I should never have expected your forgiveness, let alone understanding. But I have to, Mum, for our marriage. Karl demands—" She broke off in a shuddering sob. When she had calmed a little, she turned to Hetty with tears streaming. "It would break Joe's heart if he knew. He must never—"

"He won't know, because you won't do it, love. Trust me, I know. You will be a wonderful mother, and you will adore and enjoy your child—just as I have always adored and enjoyed you."

Nata rose hastily, then, and grasped her bag. She didn't stop to rinse her teacup or place her plate in the sink. She fled without giving Hetty the customary farewell hug.

"I hoped you might understand," she called back from the door. "But I should never have expected you could. I'll see you in a few weeks, when it's over. Someday, maybe, you'll forgive me."

Her words were punctuated with sobs, and her hands were shaking.

The door slammed and she was gone.

Two

"What on earth possessed you to tell her?" Karl's tone was taut. A worried frown sliced his forehead.

Nata shook her head, her eyes brimming with tears. She sat on the bed with her arms cradling her knees and her chin resting on them.

"What possible good can come of her knowing? You should have kept this between us and just gone and done what was necessary. Nobody ever needed to know."

"Perhaps I wanted her to talk me out of it," Nata whispered.

Karl's startled gaze jerked to meet hers. "We've discussed this, Nat."

Since the day they returned from their honeymoon, Karl had steadfastly refused to use the nickname Nata had always been known by. He persisted in calling her Nat—with a hard "a"—despite her frequent protests that she disliked the abbreviation intensely.

"Neither of us ever wanted children and we both know that even if we did, now is the worst possible time. We agreed you'd abort. It's all arranged."

"You agreed, Karl. I submitted, like the good obedient, subservient wife I was taught I must be. Like the trophy wife you wanted."

Her words cut him like a whip, and he flinched. "You're not yourself, Nat. It's understandable. Hormones. They go crazy, I'm told. Phillip warned me—"

"Phillip! You discussed this with a work mate? What has any of this got to do with him?"

"He gave me the details of the clinic. His wife's been there. Maybe you could talk to her… get some reassurance from someone who's been through it and knows what it's like… what you're feeling."

She thrust herself back on the bed and began to sob aloud. Flustered, Karl perched beside her and reached out to stroke her hair, but she pushed his hand away.

"Don't, Karl. Don't touch me."

He sighed loudly, sending her a look of mingled pity and exasperation. He rose to pace the floor.

"Natalie," he said, sitting again, but with his back to her and his forehead cradled in his palms, "I understand this is painful for you. Regardless of your ambition, our plans, I guess all women have moments of—"

"Our plans? They were your plans, Karl. I wanted a career, but lots of women have both. Lots of husbands support their wives, help with housework, care for the kids. We are luckier than most. We can afford household help, a nanny. Hetty and Joe would have helped. But oh no! The great and insightful Karl Albrecht mapped out our lives and—"

"And you agreed. Remember?" he snapped, raising his head to turn and glare at her. "Said, in fact, that you had never wanted children. Said your career was what mattered most to you, and you could not let pregnancy and commitment to raising kids get in the way of success."

"I also said I didn't want a man in my life; that I would never let a man touch me that way; that sex was not an act of love, but a concession to the disgusting animal desires of men. But you were confident you could change my thinking about that."

"And I did."

"And conception changed my thinking about career versus motherhood. Conception that happened because I let you convince me that sex was an expression of love. Well, love made a baby, Karl. Your baby. Our baby."

He stared at her, eyes wide and anxious. The clock on the cedar bedside table counted the minutes of silence.

"You changed my thinking, Karl. And you should have taken appropriate precautions."

"Oh, come now, Natalie. Honestly! We don't have sex often, but I assumed you were protecting yourself."

"And why do you consider that my responsibility?"

"Because it's you who must suffer the consequences of unplanned conception. It's your body."

She glared at his back, seething, but his attitude shouldn't have surprised her. The signs were always there, if only she hadn't been so blind to them. He was a charmer: handsome; rich; ambitious; successful. He was generous and attentive when it gained him what he desired, but egotistical and demanding; manipulative, often.

She was raised with precisely the beliefs Karl wanted his wife to hold: that the man headed the household. Women vowed to love, honour and obey. Good women did as Hetty did, but in Hetty's case it was not an onerous obligation. Joe Dreyer worshipped his wife and would do anything necessary to ensure her happiness. Joe was boss with Hetty's consent and on Hetty's terms. He asked nothing of her that she would hesitate to give. His love was unconditional, and his attention to her wants was unstinting.

Karl was different. His love had to be earned. She had earned it. He told her, often, she was everything he wanted in a wife: beautiful, classy, intelligent… successful and admired by everyone. He was the envy of his friends when he won her hand, and he delighted in their grudging admiration, just as he delighted in their grudging respect for him as a prospective partner in Melbourne's most prestigious law firm. But now, she had failed him. And it seemed he could withdraw his affection as quickly as he had bestowed it. He had made it quite clear what she must do to win it back. He had given a command, and he expected unquestioning compliance.

"This situation is of your making, Natalie. And you are the only one who can fix it. I've done what I can to help. What more can I do?"

"You could ask me what I want. Listen to me. Care about how I feel."

"Of course I care how you feel, darling. But you're not yourself. When you think about it rationally, you'll see that I'm doing what's right for both of us… what has to be."

He paced a while, then returned to sit beside her and gaze at her. His look was loving.

I'm being unfair to him, she thought. He cares. And it's true, we did agree, long before he signed Max Knight as a client. And I know what this case means for him. It really is the worst possible time to be pregnant.

"I'm sorry, Karl. I know we discussed this. We agreed. But pregnancy changed me."

He was right. Motherhood was never part of her life plan, and she always knew fatherhood never figured in his. So why did she feel such delight at seeing a little pink line on a test strip a few days after her period was due? And why did Karl's stance, now, produce such intense resentment? And yet, a part of her embraced his thinking—shared his determination to return to the life they had planned. A part of her wanted nothing more than to be free of this encumbrance.

"I'm sorry, too, Nat." Karl mumbled. "It's hard for you, I know. But we have to be strong in our resolve, darling. It's an impossible time for us, with a partnership offer pending. I can't afford the distraction. What we planned to do is for the best.

You'll see that when it's over."

The guilt demon plagued her now. A sharp voice stabbed her conscience, reminding her that there was a life inside her… reminding her of what the priests and nuns had taught: that human life was sacred; that if God blessed you with the ability to reproduce, you had an obligation to Him to protect and nurture, to give thanks, to raise your child to love and honour Him and to embrace His word. The voice reminded her of her ecstasy at the discovery of what their love had produced.

" 'Thou shalt not kill', Karl. It's a grave sin. We are Catholics, you and I."

"Lapsed Catholics, my dear," he laughed. The laughter cut her deeply. He should be angry or sad, not amused.

"I forsook religion, but I kept my conscience."

"It's not a life yet, sweetheart."

"We made love, Karl, and our lovemaking made a baby. Nothing magical happens at six or ten or twenty-four weeks that transforms it from a nothing into a life. The act of lovemaking makes the life, according to God's law. Man just makes up illogical rules for his own convenience. But men can't even make up their minds what they want to declare right and what should be said to be wrong. Until a few years ago, abortion—at any stage—was illegal. We change the rules whenever it suits social convenience, and then we try to claim superior knowledge and the right to discard God's law on the subject. Even the church does it. That's why I withdrew. Too much hypocrisy."

Clearly uninterested in her dissertation, Karl had begun to undress. She watched, annoyed, as he peeled off his shirt and exposed sculpted shoulders and a tight, lightly rippled torso. Unlike most men his age who worked in sedentary jobs, he kept trim and fit. He turned to the mirror and lifted his shoulders, admiring himself. It was a habit that always irritated her intensely, though he had a body any woman would admire. Tonight, she wished there were nothing admirable about him… that his looks were as unattractive as his current demeanour.

He turned to study her for a moment, then moved toward her. For an instant, she feared she saw lust in his expression. The thought repulsed her. But as he stood gazing down at her, his expression turned hard and cold. Momentary relief gave way to fear.

"We've done enough talking," he said, adopting the commanding professional tone he used when annoyed with a difficult client or an unbending opposing lawyer. "It's time for action. Get up and pack your things now. We'll leave for the clinic at noon tomorrow."

"No," she whispered, and pulled away from him, fearing he might strike her for her defiance. There was fire in his dark eyes now and a burning red rising from neck to cheeks and reaching to the tips of his ear lobes.

She struggled for fresh resolve. "You are right about one thing, Karl." She was stroking her belly; making little circles with her palm. "It's my body, so it's my decision. And I haven't made it yet... not for certain."

"Then take your time, Natalie," he replied icily, his lips thinning to a cruel line. "But understand this. If you keep this baby, you raise it alone. I won't be part of any child's life, nor of its mother's."

He strode to the dressing room then, and he returned clad in shorts, T-shirt, and running shoes.

"I'm going for a run. When I return, if you've not come to your senses, I'll pack an overnight bag and go to Phillip's. This issue is not open to further discussion, Natalie. I've made my choice. Make yours."

The door closed, and she was alone with her indecision.

#

Life had been so perfect. How had it come to this?

Natalya Popovich, at age nine, had changed her name to

Natalie Dreyer and left a sordid past behind. She forgot the woman who had brought her into the world and the woman and man who raised her for the first eight years of her life. She forgot the older sister they had sent away a year before and the twin brothers she had known only through photographs and her mother's stories of better times. She forgot the squalid little cottage in the Melbourne suburb of Newport, where her birth mother and father danced the Barynya and sang Russian folk songs. She forgot the ever-present fear and pain and the frequent abuse that caused it.

As Natalie Dreyer, she blossomed, loved and nurtured by foster parents who adored her.

Gottfried Johannes Dreyer and Henriëtte Elke de Hass Dreyer—Joe and Hetty to those close to them—were old enough to be her grandparents. Immigrants from the Netherlands, they'd related tales of how they had met in Footscray, where Joe found a job as a sheet metal worker. He had changed his name to sound more Australian, hoping to close the door on a troubled past that remained a dark secret, but that shaped a complex character. Steeped in religion and committed to an authoritarian system, Joe balanced uncompromising discipline with loyalty, compassion and generosity. His wife complimented it with untiring patience, tolerance, and deep wisdom.

Joe had wooed the cheerful, ruddy-cheeked woman he met walking home from work one September evening, and had won her affection. He bought the little cottage before proposing, and presented it to Henriëtte as a gift when she consented to take his hand. They'd set about fixing and decorating to make a home for the child they yearned for but never conceived. Then Joe had come home one evening to announce that a workmate had asked a favour. He needed someone to care for his eight-year-old daughter for a time. Joe didn't share with Hetty what he knew of the man and his circumstances, nor the reason for the request. He told her only that the man was a beast, and the little girl desperately needed someone to love her. And Hetty had boundless love to give.

Natalya had arrived at the Dreyer's confused and frightened. She understood that her parents were leaving her there for a while, but believed they intended to come back for her soon. Hetty Dreyer seemed a nice enough lady, but Nata was overcome with fear of Joe. He was so terribly tall and straight, with that dignified air and proper manners and that grave expression on his weathered face. He was not at all like Papa, but he was a man, and girls must always please men.

With her parents gone, Hetty led her back to the kitchen and took her on a tour of the tiny cottage. Joe poured tea and seated himself at the dining table, newspaper spread before him. Hetty waited patiently by the toilet door while Nata relieved herself, and after, while she washed. Mama had taught her hygiene, but she was afraid to dry her hands on Hetty's clean white towels. She tried to shake them dry. Hetty passed her a hand towel.

"It's all right, child. The towels are here to be used."

She was hesitant, but obeyed.

"We must get you some clothes," Hetty said. "Will you come to the mall with me?"

Nata nodded silently. She was frightened, but she had been taught to obey. Hetty fetched her handbag from the sideboard and leaned to peck Joe's cheek. "The child needs clothing," she said. "I'll take her to the stores now. I'll be back in time to make dinner."

Joe nodded and turned back to his newspaper. Hetty took Natalya's hand and led her out into the street.

#

"Ahhh! How pretty you look, my pet!" Hetty exclaimed. "Look in the mirror, sweetheart. Do you like what you see?"

"She looks so lovely in that," the shop assistant said, smiling. "But she doesn't seem too interested, does she?"

"Everything is strange. Her mother and father are ill, you

see. They've left her with us, but she doesn't know us well. She's frightened, poor child."

Hetty chose four pretty dresses, shorts, T-shirts, pyjamas and underwear. She asked about school uniforms and a coat. Natalya was confused and afraid. She kept her eyes downcast and her expression grave, until one new dress took her fancy. She twirled before the mirror, flicked at her hair, and even ventured a tiny smile. "Pretty," she whispered.

"You sure are, my darling," Hetty replied.

"We need shoes now," Hetty said, "but first, how about a milkshake? It's thirsty work trying on dresses."

Natalya nodded silently.

"She can wear that dress," Hetty said to the assistant. "Just remove the tags, please." They discarded the clothes she had arrived in. Hetty handed her a bag to carry, gathered up the remainder, and led her toward the cafe. "What flavour do you like?"

Nata stared blankly, her lips pressed tightly together.

"Two strawberry milkshakes, please," Hetty said. She pulled out a chair, indicated for Nata to sit, and took the seat across from her. When the drinks were placed in front of them, she dropped the straw in, sipped, and smiled broadly.

Hetty had almost finished when Nata finally pushed the straw hesitantly into her glass, but she couldn't disguise her delight at the taste. Her eyes lit as she sipped. She'd never had strawberry milkshake before.

As they started for the shoe store, Natalya quietly slipped her hand into Hetty's and smiled up at her. Hetty's kind, gentle manner had won her over. As long as Joe kept his distance, she was confident living in the Dreyer house would be okay.

#

"Won't you model your new clothes for Uncle Joe, Natalya?" Hetty asked when they returned from the stores.

She shook her head vigorously, dropping to sit on the rug and hug her chest tightly. She was afraid of Joe. She would stay in her room where she was safe from him.

"It's all right, darling," Hetty assured her. "Just put some play clothes on and we'll put the rest of your new things away for now. Tomorrow, we must get you some books and toys. Do you like to play with dolls? The one on the dresser is yours now, my dear. You can take it down and play with it, but be gentle with it, won't you?"

Natalya remained seated on the mat, staring at the floor. Hetty hesitated for a time, then lifted the doll down and placed it beside her. She quietly slipped out and closed the door behind her.

Joe tapped softly on the door to Natalya's room, calling to her. When she ignored his soft knock, he turned the door handle slowly. He pushed the door open. She was seated on the mat, dressed in play clothes now, with the doll in her arms.

"Achh! Wonderful!" Joe exclaimed. "Fount something to play wid. Mind you handle gently, now. She's precious. Aunt Hetty made a start on dinner. Wants to know what you like to eat, young lady. Spoiling you, yes? All dem nice clothes, and now wantin' to cook favourite. Tell me what I tell her t' make."

Natalya kept her head down and her lips zipped. Her grip on the doll tightened.

"No need to be afrait of us, little one," Joe said, trying to sound reassuring. "But you must answer when I ask question. It is manners. I know your papa taught you manners, yes?"

Terror and rage flooded over her then, at the mention of Papa. Her head jerked suddenly. She lifted her arms above her head, still holding the doll tightly. Then her arms came thundering down.

She hadn't meant to break the doll, but it caught against the corner of the dresser. Craaaaack! It shattered. Tiny pieces of porcelain sprayed over the rug and her folded legs. Stricken, she leapt up and pushed past Joe. She ran through the kitchen and down the hall to tug at the front door. Hetty was close on her heels, but she made it out the front gate and was half a block away before Hetty, panting heavily, caught her arm and swung her round to face her. Hetty's face was red and dripping and her neck was pulsing. She held Nata tightly.

Joe came up behind her then and scooped her up in his strong arms and carried her back to the house, back to her room. He placed her on the bed.

"That doll belong to Aunt Hetty. Meant a lot to her. An' you can't be runnin' off like dat, girlie. Aunt Hetty is too old to be chasing young girl all about de streets. You papa—"

Natalya was shaking violently, terrified. She'd heard Papa telling Joe to beat her hard if she did wrong, and she knew what she'd done was really bad. She'd heard Joe say he'd never hit her, but she didn't believe it. He'd never had a naughty little girl to deal with before.

"Shhush, Joe," Hetty called firmly, pushing ahead of him. "It was mention of her papa that upset her, can't you see? She's frightened, is all. She needs comfort."

"Can't haff her smashing things or running off, Het," he said, shaking his head. Natalya cowered and huddled close to the wall, now even more convinced he was going to beat her, or maybe send her away.

"It's all right, Natalya," Hetty whispered. She moved closer to the bed. "It's all right, sweetheart," she repeated. She sat beside her and reached tentatively to touch her arm. Natalya pulled away.

"Poor child is terrified," Hetty said. "Heard her papa, didn't we? Probably expects a beating now. Her papa would thrash her for sure."

"No need to be afrait, Natalya. No-one in dis house will raise a hand to you," Joe said, but his words didn't reassure her. She had done a terrible thing. She deserved a thrashing; she knew she did. It puzzled her why they seemed so distressed that she was frightened. Papa never cared about her fear. He only cared that she learned a lesson.

She hugged the wall, trembling and confused. Hetty reached across and touched her arm gently. "I'll clean up the mess, and then we'll leave you for a while. I'll fix something nice for your dinner. We'll talk later."

Hetty turned and nodded to Joe. He returned to his newspaper. She silently swept up the broken china, tearfully picking up broken remains of the doll's head and body. Natalya watched her, overcome with remorse at what she had done. Part of her wished they would beat her... wished they would punish her somehow. Even Mama would have said she'd earned a harsh punishment for this.

Hetty tiptoed from the room. Nata was alone for a while. Alone in that pretty room with the panda. Alone with all the lovely new clothes Hetty had bought her. Alone, and overcome with guilt and fear and a burning wish that she could somehow put the doll back together—that she could stop Hetty being upset.

Hetty stole back into the room and stood beside her. "Oh, Natalya," she whispered, "what does a doll matter when I have you to love. Please, please, don't run away, child. I only want to hold you and love you and protect you. I only want to care for you forever, if you'll let me. We'll buy another doll tomorrow, and books too, and other playthings. And I'll cook your favourite foods, if only you will tell me what you like."

Nata turned slightly to stare, bewildered, at the crying woman.

"We only want to love you, Natalya," she said softly. "Won't you please, please let us love you?"

#

Dinner was late. Hetty served up soup and left-over fish pie with ice cream and canned fruit for dessert. Natalya ate silently, but enjoyed the food. After dinner, Hetty ran a warm bath for her and left her to wash herself.

At half-past eight, Hetty tiptoed into her room and lightly touched her head as she lay stiffly, eyes tightly shut, pretending sleep. Hetty moved to withdraw, but suddenly Nata stirred. She turned on her side and reached out and put her hand over Hetty's.

"Papa said I should call you Mrs. Dreyer," she said. "You're not my aunt."

"Then perhaps I can just be your friend," Hetty replied. "I know what your Papa said, child, but 'Mrs. Dreyer' is far too formal. I really don't mind if you just call me Hetty. It is my name."

Natalya smiled. "I'm very sorry for breaking your doll, and running away. Thank you for being kind to me. I'll be a good girl from now on, if only you'll keep that man away. He musn't come into my room, you see?"

"Joe? My dear girl, Joe would never hurt you. He loves you just as I do."

Natalya pulled away from her again.

"It's all right, darling," she whispered. "I'll protect you. I won't let Joe come close again." Hetty kissed her fingers and pressed them against Natalya's cheek. "Sleep tight. Dream sweet dreams, my darling." She withdrew and closed the door.

#

Those first few weeks, Nata dreamt often that her Papa came for her. She woke sweating and sobbing.

"Come to Papa, leettle one," he called. "Come show Papa how much you love him."

"I want Mama. Where is Mama?"

They had been dancing and singing. Papa stamped and waved his arms and roared with laughter. Mama looked fearful, but he ordered her to sing louder and dance faster, and she obeyed. Papa stopped, now and then, to take another deep swig from a bottle. He'd become unsteady on his feet, and then he'd fallen. He blamed Mama. He hit her and punched her and she cried out.

Then he locked her in their bedroom, and Nata turned ashen white and started to tremble.

"Mama is unvell, my child. But Papa is here. Come, geeve Papa a hug."

"You hurt Mama."

"Mama make Papa angry, leettle one. You know vat happens ven Papa is angry? You and your Mama and Elena, you must do as Papa tell you, treat Papa with respect. Papa teach you respect. Sometimes ze lessons hurt. Papa doesn't like hurt you, but ze lesson must hurt so you remember."

He pulled her to him and she smelled his foul breath and stinking sweat. He rubbed his stubble on her face and it scratched painfully. He took her hand, guiding it over the rolls of belly fat, down... down... down...

"No, Papa. Please, no!" The tears came and she tried to draw her hand away. She hated touching him there.

"Is all right, leettle one. Papa loves you. You gotta learn how make men happy. Make Papa happy."

"Mama! Maaaa—" she screamed, but he covered her mouth with his shovel-sized hand, and he pressed his fat fingers painfully into her cheek.

"You mus' do as Papa say," he commanded. "Leettle girls mus' obey."

She struggled, but he held her tightly and huffed his hot, sour breath into her open mouth so that she tasted his foulness. "You obey Papa," he said, "or Papa beat you proper."

She learnt to avoid the beatings, though she hated what she had to do to please him. Often, he gave her sweets after. He would let Mama out and she would limp to the stove to make his dinner, her face flushed and her eyes swollen; scald marks down her cheeks. She would give Nata knives and spoons to lay out on the table, and then she would bring bowls of broth and thick slabs of black bread. When she had cleared away, she would draw Nata to her and kiss the top of her head and whisper, "My darling baby. Such a good little girl. If only Mama could protect you from him!"

#

Hetty came to her, sometimes, when she cried out in the night. She held her and rocked her and whispered that she was safe now and everything would be all right.

"Whatever did he do to you to make you so afraid?" she asked over and over. "What memories torment you, little one?"

Nata never told. She dried her eyes and wiped her nose, snuggling against Hetty. Hetty hugged her and stroked her as her Mama had done. "You are safe here, little one," she told her. "Joe and I… we only want to love you and protect you and help you forget whatever horrors you endured."

Joe never beat Hetty. He was kind to her. True to his promise, he never once beat Nata either. It took months for her to learn to trust him, but once there was trust, love slowly followed. He never made her touch him. He never rubbed a stubbled chin on her or breathed sour breath over her. His face wasn't pock-marked and ugly like Papa's. He was taller, and trim, and always well groomed. He drank wine in moderation; she never once saw him drunk. She never heard him raise his voice in anger either, though he was often stern with her. He demanded courtesy and respect, but he was always polite.

"I wish to talk please, Nata," he would say, tapping lightly on her bedroom door. "May I come, please." She knew his tone well, and she knew what that request implied. He would ask her to sit on her bed and he would stand beside it, towering over her and looking down with that grave, disapproving frown that set her to trembling. It was a different fear from the fear she'd had of Papa. Perhaps it was a healthy fear, but she never ceased to fear his disapproval, and to seek his endorsement of her choices.

"Your behaviour does not please me, Nata. I think you know what you done wrong, yes?"

She would hang her head and confess her sin, and he would lecture her sternly. The lecture invariably ended with, "You will make confession and ask de priest for penance, an' now, until you learnt lesson, you do extra hart chores insteat of enjoy free time."

He didn't punish her often, but when she incurred his displeasure she was compelled to scrub that front veranda, on her hands and knees, until the boards were snow white and her hands burned and her knees throbbed. She raked leaves in autumn until her hands began to blister. She washed windows and whitewashed the fence and picked up litter from the street in front. Hetty would tell him he was being too harsh, but he replied that life was hard. "Hart work never hurt," he would say. "Discipline child is unpleasant job of parent, but I do duty as father."

When he was satisfied that she'd been punished enough, he would say, "You done goot, Nata. When you accept punishment and not complain, and put good effort into tasks, you make me prout." He would hug her and tell her he loved her and she would glow.

He sent her to music school and dancing lessons and to deportment classes to learn the rules of etiquette and how to behave as a lady. He set high standards of academic performance, demanding she spend long hours studying. Hetty often had to make excuses for her failure to do the chores she was assigned. Joe believed in the value of work, and that idleness equated to temptation. He left her no time to contemplate mischief.

He insisted she dress conservatively. Until she turned sixteen, she wasn't permitted to have her ears pierced, to wear make-up, or to date. When she was older, he set and enforced a strict curfew. He insisted her escorts collect her from the house and deliver her right into the living room after, and he embarrassed her with his interrogations of them and his little lectures.

"You're so old fashioned," she complained to him often. "You don't understand young people. It's a different world from the one you grew up in, and you are trying to impose the same rules your Papa imposed on your sisters in the old country. It's not fair."

"Life not fair, my little one," he would reply. "I not say sorry for making you behave how I think right for girl your age. You resent it now, but someday you thank me."

But with the strict discipline and sometimes frustrating rules came overwhelming generosity. Nothing was too good for Joe Dreyer's little girl. She knew he went without a great deal of life's comforts to keep her well-dressed, send her to good schools, and give her opportunities that few girls from working class families could ever hope to enjoy. Joe Dreyer had big plans for his daughter, and he cultivated big ambitions in her. She would please him. She would make him proud. Nothing mattered to her more.

#

Tree branches bowed gracefully under the weight of new shoots, reaching and bending obligingly to shade little groups congregating on the university lawns. March was coming to an end, and the late autumn sun polished the leaves and sent tendrils of light to dance over the golden tassels dangling from the mortarboards of the triumphant alumni.

Gowned students gathered near the door of the great hall. Parents and friends took their seats inside. A group of prestigious looking men and women, some with age lines creasing their faces and hair liberally salted, mounted the stage. A gowned man approached the microphone. It crackled and popped, and then his voice rang out clearly, silencing the shuffles and merry chatter and drawing all eyes to him. Cameras danced and bobbed over the heads of the crowds. Shutters clicked.

Natalie Dreyer scanned the rows. Hetty and Joe were there, somewhere, primped and preened; dressed in their invariable "Sunday best". They would be sitting straight and tall, feet together, hands folded in their laps, faces flushed with excited anticipation.

"Appearances matter, Nata," Hetty had told her often. "You might belong to the working class, and have little, but you can still have pride. Self-respect. If you do an honest day's work, you can hold you head high, whatever your station in life. But you, my darling, will rise to a higher level. I know it. And we must ensure that we never embarrass you, no matter how high you soar."

Nata would never be embarrassed to introduce her parents. Joe was self-conscious about his accent and language. Hetty was painfully aware of her advancing age and ample figure. She wore long sleeves to hide the fleshy rolls on her upper arms, mid-length skirts to draw attention away from the angry bulging veins that lined her legs, and gloves to hide her work-worn hands. But Nata saw only the warmth in her eyes, the glow of her ruddy cheeks, and the deep dimples that framed her sunny smile. Still, she was pleased that they kept their little home neat and clean, and that they dressed with care. Their behaviour, in any situation, was always beyond reproach. The high standards they had held her to had stood her in good stead. She won respect and admiration wherever she went, and she enjoyed untiring attention and aid from teachers and mentors.

The ceremony began. Endless tiresome speeches, interspersed with unenthusiastic clapping; monotones droning on and on. The audience was restless. Graduates were bored. At last, those in gowns and mortarboards were called to line up in the aisle. The name calling began.

Someone climbed the stairs, lifting his gown so as not to trip. He stepped forward. Handshakes. A diploma was handed over. Cameras flashed.

"Next…"

Another, and then another. On and on it went.

The last name was called. The graduates lined up for the procession back to their places. More speeches. Then the prize-giving began.

"…the highest honour this university awards—" Rich with promise, the Dean's singsong voice rang out. A dozen eligible graduates froze in anticipation, eyes swimming with excitement and flesh marbled with goose bumps.

"…for outstanding academic achievement and all-round excellence, an award presented only to students whose conduct and character is exemplary in every respect… a student who has set the bar high for those who will follow her… a graduate who, I predict, will make her mark in the heady world of corporate law…"

The atmosphere was electric. Nata barely dared to breath. She feared her pounding heart would drown out the Dean's announcement. And then it came…

"Congratulations, Natalie Dreyer…"

The sense of triumph hit her as would a chill wind gust on a sizzling summer day. The crowd roared approval as she made her way to the dais. Happy tears streamed down lightly freckled cheeks. The floor seemed to sink away beneath her, so that she waltzed on air.

"Thank you…" she said mechanically. She stared, mesmerized, at the audience. A huge lump of emotion lodged in her throat, locking it. For a heartbeat of time, the words refused to form. She panicked. Then the lump exploded in a spasm of ecstasy. She gripped the microphone. The clapping lessened. She found her voice.

"I want to thank each and every one of my tutors for their unfailing patience, their generosity in passing on all they know, and the sincerity of their encouragement and reassurances—

"The executive of Adams, Bryant and Company—to whom I was assigned as an assistant for work experience—for giving me the opportunity to learn from some of the most accomplished and respected lawyers in this state; and their staff for their patient help and guidance, and their friendship.

"My fellow students—whose companionship has

brightened my days here. And all the wonderful friends who have supported and encouraged me, and who, I know, today, will unselfishly join in celebrations of my success.

"Most of all, I want to thank my mother and father, Joe and Hetty Dreyer, the world's best parents. This achievement would never have been possible without their amazing generosity, their untiring support and encouragement and, most of all, their deep and unconditional love. From the bottom of my heart, Mum and Dad, thank you. I love you."

The crowd erupted in cheers and thunderous applause. Natalie floated from the stage, joy clapping in her chest and roaring in her brain and her face split in a mammoth smile that she was certain nothing could ever erase.

Later, Hetty and Joe hugged her so hard she feared she might break. Hetty's happy tears wet her gown. With his shoulders thrust back and his head high, Joe seemed to have grown a full inch, and Nata was certain at any moment his swollen chest would cause his shirt buttons to pop.

"What you like us to buy you for reward dis time?" Joe mumbled, his salt and pepper eyebrows working vigorously. It was their custom to let her choose a special gift each time an achievement was recognized. Every favourable report card and parent-teacher interview had been richly rewarded.

She felt a sharp pang of guilt. She knew he borrowed money to pay her fees and buy her textbooks. She'd wanted to work, but Joe insisted she must devote herself entirely to study.

"You have given me everything already," she replied. "Now it's my turn to reward you."

"Ach!" Joe said dismissively. "We want a chilt. You were gift from Got. You are our rewart, Nata. Beautiful, smart, wonderful daughter who get up on stage and call us 'mum' and 'dad'. What honour! Now, show me certificate. Let me read…"

Karl came over, offering a handshake and asking if he might be introduced to her parents. She had talked with them about him often, praising his skill and telling them how he had mentored her through her months of work experience. Joe thanked him profusely for the effort he'd invested to aid their daughter's success.

"She is beautiful girl, yes?" he said, and Nata flushed crimson. "She has many talents also. Not just academic ability."

"Hush, Dad," she mumbled. "Mr. Albrecht is not interested in my looks or my talents."

"Ah, but I am, Miss Dreyer," Karl replied. "I am interested in everything about you."

"And excepting in a professional capacity, I am not the slightest bit interested in you, sir. So I would be grateful if you would restrict your interest in me accordingly," she snapped.

He nodded to her parents, his lips twitching in a half-smile as he departed.

Joe chided her—after Karl had gone, thankfully. He warned her sternly that courtesy and appreciation are as essential for professional success as ability and endeavour. "Look to me like Karl Albrecht able to help your career success, young lady. An' wanting to."

"Besides," Hetty added, "he's an attractive and charming man. You could do far worse. You might be focused on your career for now, but eventually you will want the attention of a suitor."

Pigs will fly. Nata accepted the rebuke with pretended contrition. She refrained from telling them, again, that she had no intentions of ever taking a romantic interest in a man. Joe Dreyer—her foster father—was the only man she ever intended to regard with affection. Her foster father was the only man she would allow to address her using terms of endearment.

Despite her protests, Joe and Hetty rewarded her: a three-month tour of Europe. London, Paris, Athens, Rome. She cruised down the Danube and took a gondola through the streets of Venice. She visited the world's most prestigious art galleries; craned her neck to see the top of the Eiffel Tower; skied in the Swiss Alps; and watched the changing of the guard at Buckingham Palace. It was an amazing holiday, and far too generous a gift; one she protested was well beyond her parents' capacity to afford. She swore, secretly, that she would repay them, someday soon. They had made such sacrifices for her. But they would live in comfort—no, luxury—in their old age. She would see to it. She owed it to them, and she hungered for the day when she might be able to honour the debt.

Perhaps she would send them to Europe someday — or to America or Asia — or just on a romantic Pacific island cruise. She wondered if they would want to travel and to where. Did they ever crave to return to the "old country"? They never spoke of home-sicknesses, or of family. She asked, once. They answered merely that this was their home now. They had a good life here. They were content. Hetty Dreyer was the kind who was always content with whatever lot fate dealt her.

Perhaps it was Joe's influence that made Nata a different breed. She wanted to conquer the world. She wanted greatness. She had her future mapped. The route ahead was crystal clear, and no man would ever stand in her way. Most of all, though, she craved Joe's approval. He had nurtured her ambition, and she wanted to fulfil all his aspirations for her. She wanted to make him proud.

THREE

Natalie returned from her holiday to an interview with the partners at Adams Bryant & Co. They offered her a position, and she accepted it eagerly. She continued with her post-graduate studies, while throwing herself into her work with enthusiasm and resolve. She intended to excel. Joe had taught her she could be anything she wanted to be, as long as in whatever she chose to do, she gave her all.

"Never rest, Nata," he would say, "until you done the very best you can do."

She knew his work was menial and unfulfilling, but he took great pride in doing his job well, and in never taking a day—or even an hour—of sick leave. He had always arranged his holidays so that he had leave entitlements to use if he needed time off to attend parent-teacher interviews or school concerts. He never missed or was late for even one. But he demonstrated uncompromising diligence and unfailing loyalty to his employer. He reminded her, often, that she must be grateful to her employer for the opportunity he provided and repay that kindness by always holding herself to the highest standards of performance in her work.

Within five short years of her graduation, she had achieved all that Joe had encouraged her to aspire to. She was Ms Natalie

Dreyer, junior associate corporate lawyer in a leading Melbourne firm, with money to buy whatever took her fancy. She worked, often, on satisfying briefs for Melbourne's corporate high fliers. She loved her work. When she had time off, she took ocean cruises and enjoyed holidays in exotic places. She spent her Saturdays bush walking with friends, sipping wine at art exhibitions, or attending symphonies and operas. On Sundays, she returned to the humble worker's cottage in which she'd spent a magical childhood, spoiled and adored. She dined on Hetty's succulent roast lamb and sweet jam puddings. She took delight in showering Joe and Hetty with gifts to thank them for the sacrifices they had made to help her achieve her dream. Hetty danced and squealed with delight. Joe protested, but she knew he was grateful.

She hadn't needed a man. She hadn't wanted a man—not after what Papa made her do. Nata was happily single, a career girl. She worked with charming and successful men—mostly married. She dined and drank and partied with a merry crowd. Men sometimes drove her home and she asked them in for coffee, but then she said good night with a quick peck on the cheek and retired, contentedly alone.

At first, Karl was one of many casual friends, and he seemed content with that status. But in time, he began—more and more frequently—to express his admiration and to seek her company. His attentiveness flattered, but she kept her distance. Finally, he could restrain himself no longer.

"I love you, Natalie," he said wistfully. "I enjoy your company, but I want more. Why do you always push me away?"

She felt the colour draining from her face and a familiar lump forming in her throat. Her heart lurched against her ribs.

Up and down. Up and down. Good girl. You must learn to please...

Nata's past was far behind her, but there were some things she could never forget.

"It's complicated, Karl. I just don't want a man in that way, that's all. I don't want to offend you, but you might as well know how things stand between us. I like you, a lot. But it stops there. It can never be more."

His face fell. A desolate slump of the shoulders replaced the usual jaunty, confident air. His look of hurt confusion stirred the old guilt demons, and she wanted to swallow her words back. She longed to unburden herself, to trust him. But fear and shame prevented her from sharing her feelings.

He persisted, gently. He continued to pursue her, saying he was content with her company. He said he was fine with seeing her on her terms, promising faithfully he wouldn't pressure her for more.

#

The week before Christmas was long and stressful. She finished late, and exhausted, on Friday, but they had had a major victory. She and Karl were the toast of the firm. Their client sang their praises from the rooftops and endowed them with gifts.

"A good wine," Karl whispered tactfully, observing her refilling her glass again. "It goes to your head if you don't eat. Please, let me take you somewhere classy and buy you a fine meal. You deserve it."

When she took Karl's arm and strode beside him into the exclusive Vue de Monde for dinner, she felt lighter than air. She let him order for her and she picked at her food distractedly, but drank the expensive wine with gusto. When he led her out, her head was spinning and she felt strangely disoriented, but enraptured. He carried her up the stairs to her apartment and laid her on her bed. He gently removed her shoes, her skirt, her blouse, and then her stockings. He unclasped her bra. Somehow, she hadn't the strength to resist. The room was spinning. She was drifting on a cloud. She was sleepy now… dozing. He was fondling her breasts, sucking her nipples, kissing her belly. He was inside her, and she was giving herself to him. A fragile bubble of joy shimmered and her heart bumped against her ribs seeing the smile that lit his eyes.

Uuu...p and dooo...wn...

Papa's voice faded away. He was dead. Papa Popovich was dead. Natalya Popovich was dead.

"You are so beautiful, Natalie. God, how I love you!" Karl's voice. Wonderful, adorable Karl. Natalie Dreyer was in love. The demons were gone, and nothing, now, could dim her smile.

#

She lifted a thundering head from her pillow, next morning, to inspect the small blood spot between her legs. She had, she concluded, at last succumbed to temptation. Her perfect life was over; her private battle lost. She fell back on the pillows with a soft groan and relived her descent from grace.

She had met him, first, while studying. Seconded to a prestigious law firm to gain work experience, she had been assigned to work with him. He was everything most girls look for in a man: rich, successful, good looking, charming, and attentive. He challenged her. He introduced her to the most promising clients. He educated her on the politics of the firm and the legal fraternity. He fed her ideas for her thesis and he proof-read and commented on her writing. Ultimately, though she'd never admitted it, much of her achievement in her final year of university should be credited to Karl Albrecht.

She guessed he felt affection for her, but she fought to ensure he understood that she felt gratitude, nothing more.

She replayed a memory of him at her graduation. He had offered his congratulations, then—firmly and quite publicly rebuffed—he had slipped quietly away. Despite Joe's stern instruction, she hadn't sought him out to apologise. And he gave no hint afterwards of any continuing interest in her, personal or professional. She told herself her interest in him was strictly the latter. If he could assist her career… but only if he did so with no strings attached.

Her friends berated her foolishness, of course. Most craved the attention of a desirable man. they included marriage and children in their plans for the future. Not her. There was no room for men in her life, except as occasional companions when the absurd rules of society demanded the accompaniment of one of the opposite gender. Her past experiences precluded sexual activity, and she had long ago accepted that she would remain a spinster. Her career was her life.

Karl had re-entered her world just weeks after her return from Europe. His signature was at the bottom of a formal invitation to meet with the partners of Adams, Bryant and Co. for a job interview. Joe was thrilled. Hetty was excited. Natalie was hesitant. The job opportunity was promising, for the firm was perhaps the most prestigious in the State, but Karl Albrecht was a fixture in the corporate law department. She would be working alongside him. No matter. She would focus on her job. She would tell him firmly, but politely, that she had no interest in him and would deeply resent any advance. He had plenty of female admirers. Once convinced that he had no chance with her, he would seek the company of women who would appreciate his wit and charm.

She accepted the firm's offer, and she threw herself into her work with an enthusiasm and determination rarely seen in the world of corporate law. She excelled. Granted her Practising Certificate, she quickly won the confidence of her superiors, earning a reputation as one of the most talented young corporate lawyers in Melbourne. Only Karl rivalled her, and she was astonished to note that he showed no resentment. He applauded her successes. He offered assistance when she struggled. He offered comfort and reassurance when she stumbled.

Then Karl had begun to court her. Handsome, charming, perfect Karl. Senior Associate. Ambitious and successful, like her—needing no-one—but enchanted with her. Determined to seduce her.

She flirted with him. She let him escort her to social functions arranged by the firm. But she held him at arm's length. As an evening in his company drew to a close, she would peck his cheek casually, thank him for his attention, and say good night. If he tried to draw her closer, she would pull away, laughing.

"We are friends, Karl, not lovers," she would say with a smile. "Save that for your girlfriend."

"You are my girlfriend," he replied one evening.

"Ah, but you didn't consult me about that," she said lightly. "I think such a claim requires my consent. And in case I offend, be assured that I'm nobody's girlfriend, and never shall be."

She shared his tastes in art and music. They liked the same plays and films. They favoured the same restaurants. He played the role of escort perfectly. He was well-dressed, well-groomed, charming, and attentive. And he asked nothing more of her than that she allow him to summon a taxi for her, though eventually she conceded that since he passed close to her door going home, it was far more sensible for him to drive her home. And on occasion, it seemed rather ungracious not to invite him in for coffee, but only for coffee

When the gifts began, Nata was nervous. When he bought her fine jewellery and silk blouses, she decided the friendship had progressed too far. It was time to remind Karl, firmly, of the terms of the association. He accepted her rebuke, acknowledging that he had overstepped the boundaries and promising, in future, to respect the limits she had set. But then came that triumph and the night of celebration. In her inebriated state, she had allowed Karl to seduce her.

#

Blinding light streamed in through the tall windows. The clock showed 8 am. Nata leapt from the bed and stumbled to the bathroom to splash cold water on her face. There was a dull throbbing behind her temples and her mouth was dry and tasted evil. She glanced back at the ruffled bed. Empty, just as she should have expected. Karl had gone... slunk away while she slept. Like a guilty intruder, he had taken what he wanted, then left her.

She wrapped a robe about her and stumbled to the kitchen. The smoky smell of bacon mixed with the warm, homey scent of fresh toast.

The shrill whistle of the kettle ceased and she heard music playing... a love song. She stopped to listen, then ran her fingers through her hair in a vain attempt to tame her tangled curls.

I must look dreadful. I should...

"Good morning, my beautiful lover."

He was bright and cheery; fully dressed and groomed. There was no sign of remorse in his expression, but neither did he look triumphant. His smile was warm, his eyes wide and candid. He took her in his arms and kissed her forehead lightly.

"Eggs and bacon? Coffee? Juice? You slept well, my darling."

She let him guide her to a chair. He placed steaming coffee before her and bent to kiss the top of her head. Thoughts stumbled over one another in a confused stew. Should she be angry... afraid... relieved... happy?

I do not want a man this way. But he says he loves me. Can any man be trusted? Could I be in love with him?

Hetty's words replayed in her head. "Some men are good, Nata. Some men treat women with respect... love them... care for them. Like Joe. He's a good man. You know he is. He would never hurt a woman... never betray a woman's trust. There are others like him. Maybe Karl is among them? If you give him a chance..."

Mama gave Papa a chance. Mama believed him... trusted him. But that was Papa. Joe showed me that men are not all like Papa.

Her head pounded. She sipped the coffee and commanded the voices to be still. Karl was buttering toast. He was smiling at her… a victor's smile? It should annoy her, but her resolve had flown. She quivered with delight at the cajolery in his deep, dark eyes.

He dropped a plate in front of her and the smell of bacon tickled her nose. Suddenly, she was ravenously hungry. She tackled the eggs with gusto. The soft music filled her head and chased the pounding away. Karl sat opposite her, face sparkling with exhilaration and brown eyes shining into hers with transparent adoration.

"I love you, Natalie," he said softly. "I know you struggle to trust me. Someone has hurt you, badly. I want to take care of you, chase all the memories away. I swear to you, darling, I will never hurt you, never let you down."

He rose again and rounded the table. He was beside her now. He dropped theatrically to one knee and his palms met in supplication.

"Natalie Dreyer," he said with a reverence that tempted her to giggle, "I, Reinhard Karl Alaric Albrecht, do hereby swear my undying love for you. I promise faithfully to love you, to honour you, to cherish and protect you, and to be faithful only to you until the day of my death, if only you would do me the enormous honour of becoming my wife."

#

Six months later, Joe Dreyer combed his bushy eyebrows, donned a rented tuxedo, pinned on a bow tie, and proudly marched his beloved daughter down the aisle. Resplendent in a gown of ivory satin, trimmed with layers of exquisite imported lace and hundreds of tiny pearls, Natalie read her pledge of everlasting love and commitment. She waltzed to the door of the opulent reception hall to be introduced as Mrs. Karl Albrecht.

They honeymooned in Hawaii, staying at the exclusive

Hilton Hawaiian Village. They snorkelled, surfed, and sun-baked. They feasted and danced the hula at a luau. Nata bought Karl Hawaiian shirts. He bought her a stunning coral and diamond pendant.

At night, they retired to the hotel's elegant bridal suite, overlooking the famous Waikiki Beach, where he massaged her neck and shoulders, fondled her silky hair, kissed her lips and breasts and belly and told her, over and over, how he adored her. She bid the voices be silent and embraced him, and when he penetrated her, she dutifully feigned pleasure.

They returned home to settle, as a couple, in Karl's luxury apartment in upmarket Toorak. Nata was in heaven. For so many years, she had struggled to fool herself; to believe her own lies, convince herself that she had it all. But now, she was sure her perfect world truly was complete.

#

Five months later, on December 10, 2007, Natalie wrote in her diary:

> *My period was late. It's started now. Thank God! I do not want to be pregnant. My job demands all my energy. I haven't got the personal resources to devote to a child.*

> *Hetty can't understand, of course. She had so desperately wanted an infant to hold. Her barrenness caused her pain far beyond the comprehension of most women—pain so intense that when she was asked to care for a pathetic little pauper girl, she was thoroughly enraptured and gave her everything. Now, that ungrateful waif is refusing to make her a grandmother. Who can blame her for struggling to hide her disappointment in me? Oh, she tries hard. But she can't disguise her feelings. She hurts, and I know it.*

> *But I have no desire to be a mother. And yet—it's weird—*

for some reason, part of me hoped I was. It's insane, I know. I actually found myself feeling mildly disappointed when my period started. My heart skips a beat whenever I see a mother pushing a pram. And my breasts tingle when I see a mother feeding a baby.

Hetty says there's a part of every woman that aches to grow an infant inside her. She says it's nature. The species needs to reproduce to survive, so women are made to want to bear fruit from the womb. That's their purpose in life.

Poor dear, sweet Hetty! She allowed Joe to sacrifice so much of their comfort and security to educate a waif. And now all she wants to hear is that I'm happy to throw it all away and spend my life in the kitchen and nursery. Barefoot and pregnant. Infant sucking at my breasts. Not a concept Karl would embrace enthusiastically, and certainly not a way of life I would ever choose. No! Motherhood doesn't fit with my vision of a perfect life.

A year later, on December 19, 2008, she wrote:

Yesterday, Gilbert told Karl they were considering offering him a partnership. We are over the moon. Life just keeps getting better and better. We celebrated, of course, and I did it again. I got a little drunk. We had another wild night of passion. It was amazing. To think I never wanted a man to touch me. I used to be so afraid of sex. Not that it's like last night all the time. Only occasionally. We work too hard and get too tired, so we don't do it often. And when we do, Karl usually satisfies himself. But nights like last night...!!!

That must have been when it happened. I was careless. And now?

Karl had it all worked out, of course. That was his way:

to calmly deal with situations; to conceive practical solutions, without fuss or emotion. He was right, of course. They had agreed they didn't want children, and abortion was the logical solution. So why was she so confused? Why had her previously firm resolve left her?

Conceived in an evening of passion, the confirmation of her baby's presence brought such a thrill. That she and Karl… that their love could create a life. She had floated on clouds until she told him. She was filled with such rapturous joy, such consummate happiness, that until he brought her back to reality, she had not considered the complications pregnancy would cause. She totally forgot how opposed she had been to becoming a mother.

He had questioned her certainty at first… reminded her that home tests were prone to error. Then he added that, in the early stages, abortion should be relatively simple. Of course there was no question of having the child, and he reminded her firmly of all the reasons why. That first night, he maintained a cool dignity, though she had detected a faint air of reproach and an underlying threat in his dulcet tones. Then she had consulted her doctor, and come home weeping. And now he was asking her to choose: marriage, career, perfect life—or child.

He was right, of course. It was the logical choice. She had made that choice a long time ago. Except that back then, there was no tiny life growing inside her.

She threw herself down on the satin sheets and buried her head in her pillow to silence her sobbing. The room darkened. The city donned its night attire, neon lights blinking merrily. Traffic lights blazed and lines of headlights snaked along the avenue. She drew the drapes, then wiped her face and went to the kitchen. She switched the kettle on to boil, and then she dropped onto the window seat and gazed out at the night, recalling his last words. Her head throbbed, and her stomach churned.

"Oh, Karl!" she said aloud. "However can I make you understand? I've agonized over this. I honestly thought it was the last thing I could ever want. I almost convinced myself I wanted to abort. But even if it means losing you, I cannot rid my body of the life that grows inside it. Whatever it might mean for our marriage, and for my career, I will not murder our child."

FOUR

Her words replayed in his head, over and over. Karl drew himself up, thrust his shoulders back and told the voice to be still. He could ill afford to let domestic problems distract him. He deposited his brief case, belt and wallet on the conveyor belt and stepped under the metal arch. A uniformed guard nodded to him as he gathered his possessions. A colleague, following him, raised a hand in casual salute.

"Morning, Karl. Progress?"

He shook his head. "None. And none likely." His tone was flat. "Cases like this make lawyers rich. Do nothing for their reputation."

He strode toward the lifts and pressed "Up". There was a ting and a hiss. A light flashed and the doors slid open. He stepped in and pressed "13". As the lift closed and began its climb, he leaned against the wall to ponder what he would say to the judge. There was no easy way to tell him his client wouldn't agree to the suggested settlement. Nor was there any easy way to tell a client who is losing two million a year that the courts aren't going to help him, no matter how right his cause and no matter how much evidence might be produced. Some things are beyond the capacity of lawyers to fix.

But where does Judge Shawdforth stand in all this? It

would be nice to be able to identify the enemy.

God, I'm glad Natalie is no longer involved in this one, he mused. *Natalie! There's a far bigger problem than a client waging an un-winnable legal war.*

He forced himself to focus on the matter at hand. It presented a conundrum he'd never faced before. Karl could live with the occasional defeat, but he was decidedly uncomfortable with the way the judge was handling this case. It wasn't as though Karl was above using the process on occasions. Nor was he naive. The legal system was elaborately constructed to serve white collar criminals—the ostensibly respectable ones: esteemed and titled judges, politicians, senior bureaucrats, and their mates.

Does their power corrupt, or do they seek power with corrupt aspirations?

Karl had no illusions about the motives for decisions and appeals. Lawyers knew how the system worked and whom it served. But when little people got hurt, Karl's principles prevailed over collegiate loyalty and hunger for fees. The crooks could run their scams, but leave the little people alone. And just what was this scam? It smelled of something far more sinister than fraud. If it's dirty, leave Karl Albrecht out of it. He didn't need the aggro. He berated himself for ignoring his instincts. His crap detector had wailed the instant Max Knight had entered the room. But the guy was 82, a successful and well-respected multi-millionaire with sixty years of business experience under his belt and a seemingly quite genuine complaint. He needed a good lawyer, and he could pay well. On the face of it, the matter had seemed simple enough. And the dynamics of the case had interested him. Who could have guessed where signing Max as a client would lead?

Who could have guessed he and Nat would be in the situation they were in now?

Life, for them, had been so perfect. He had never had a second of doubt that the perfection would last forever. But lately, marriage problems occupied his thoughts more often than work, and that was a situation he had promised himself, over a decade ago, he would never permit to happen again.

#

Karl was 12 years older than Natalie, and he'd been married before. That had worried her parents at first, but they had become enamoured with him long before Nat succumbed to his charms.

Nat had seemed the ideal partner for an ambitious, highly successful corporate lawyer. Raised by an older European working-class couple, steeped in traditional values, she had been taught that the husband was head of the household and that a wife must be appropriately subservient to him in domestic matters. Indoctrinated with that view of domestic life, she had repeatedly insisted she would never marry… that she neither needed nor wanted a man in her life. The idea didn't fit with her ambitions and determination, nor with her feisty personality. Karl had invested considerable time convincing her that taking the title of "Mrs" didn't necessarily mean losing the independence she valued so strongly, but eventually he had won her over.

Neither of them wanted children. They had agreed on that long before there was any hint of her responding to his advances. She was a career girl, destined to make her mark on the world of corporate law and equipped with the brains and the skill to achieve far more than she aspired to.

He was ambitious, but he'd already achieved substantially, and at forty-four, he was ready to slow down a little and enjoy the good life. He'd earned it. Now his focus was on ensuring his success was recognized, and his years of effort appropriately rewarded. He wanted to be greeted by name at exclusive restaurants and shown immediately to the best table. He enjoyed instant recognition and diligent attention to his every need when he travelled… first class, of course. And he delighted that bell boys and maitre ds excused themselves from whatever they were doing and hastened to attend him when he entered fine hotels.

He wanted his name on the firm's partner list, wanted to go home to the multi-million dollar mansion with a brand new Porsche parked beside his Ferrari. It thrilled him when people saw that he drove a vehicle worth more than an average inner-city house.

Most of all, he wanted to prove himself to the tyrannical father he so detested. Karl had declined the offer of a position in the firm his grandfather had founded. Determined to prove he could make it on his own, he had sacrificed the prestigious position he stood to inherit for freedom from his father's dominance and demands. But despite his considerable ability, evidencing his worth in a firm where the Albrecht name didn't impress had proved more difficult than he had anticipated.

Natalie Dreyer had qualified as the perfect associate. She was beautiful, smart, and talented—never snobbish or pretentious—and her ability was readily recognized. She had quickly demonstrated a capacity to add substantially to the number of A-list clients on their books and to achieve results that impressed them. She respected Karl's professionalism and skill, admired his ability to charm, and, as well as performing her assigned tasks diligently, was a perceptive researcher and interviewer and quick to offer fresh ideas.

She had appeared to qualify as the perfect life partner, too. The only daughter of respectable working-class people whose doting, discipline, and faultless example, along with the excellent educational opportunities they had scrimped to provide for her, had produced one genuinely classy lady. She shone in upper-crust company. She had impeccable taste in clothing, furniture and decor; appreciated the same authors and literary genres; and shared his love of fine art, opera and travel to exotic destinations.

Their physical relationship had always left much to be desired. Something in her past had made her afraid of intimacy. She harboured a deep, dark secret—one Karl worried might damage his image if ever revealed. But she held it close. And Karl was content with their occasional lovemaking. Her less than passionate responses didn't distress him greatly. She was submissive.

When Gil had announced Karl was in line for a partnership offer, they had celebrated... a wild night of drinking, followed by passionate love making. She'd failed to take precautions. Two weeks later, she was worrying over a missed period, and then over a pink stripe on a test strip, and then she'd consulted Dr. Mansel and she'd come home ashen and weeping.

The solution seemed simple enough. He was prepared to pay whatever it cost... send her anywhere she needed to go... the very best attention, of course. He had expected her to welcome the suggestion, and at first she seemed to accept it. Then she'd gone and told Hetty, and the damned woman talked her out of it.

"I'm Catholic, Karl," she had said. "We were married by a priest... remember? We took vows."

"A lapsed Catholic, my love," he had reminded her. "And even devout Catholics exercise common sense when it comes to matters such as this. I'll warrant the priest has aided the occasional abortion. The orphanages that housed nuns' bastards are a relic of the past, thank God!"

They'd argued. He'd stayed at Phillip's for a few days, thinking to give her time to come to her senses. But when he returned, she'd declared that she intended to bear and care for his child, with or without his help.

"Practical considerations necessitate that we remain business partners," she said, with an uncharacteristic calmness that alarmed him. "There's nothing requiring us to continue as sex partners, or to share either material possessions or the responsibilities of parenthood. You are welcome to go your own way if it suits. I'll go mine.

"We both know motherhood never figured in my life plan, Karl, but now... I intend to apply myself to the task of mothering with the same passion and diligence I have always applied to my career. I'll learn to love our child and to love life as a mother."

Her confidence frustrated and frightened him. He was accustomed to getting his own way. He was head of his household. He made the big decisions, and she had never previously questioned his authority. But she made it clear there was no compromise on this issue. She was having this baby and keeping it. He could go along with that, or they could part.

He had tried reminding her that Catholics regard marriage as sacred.

"You divorced your first wife," she replied, "and you used the claim that we were 'lapsed Catholics' to justify proposing abortion." She retreated into glowering silence while he fought desperately for an answer.

"No rebuttal, counsellor?" she had asked. "How unusual."

He had stayed, but slept in the guest room. He needed time to consider his options. There was a cold tension between them that made being together—even at work—decidedly uncomfortable. Three weeks now, and neither would bend. It was distracting him, and he couldn't afford that with a partnership offer pending. She was struggling too. She'd taken some time off. Stress leave, though they'd taken care to ensure nobody knew the cause of her anxiety.

#

He exited the lift and strolled into the courtroom, nodded to the opposing team, unloaded his papers, and sat down to wait for His Honour's entry.

Thirty minutes later, he bundled his papers into his briefcase, nodded again to the opposing team, and left. It had gone exactly as he expected. They had been called to chambers and cautioned that this was a battle neither side could win. It would be hideously expensive and time-consuming. Ultimately, the matter would most likely be buried by procedural bureaucracy. In layman's terms, it meant: I'm going to ensure there are repeated lengthy delays, and your opponent will no doubt competently assist that endeavour.

"There are complex technicalities of law that must be considered," the judge had said. "It's by no means a simple matter. If it was, the Member would have resolved it."

Ah yes! The esteemed Member—charged with efficiently resolving body corporate disputes. She was noted for her procrastination and arrogance, and she had demonstrated a complete lack of integrity on this one. Disallowed his petition; cautioned him that she regarded his client's conduct as vexatious. Evidence of fraud, destruction of records, manipulation of voting processes, and perjury were apparently not sufficient causes to justify legal complaint.

"The Member ignored the evidence. Whatever her motive, she had no interest in resolving the issue appropriately. That's why we are here," he argued.

"I caution you, Mr. Albrecht, not to denigrate my colleague. I am confident Ms Ross was diligent and had sound reason for her findings."

"And my client has sound reason for making this appeal, sir," Karl protested. "He is losing millions, but he can sustain the loss. His primary concern is for the small investors who bought his units. They are suffering. There have been repossessions. My colleague's clients are picking up great bargains, unfairly. This will end in tragedy." He had paused for a minute to ponder possible motives for wanting the matter closed down quietly. "My client has no interest in uncovering his opponents' motives," he added, "nor in seeing them punished. He just wants order restored."

"We all want order restored, Counsellor, and the way to achieve that is for your client to agree to settle. Offers have been made. He should consider them carefully. Otherwise, I can make rulings that will influence his thinking. I'm granting the petition for a stay. You and your esteemed colleague have fourteen days to reconsider your positions, counsel your clients and hopefully come to an agreement."

The message was clear enough, and Karl now had the unpalatable task of telling his client that, despite copious evidence that the opponent's deposition was blatantly dishonest, there was no way this case would be won with these tactics. This particular court had no interest in truth.

#

"I don't think our petition is going to fly." Karl spoke slowly. Seated in a leather armchair in Levi Wyman's office, on the first floor of Max Knight's upmarket backpacker hostel. He had been silent, surveying his surroundings, long enough to start Levi fidgeting. He knew Levi noticed him appraising the art works hanging on the wall. All commissioned originals, of course, and quality pieces. The Turkish carpet square was hand-woven silk. The floor tiles were marble. Great goldfish-bowl windows looked out over vast expanses of lush green lawn that rolled gently down to the river bank. Beyond the lawns, there were views of the bay. This was rare and valuable inner-city real estate, and no expense has been spared developing it.

Max and Levi were seated side by side on a settee across from Karl. They had been silent, watching him.

"It might be wise to consider the settlement offer." Karl's tone was apologetic. He didn't often feel inadequate in the presence of clients, and he was decidedly uncomfortable.

"Eighty thousand is still an awful lot of money," Levi replied. Max's right hand man seemed to speak for him most of the time. On the rare occasions Max spoke, everyone took notice. His comments were always curt and pointed, and he never said anything that left room for debate. He let Levi offer needed explanation or clarification.

"It's a lot less than half a million." Karl searched Max's

face for a hint of his response to the offer, but he was giving nothing away. The guy had a face like a shrivelled almond, with dark beady eyes and tight lips that seemed to get lost in the wrinkles. His expression was nearly always inscrutable, and he'd clearly studied the effective use of body language.

An experienced poker player, figuratively speaking. He'd do well as a lawyer.

"I can't believe you'd favour us paying a large sum of money we don't owe," Levi replied. Karl noted the "we". Levi was on salary, but obviously, after twenty years on the payroll, he felt a strong investment in the business. Max was lucky.

"The offer is only a starting point for negotiation. We can press for a further reduction in the sum, or even removal of that clause if our counter-offer gives them something of value. Let's talk about the second half of the petition," Karl said. "Can we at least agree to withdraw the demand for the committee to be removed? Does it matter all that much?"

"You have to understand how much damage they're doing to the business. They have a vendetta, Karl. They're out to destroy the enterprise, and they don't care who they hurt in the process."

"Why on earth would they want to do that, Levi? They bought investment units, like all the other owners. They want tenants, surely?"

Levi flushed and his eyes dropped to stare at the floor. "They don't want tenants," he replied quietly. "They have another source of income, one that they wouldn't want exposed. One they would probably not hesitate to kill to cover up. Certainly they've already resorted to bribery and blackmail, and judges and investigative journalists have been happy to take the brown paper bags and play along."

Karl's forehead pleated. "I think you need to tell me all." He gazed meaningfully at Max. "You've been in your share of stoushes, Max. Surely you understand that a lawyer can't help you if you only tell him half the facts?"

"We hoped there was no need to venture into the murky waters," Levi replied. Max was gazing at him furtively. "It really didn't seem relevant to what appeared to be a very simple commercial complaint." He was silent for a moment, thinking, perhaps evaluating Karl, measuring his trust in him.

"What we'll have to tell you—if you insist on knowing—is un-evidenced, and really quite incredible. And there's no way you want to get involved in trying to either prove it or expose it, I assure you."

"You'll have to let me be the judge of that." Karl was back in control now, and rebuking. He shouldn't be compelled to enter into a battle with only half the facts, and he was furious at his client's omission.

Max and Levi exchanged questioning glances, clearly deeply disturbed.

"Rush, the building manager, is in a partnership with the committee members, running a business in the building. A very sleazy business," Levi said quietly. "Using girls and young boys."

Karl sucked in a breath. Levi's face puckered in anxiety. Karl had a sudden flash. *Headlines... how long ago? Three years? More? It was big news at the time, but after the initial burst, the press went curiously silent all of a sudden.*

"I hesitate to ask," he said in an apologetic whisper, "but that press exposé about Max and the girl. Was there any substance to it at all?"

An awkward silence stretched out between them.

"No," Levi replied at last. He was looking directly at Karl now, and his face was working in a contortion of fear and anger. A dull tide of redness crept up Max's bull neck and across a face liberally creased with age and worry lines.

"I need the truth if I'm to help you," Karl said. "All of it."

"It's a long story."

"Then can I suggest you ask Sarah to bring us coffee, and to hold any calls?"

#

An hour had passed, and Karl's stomach was rumbling when Levi finished his story. He had detailed how the building was originally constructed for Max's company, but half the units were later sold to small private investors who were invited to place their units in a letting pool managed by a contracted on-site agent.

Max's company marketed upmarket backpacker accommodation overseas. When Max's units were filled, his marketing team referred surplus customers to the on-site agent, who booked them into rooms owned by the private investors. The agent took a commission on each letting—plus cleaning and maintenance fees—and paid the balance to the unit owner.

Unit owners paid levies to an owners' association that regulated and supervised maintenance of common areas of the building and enforced certain rules regarding unit usage. Run well, the venture promised strong profits for both letting agent and owners, as well as for Max Knight.

"John Rush bought the letting rights a few years ago and took over as on-site agent," Levi explained. "But he had little interest in letting units. He set up a sex business on the fourth floor, which featured premium units and some excellent leisure facilities.

"Max's marketing team was unwittingly supplying young, money-hungry travellers who were happy to indulge Rush's wealthy clients."

Karl nodded thoughtfully. "Foreigners, with a poor command of English and no understanding of our laws, would obviously present minimal risk. Unlikely to talk; less likely to be believed—."

"—And with no comprehension of any laws that might protect them, much less knowledge of where to go for help to enforce them," Levi agreed. "To silence any complaints from the owners' association, Rush offered committee members a share of profits from the sex business. He used their units to accommodate his sex workers. Anyone whose conscience led them to refuse the offer was quickly removed from the committee using false claims of improper dealing, and replaced with owners who would co-operate. Rush and his mates used vote manipulation and bribery to ensure every committee member was a Rush supporter.

According to Levi, Rush had quickly lost interest in the genuine side of the business, leaving units empty and investors losing buckets of money, while he focused on the sex business. Foreign agents quickly recognized that Rush wasn't doing right by their clients and bookings fell away. Max's units, like those owned by honest private investors, stood empty. Business losses escalated.

Levi said Max had sought to have Rush's letting rights cancelled for misconduct, but Rush responded by allying with the committee to falsely claim Max had not paid levies, and to file suit for business damage claiming he was sullying their reputations with false claims. They also claimed Max's attack on Rush had caused owner association disruption that reduced the attraction of the units and thus the sale price. Of course the converse was true. It was Rush's neglect of the legitimate business that was causing disruption and loss of value, and Max needed Karl's help to evidence that conclusively.

"So you're suggesting the story about Max and the girl was fabricated by Rush and his friends to discredit Max and force him to remain silent about the business?" Karl's tone was doubtful. "But surely, knowing what was going on, you could muster enough evidence to make a credible report?"

"Clients of Rush's sex business, known as 'The Fourth Floor Gentleman's Club', include some powerful people, Karl. There's politicians, senior bureaucrats, judges," Levi cleared his throat, "…and lawyers and barristers. Rush and the committee were able to blackmail judges to breach court procedures and make dodgy rulings… by threatening to release the customer list."

"What you are suggesting," Karl said thoughtfully, "is that there was an extraordinarily well-constructed plan, brilliantly executed over a period of several years, and involving a lot of people in high places. A plan to cover up the use of backpacker rooms and the recreation facilities in this building for entertaining perverts and paedophiles."

Karl stroked his chin, searching Max's expression. "You came to me with a complaint about Rush damaging your business by abusing guests, and a fraudulent claim by a committee led by someone Levi referred to as 'Idiot Dunce'—a Mr. Elliot Munce. But the case you asked me to take on was ostensibly a relatively simple matter of misconduct by Rush, and false claims of debt by the committee.

"Now you want me to believe Rush is a pimp, and this Munce—who, it seems, is anything but an idiot—constructed an elaborate plan to cover up sex crimes, having first taken steps to compromise Max's reputation so he would have no credibility if their commercial attack strategy failed?"

Karl's eyes fixed on Max. When Max replied, his voice was tight with anger. "Everything Levi told you is true, but if you choose not to believe it, we should part company now. And if you do choose to believe, you should understand that knowing puts you in harm's way. There are well-connected people involved, and I'm not referring to the pimp and his madam. It's his clients we need to worry about."

"Munce is every bit the dumb idiot we branded him," Levi added. "He didn't orchestrate this. He's a mere puppet. We think we know who the mastermind is, but he's cunning, and so is the lawyer bitch who guided the campaign, Munce's wife."

Karl's startled look demanded clarification.

"A bureaucrat. Junior barrister, I believe, with the federal tax office. She's wily, but I doubt it's her expertise winning the war. And it's not the lawyer you faced in court yesterday either. He's a rookie, but I'll warrant they've got some big guns advising them behind the scenes."

"And neither any payments to lawyers nor any payments to Rush, Munce and his crew show in the records?"

"Well, they wouldn't, would they? They've engaged a dodgy manager and a dodgier auditor. They've got friends in the Tribunal, probably including the President himself. The owners can't even get access to the files or detailed financial reports. Nobody knows who is paying what to whom. And I'll warrant they never will." Levi's tone was bitter.

"So there's no solid evidence at all?"

"Oh, there is," Levi replied. "In abundance. It's just that it's all in the possession of authorities and power brokers, who choose to bury it."

"Not quite accurate," Max interjected, looking less wounded now and more aggressively defensive.

"A few owners accumulated files of evidence," Levi continued for him, "but they've also been attacked, and in many cases they've simply sold out of the scheme at a loss and gone silent. Whether or not they retained their files, we'll probably never know. But I doubt they'd co-operate if we tried to involve them, and we wouldn't want to. People are getting hurt. We want to protect them as far as we are able."

"I don't suppose there's much point to me asking you to name your key suspects?"

Levi shook his head. "Better that you now forget what we just told you. But perhaps you understand now that a settlement on their terms isn't going to put an end to our woes. It's more likely to invite a more ambitious demand."

"I fear that's true. But I'm not sure where that leaves us. I have instructions from a judge whose orders are not easily ignored."

#

"There's a man waiting to see you." Renee's expression was

puzzled. "No appointment. Only gave his first name—Roland."

Karl had returned to the office irritated, and the city traffic hadn't helped. He didn't deal well with not having answers for his clients, and he was particularly peeved at not having a ready solution for a client as prestigious as Maximillian Knight. He snapped at Renee. "No name, no access. You know the rules. You should have sent him away immediately."

"He was very persistent," she replied calmly. "Said he didn't mind waiting… as long as it took. And if you won't see him today, he'll be back tomorrow and the next day."

"Did you ask him what it was about?"

"Of course. He wouldn't say. Just said it related to a matter you were handling."

"Tell him I might see him if he gives his surname and tells you what kind of advice he's looking for."

"I've done that already, Mr. Albrecht," she said. "I was quite insistent. He won't bend, I'm afraid. And please don't bark at me. I do my job well, but I can't compel someone to talk if they are determined not to."

Karl shrugged. "Sorry," he said, without sincerity. "Tell him I'm too busy, and not to bother coming back because I'll be too busy tomorrow and the next day too. And bring me a cup of coffee and a sandwich. I missed lunch."

"Coming right up, sir," Renee said, offering a mock salute. Neither tone nor expression implied servility.

Renee had worked for him for nearly two years now, and she was one of the better secretaries he'd engaged. Willing, even to do things that weren't in her job description. Not uppity like some of the girls. She mostly tolerated his impatience without complaint, though he knew she had remarked, behind his back, that his abrupt manner often bordered on outright rudeness.

She hurried out. He stepped into his office, shrugged off his jacket, tugged at the knot in his tie and settled himself at his desk, leaning back in his chair to think. Suddenly, the door was flung open and a short, thin man with beady eyes and a hook nose stepped confidently in, kicked the door shut behind him, and dropped into one of the two visitors' chairs that faced Karl's carved oak desk.

"Nice office," he said, nodding at the glass wall overlooking the river. "Good view from up here. And pretty classy furnishings."

"Who are you and what do you want? " Karl snarled. "You don't have an appointment and I believe my secretary told you quite clearly you were unwelcome."

"Tut tut, Mr. Albrecht," the man said, pursing thin lips and shaking his head. "Not polite. I expected better from someone of your breeding."

"And what do you know about my 'breeding'," Karl barked, leaning forward.

"I know a lot about you, Mr. Albrecht. I've done my homework, see." He broke into a sardonic smile. "Name's Vance. Roland Vance." He stood and extended his hand. Karl ignored the gesture. Vance waited a moment, then shrugged and sat down again.

"All right, I'll tell you my business and I'll make it brief," he said. "I can see you're a busy man. I heard you tell the young lady out there you were hungry. Men don't function well with empty stomachs, do they? She'll be back any minute now with your lunch, and I wouldn't want you to get indigestion on account of having uninvited company."

Karl was fuming now. The man was not only unwelcome, but a decidedly loathsome individual. "Mr. Vance, if you don't leave, I will be compelled to call security," he said.

"Don't," Vance replied. "Your boss wouldn't like it. Gil and I are friends… sort of."

"I don't believe you."

"Ask him. Meanwhile, I told you I would make it brief. So here's the thing, Mr. Albrecht. You met with some acquaintances of mine this morning, and I'm quite concerned that they might have told you things that my friends would rather nobody know."

"What do you know of my confidential conversations with my client, Mr Vance?" Karl asked, squinting at him.

"Some powerful people are very worried nasty rumours might start to circulate about that building. And the last thing we want is for police or journalists to come poking their noses about. Reputations are at stake. Politicians. Senior bureaucrats. They are just like the rest of us, Karl. They like to pursue certain pleasurable activities… you know, satisfy physical desires. And they like to keep their indulgences private. How they choose to conduct their private lives—what particular pleasures they choose—is neither your business nor mine."

"If it's illegal—"

"Shhh! Karl, I know you respect the law. I also know you value your reputation and your career prospects. And you have a gorgeous wife."

"Are you threatening me?"

"No. I'm offering a friendly caution. A little advice. What you need to do is make sure there are no investigations into Max's business. Nobody asks questions. Nobody interferes with the little sideline business he told you about. You convince Max to let things continue as they have been… maintain the status quo. If he won't do that—if he insists on pursuing the course he's been on—you just stall. Lawyers do that well when it suits them, don't they? Take his money. He's got plenty. Create the impression that you're working for him. But don't upset the apple cart, if you know what I mean."

"He told me he'd sacked two lawyers already. Both did precisely what you are asking me to do."

"Yes, and he'll probably eventually sack you and move on to another. Meanwhile, I want to see you profit handsomely from your association with Max, and I want your assurance that my good friends won't have to worry their little heads about investigations or media exposés. Not too difficult?"

"I don't operate that way, Vance," Karl said, making little effort to hide his annoyance. "I win for my clients. That's what they pay me for, and that's why I have a good reputation and career prospects."

"And I respect that, Karl. I do. But this case demands a different approach, because of the people who might be put at risk if you were to achieve what Max wants. Understand? I think you do, and I suspect your lunch is on its way, so I'll bid you good-day. Thank you for your time."

#

The light outside was fading. Karl watched through the glass wall as an orange sun dipped slowly into the river and both sky and water took on a coppery glow. He'd wasted almost an hour pondering Vance's purpose, and then brooding over the recent changes in his wife. It was disconcerting, seeing her each day without her business suit and brief case. With flowing smock draped over her belly and the hair hanging loose over her shoulders, she was turning into his mother, and he feared the implications of the change. He worried that he might become his father—guilty, resentful, lonely, and bored. With nothing in common with a creature obsessed with domesticity and small people, his father had withdrawn from family life. For a time, he was distant and uninterested, and he ignored both the mother and the child. But as Karl grew, his father became increasingly concerned with his education and development, and increasingly harsh and intolerant in response to the flaws he seemed to believe resulted from the woman's doting.

Karl needed his associate back—and focused. He needed some assurance that she wouldn't morph into Hetty—that she wouldn't fill her brief case with scone recipes and formulae for stain removal and carpet freshening. He needed her stimulating conversation, her bright ideas, the arguments and challenges when she played devil's advocate in play-acts of courtroom scenes. He relished the admiring glances of clients and colleagues when she strutted into a room, hair pinned up; long, straight skirt hugging a firm and shapely derrière; collar buttoned high under a crisply tailored woollen blazer; carrying files neatly packaged in a leather folio and with a folded silk handkerchief and a gold pen peeking from her top pocket. She would extend a graceful hand, displaying short but perfectly groomed nails on the tips of her long elegant fingers, and she would introduce herself with a self-assured half smile and a tone that was honey-sweet, yet laced with a "don't mess with me" firmness. She would fire at the opposition with silvery politeness, but with an unmistakable hint of steel in the words she chose.

Karl marvelled at the magical glow that so enhanced her beauty now and at the gentility in her touch and tone. But he wanted assurance of a temporary change. He loved to watch her, in the evenings, releasing her hair and arranging clips and pins beside her brushes, then wiping away the make-up and lathering her skin with lightly perfumed night cream. But her soft look and seductive scent was exclusively for him, at bedtime, or for their kitchen or lounge on a lazy weekend afternoon.

Aware of the fading light, Karl checked the gold Cartier watch she had given him as a wedding gift. Almost 6 pm. He stepped out and locked his office door. A ribbon of light shone under Gil's door. The chief was working late. Karl tapped tentatively.

"Got a minute, Gil?" he called. The reply was welcoming. Karl stepped into the vast executive suite, shed his jacket, loosened his tie slightly and dropped into the comfort of a plush suede settee positioned near the window wall. He laid his arm over the backrest and crossed his legs.

"I had an uninvited visitor today. Vance...Roland Vance... Said he was a friend of yours, Gil."

Gil's gaze was pensive. He gave no reply.

"Decidedly unpleasant type, and what he had to say appeared to be in the nature of some sort of mild threat. Mentioned a matter I'm working on for Maximillian Knight."

Karl didn't speak of the business Max and Levi had described, or even hint at knowledge of any scandal or illegality. He told his boss only that Vance seemed to know rather more than he should about the matter and about Karl, personally. He'd alluded to knowing of confidential conversations between lawyer and client.

Gilbert Bryant leaned back in his chair and tapped a pencil on the desk thoughtfully. It was a habit that irritated Karl, but Gil was the senior partner in the firm now and looking for a replacement for his recently retired partner, Ewan Adams. Karl wasn't about to say or do anything to damage his prospects, and if that meant tolerating both Gil's annoying habits and the occasional visit with Celia—Gil's insufferably ill-humoured wife—he would do so silently and, to the best of his ability, with good grace.

"I wouldn't refer to him as a friend," Gil said, "but I've met him somewhere. And I have some knowledge of the matter in question. I am quite friendly with Judge Shawdforth."

Karl struggled to suppress a gasp, but couldn't halt a slight expulsion of air. He'd been almost convinced Shawdforth was dirty. And why would Shawdforth discuss the matter with Gil? It was unethical. He remained silent, hoping his dismay wasn't too apparent.

Gil put the pencil down and stood up. With his hands now clasped behind him, he paced a little. He walked to the glass wall and gazed out at the view. Karl waited in silence.

"My second son thinks he wants to leave school and be an actor. I told him he'll not only complete high school, he'll apply himself sufficiently to his studies to gain admission to university, and then to achieve, at very least, a bachelor degree. And not in the arts. He can be an actor after he has gained some useful qualification that will stand him in good stead long term if acting doesn't."

He turned and walked back to stand at the corner of his desk, facing Karl. "I've engaged a tutor, cut his allowance, and withdrawn privileges until his grades improve to my satisfaction. He thinks I'm an ogre right now, but some day he'll thank me."

Karl studied his boss in silence, wondering about the relevance of his dealings with his son to the issue at hand. Gil was usually focused and succinct.

"You're a winner, Karl, and I admire that. But sometimes the best win is figuring out what's best for your client and convincing them it's a better outcome than the result they thought they wanted."

It was a concept Karl was very familiar with, and it was a strategy he employed often. He'd actually tried it on his wife in response to an unplanned pregnancy, but it had failed dismally in that instance.

"Shawdforth insists Max should settle, but Max says it's out of the question," Karl said.

"Might be his wisest course. Our Maxy has a history, Karl. Not one he should be proud of. You know about the scandal?"

"He claims he was falsely accused."

Gil chuckled. "Isn't anyone who's caught with their pants down? Look, he doesn't need a dirty fight. Who knows where it might lead? Shawdforth wants the matter settled. Maybe you need to persuade Max. It's not as if it's a critical matter for the firm, Karl. You've got much bigger fish to fry."

"And the investors who are getting hurt? It's bad, Gil. And it's going to get worse. Repossessions. Bankruptcies. These are ordinary working people who bought backpacker units expecting a fair rental return—a little extra to cover the cost of their kids' education or expensive medical care, or a retirement nest egg. They—"

"I feel for them too, Karl. I hate to see decent people getting hurt. But their protection isn't our responsibility." He sat down again and leaned back, thinking, then leapt suddenly to his feet. "I know where I met Vance. He was with a fellow named Munce at a do I attended. Shawdforth was there as well. He seemed to know them both quite well."

Karl rose and turned to the window to hide his alarm. Gil surely wouldn't be involved in anything grubby. But there were some serious questions here about that judge.

"I agree Vance seems a nasty little creature," Gil continued, "but I'm sure he's quite harmless. I wouldn't stress too much over his visit. I'm sure you'll do what's best for all concerned, Karl. By the way, how is the charming Natalie? Keeping well I trust?"

Karl felt a twinge of suspicion. *Common courtesy,* he told himself. *Nothing more.*

"Better. Enjoying her little break."

"Let's ensure she stays safe and well, shall we?" Gil cracked a wide smile. He lowered his voice to almost a whisper. "Look after your family and your future, Karl. And for goodness sake, keep Natalie out of this. Tell her nothing."

He rose and extended a hand. "Good night, Karl. Give the lovely lady my regards."

Confused, and weighed heavily with an unaccustomed sense of powerlessness, Karl eased the Ferrari out into the city traffic and headed for home. He would call Max on the way. Tomorrow was time enough to argue the merits of withdrawing. Tonight was for working on his damaged marital relationship. However unpalatable the life Natalie seemed to have chosen for them, separation was not an option. Divorce damaged professional reputations, and was expensive. He'd been there once, and two decades later it still hurt when he recalled what it had cost him. But he was young then. There were no children involved, and minimal assets. A marital breakup now would be ten thousand times worse.

"Get a grip, Karl," he told himself. "Take control, man…

of your client and your wife."

Ever since he left his father's house, Karl Albrecht had always been in complete control of every situation. Failure was as intolerable as subjugation, and Karl was determined never to endure either again.

#

Entering the apartment the following Friday, Karl reminded himself again of the reasons he had eventually chosen to concede. This was a victory, not a surrender. He was assuring his future. The partnership offer would be withdrawn, he knew, if he and Natalie parted. The last thing the firm needed was a partner distracted by a marital dispute with an associate. Besides, a smart, beautiful wife was an asset for a man of his stature. As much as he'd resisted the idea, he had to acknowledge that a family was also, in many ways, an asset. Being a father seemed to earn a man greater respect.

Yes, he'd decided, *there could be advantages to fatherhood, and maybe to a move, now, to a family home—a mansion in a quality beach-side suburb, with accommodation for a live-in housekeeper and nanny. Hetty and Joe might even move in, if the house were large enough. With them in permanent residence, the child would be cared for and disciplined, and a minimal imposition on busy parents. Natalie would be confident that her infant had the best of care.*

The more he'd considered the option, the more perfect it had seemed. It was a win all round. He could save face... put an end to the tension between them... maybe even move back into her bed. Despite her coldness to him, he desired her. Emotional distance hadn't stopped his physical urges.

He deposited his brief case, carefully laid the bunch of roses he'd purchased on the hall table, shed his jacket and tie, and went to the kitchen. She was on the window seat, sipping coffee. He took a seat opposite her and gazed out at a warm tangerine sky, streaked with deep orange and copper red and the ever-so-faint touches of light purple. The sinking sun seemed somehow symbolic, but the city was lighting up. And the sun would rise again. He reminded himself again of the advantages of reconciliation, mentally rehearsing the little speech he must make.

Please let it sound suitably sincere.

Contrition was always a significant stretch for Karl, and indeed, he was not at all sorry for the stance he'd taken. His concession was motivated solely by practicality. He swallowed hard, ordering his throat muscles to unlock.

"I've made a decision, Natalie," he said.

She opened her mouth to speak, but he held up his hand to silence her.

"Please, darling, let me say this without interruption."

He caught the look of surprise at the endearment.

"I've been wrong. The life we had planned... I thought it was perfect... everything I'd ever wanted. I worried that motherhood would spoil what we had... spoil your gorgeous figure... tire you... distract you... leave you no energy for the things we love doing together in the little free time we manage to claim for ourselves. But that maternal glow suits you. I've talked to Gil and Phillip, and to Joe. Fatherhood involves some sacrifices, but it also brings rich rewards, it seems. There are ways for women to reconcile the obligations of parenting with pursuit of a career, especially when there's ample money to pay for the right kind of help.

"What I'm trying to say, my darling, is that I love you, and if having this child will make you happier, then we will make it work."

He went to her, then, and sat beside her and tentatively wrapped an arm about her shoulders. He sat for a moment admiring the finely sculptured face with its high cheekbones, domed forehead and pointed chin. Even seated casually, her pose was regal.

"I've been a jerk," he said, chafing at the requirement to affect shame. "Can you ever forgive me?"

She turned her face to him, a glimmer of tears in those deep green cat eyes, but her rich full lips curved in a relieved smile that deepened her dimples.

"There's nothing to forgive, Karl," she said. "I understand. I do, really. Hetty said it might take some time for you to adjust to the idea of a child. She said I must be patient. But I can't tell you how happy you've made me."

"Then let me take you out to dinner, my love, to celebrate. And in the morning, we'll call an estate agent and register our interest in buying a home suitable for the family of a partner in one of the nation's most prestigious law firms. But first, you must excuse me for a moment."

He withdrew his arm, stood, and went to the hallway to retrieve the roses.

"Beautiful roses for my beautiful woman," he said, passing them to her.

She laid them on the table, read the card, then embraced him. "I love you, Karl," she whispered. "Let's not go out. Let me cook for you. Let's spend a quiet evening at home, and we'll see where it leads."

Well done, Karl. It wasn't as difficult as you anticipated, was it? Sometimes a loss is actually a win, old man. It's just the perspective you choose to adopt. Maybe—just maybe—you'll find aspects of fatherhood enjoyable. Gil and Phillip do. Their wives are working professionals too. If they can make it work, so can you. It doesn't have to be like it was in your childhood home.

Karl's father was a lawyer, and his grandfather before him. The family was rich—inherited wealth. Both father and grandfather were tyrants, and miserable, virulent men. His mother was a mouse, afraid of her own shadow and mortally terrified of incurring his father's anger. He gave an involuntary shudder as his memory replayed an often recalled scene.

Karl, aged seven, sat pressed against the wall, hugging his knees. He fought back tears. Father disliked cry-babies. Mother's face was ashen. She quivered as she swept up the broken pieces of the vase.

"How many times have you been warned not to run in the house," his father bellowed. "You will spend the afternoon in the cloak closet. And there will be no dinner for you this evening. You will learn obedience. Do you understand?"

"Yes," Karl replied, in a nervous whisper, dreading long hours locked away with a bursting bladder or raging thirst. More than once, his father had left him there all night, and he'd suffered further punishment, in the morning, for soiling himself.

"Yes, Father," his father shouted. "And speak up so I can hear you. Learn to show respect, boy."

"Yes, Father."

He stepped into darkness and huddled among the shoes and bags, trembling as he heard his father turn the key in the lock, yet secretly glad to avoid watching what he knew would follow. But he heard it. He always heard it.

Whaaack! The dustpan clattered to the floor and china pieces spilled over travertine tiles.

"Leave it, woman. The boy can clean it up this evening while the rest of us eat dinner. You would have cleared it away and not told me, had I not come in early, wouldn't you? And you wouldn't have punished him. You spoil him. And you neglect your wifely duties, wasting too much time indulging that undisciplined brat."

"I'm sorry." Her voice wavered. "I'll try harder to teach him." And he heard her hesitant shuffle as she made her way to the kitchen. He heard his father's heavy tread, and then the slamming of the study door.

Mother came to him that night, after Father had ordered him to bed. She didn't hug him or kiss his forehead. She didn't tuck the covers around him.

"You must try harder to please your father, Karl," she said. "You must obey him. He makes it hard for me when you don't. There is so little happiness in my life. I had to give up my work to care for you, and now you make life hard for me by displeasing your father, and he blames me. Do you see the trouble your disobedience and disrespect causes?"

"He is too much like you, Laura," his father had said often. "Weak and fragile. I had hoped he would have been more like me, and like my father. He needs discipline and training, not indulgence, to shape him into someone worthy of the Albrecht name."

Karl had learned to obey. He became almost a model son: obedient, respectful, and a high achiever in everything he did. He tried hard to please his father—more for his mother's sake than his own. She seemed always so tired and unwell. He craved her affection, but she withdrew from him and—more and more as he grew—let his father raise him.

His father, while stern and judgemental, declared him brilliant and therefore in need of education at the very best schools. He frequently commented that the boy was extraordinarily handsome, like his father and grandfather before him, and demanded that he be always expensively and tastefully dressed— rarely allowing casual attire. He paid for sports training and demanded that Karl pursue an intense physical fitness program.

Grandfather regularly lectured Karl about his social status. "You are of the upper class, Karl," he said often. "Never forget that being of that class confers responsibilities as well as privileges. You must behave in a manner becoming of men of our stature. We are admired and respected, but also often resented. Those beneath us relish any opportunity to denigrate us and make us the subject of gossip. In public, your dress must always be impeccable, and your conduct above reproach."

When Karl was eighteen, his father cast him out for a year. He ousted him from the family home with a few changes of clothing, a handful of change, and a minimal stipend to ensure he wouldn't starve. "To appreciate opportunity, and make proper use of it, you must experience the pain of poverty," he told him.

Karl went out a materially indulged boy, believing his heritage entitled him to security and comfort. He suffered, but he fought to prove himself. His father welcomed back a man—bitter, resentful, but capable, and nursing a savage thirst for career success and independent wealth. He applied himself to university studies with diligence and determination. His father had cultivated in Karl a burning ambition to achieve, an unwavering belief in his innate superiority, and confidence in his entitlement to a life of luxury and the admiration of his peers.

He was superior. He would achieve all his father's ambitions for him, and his own. As long as this affair with Maximillian Knight could be handled with finesse—he would take another step up. But he would not do it Gil's way. Gil's was the easy way. Karl wasn't one for easy solutions. There was potential here: important people with reputations to protect; people willing to toss fat brown paper bags about to cover their sins; people willing to make threats, and execute them. If he succeeded in thwarting their game, he could make his mark. He could net a whopping fee and he could establish himself as a lawyer to be feared… respected even by those in the most exalted places.

He would be a partner, like his father. But he would do better. He would earn his own fame and fortune. And at the same time, he would prove to the world that he could achieve what his father had not: that he could be a respected and admired family man, with an adoring wife and a child who would revere him. He would out-father Father.

Five

The path had been swept and the glass in the front door polished. Natalie smiled remembering all the times Hetty had fussed and ordered her and Joe about as they prepared to entertain a guest. It was a humble little cottage, but Hetty took such pride in it.

Joe flung the door open and smothered her in a hug. He shook Karl's hand, then embraced him. The warm scent of roast lamb wafted from the kitchen. Nata heard the clanging of the oven door closing. Hetty erupted into the hallway wiping her hands on her apron, her cheek smeared with flour.

"Karl, Nata!" she exclaimed. "Welcome. Ah, what a day this is! And I've cooked all your favourite foods to celebrate. A baby! How wonderful! Joe and I... we've been so anxious for this day... for a grandchild to love. Nata, are you keeping well? Are you bothered by morning sickness? Karl, are you taking good care of her?"

"Stop, please!" Nata laughed. "You are prattling. Calm down for heaven's sake. I'm perfectly fine, Mum, and quite capable of taking care of myself, thank you."

"Nevertheless, a husband should spoil his wife a little when she is carrying his child. You need plenty of rest, Nata."

"Karl, don't you let her work too hart," Joe ordered, "and make sure she not suffer stress. Not goot for baby. Will you be stopping work, soon, Nata?"

"No. I plan to work until I'm seven months gone, at least. And I'll be returning to work when the baby is eight weeks old. Four months' leave is quite an ask. It will be a challenge for the firm to have me off for that long."

Hetty looked concerned. Joe's frown was disapproving. Nata knew that look well.

"Surely you stop work. A baby neets its mother," Joe said.

Nata gave him an indulgent smile and shook her head. "You borrowed money to give me an education, Dad. You encouraged my ambition... urged me to study hard... rewarded me for doing well. You went wild with delight when I got my Practising Certificate. Said I'd fulfilled all your dreams for me. And now you want me to trade my career for an apron?"

She glanced at Hetty and felt the redness creeping across her cheeks. "Sorry, Mum. I'm not devaluing the life you chose. But it's a different world. Karl and I are not like you and Dad."

"We're fortunate that we can afford the very best child care and household help," Karl cut in. "Nat loves her work. She finds it deeply rewarding."

"Being a mother is deeply rewarding," Hetty said. "You will see. When the baby comes, you might rethink how you want to spend your days. You might not want someone else to see its first smile and hear its first words."

"Come out back, now," Joe said, keen to defuse any argument. "I show you what I making."

They followed him to the little workshop he'd set up on the back veranda, and he pointed proudly to two shaped pieces of wood. A sheet of timber was marked with shapes, and a jigsaw rested beside it.

"A cradle," he said proudly. "Beautiful old style rocking cradle."

Nata's face shone and her eyes sparkled. She threw her arms about Joe and hugged him hard. "Isn't he wonderful, Karl?

He was the world's best dad, and now he's going to be the world's best grandfather."

"Ach!" Joe exclaimed. "You always know how to wrap me around you small finger. Sing my praises, then ask for what you want."

"Not true, Dad," Nata laughed. "I never had to sing your praises. You rewarded me because I was polite and obedient. And I didn't dare be anything but. You were the world's most generous father, but you were also the strictest."

"I raise a goot girl," Joe said, his chest puffing. "You are lucky man, Karl. You agree?"

"Absolutely, Joe. You might have to give me some advice," Karl said indulgently, and Joe's face split in a wide grin.

"Come inside now," Joe said. "Hetty prepares a feast for us. You see what she needs help with, Nata. Karl and I, we have a small brandy."

"So, did he show you his leg?" Hetty asked, shovelling baked potatoes onto a platter.

"What about his leg?" Nata asked.

"Silly old goat slipped with the saw and gave himself a nasty gash. He had a lot of stitches, but the doctor said it's healing nicely and there'll be no permanent damage."

"He shouldn't be doing things like that at his age." Nata's voice wobbled a little, and her eyes watered. "He could hurt himself badly."

"I've never seen him happier. Not since he made that doll's house for you for your ninth birthday. He spent ages searching for just the right type of timber and a pattern that pleased him."

"After I make cradle, then I make rocking horse," Joe said, returning to the kitchen with a filled spirit glass in hand. "And don't you dare call me old, young lady."

"I didn't. Mum did," Nata protested. "All this activity is a bit premature, isn't it? It will be a while before the baby is old enough to ride a rocking horse."

"It will be a while before I finish," Joe replied. "But I make sure it ready when he is."

"Who said it was going to be a he?" Hetty said. "It might be a beautiful little girl, just like our darling. Now, let's eat."

#

The clock struck four as they re-entered the apartment. Natalie had driven home. Karl had taken a bottle of good wine for his hosts, but Hetty was a non-drinker and Joe drank only moderately. Nata, of course, was abstaining due to pregnancy. Karl claimed it was a sin to re-cap a bottle of quality liquor. Nata thought that a poor excuse for over-indulgence, but she observed with silent pleasure that either the wine, the good food, or good influence had improved his disposition considerably. She was tired, but feeling blissfully contented. She flopped across the half-round king bed and gazed up at the ornate plaster ceiling.

"I'm stuffed," she said. "I ate far too much."

"I thought pregnant ladies were supposed to moderate their eating habits."

She poked her tongue out at him and changed the subject. "Isn't Joe sweet, making a cradle."

"Silly old man, I'd say. Could've done himself permanent damage, and for what? To save a few dollars? It's not as if we can't afford to buy any damned cradle we fancy."

"You really don't get it, do you Karl?" Nata sat up and frowned at him.

"I get that he's a sentimental old fool," Karl replied. "Lovable. But a fool nonetheless. I just hope he doesn't hurt himself badly pursuing these silly sentimental notions."

Poor Karl! How often, in her youth, had Nata wished her parents were well-to-do; wished away the guilt when they sacrificed their comforts for her; wished Joe wouldn't insist her dates pick her up from that humble little cottage but would let her meet them somewhere and pretend. Joe and Hetty had given Nata everything but money. Karl's parents had given him little else.

#

"I think I've found our new home, Karl." Natalie's voice quavered slightly. "I know you warned me not to get too into house hunting until you could find time to arrange inspections, but you're always so busy, darling. And I don't want to be moving when I've got a belly the size of a basketball."

She pushed a brochure across the table. "It's Saturday. Surely you can find time this afternoon to drive out to Black Rock and take a look? You're working way too hard lately. You're neglecting me."

"Oh for pity's sake, Natalie. I'm working to secure our future."

"I should think our future is quite well enough secured already, Karl. But we have to live a little as well. There's more to life than work and money."

"Yes, all right. I'll look at the brochure and if it appeals, we'll go and look. I presume you've set it up already with the agent and she's made arrangement with the owners?"

"Of course. There are actually two houses I asked her to show us. I like that one best." She pointed to the brochure she had given him.

"Sometimes, Natalie, I feel like I'm no longer master of my own home. And I don't like it. I wish you wouldn't arrange these things without my consent."

Nata inhaled sharply, but bit her tongue. *Save it for the big issues, she reminded herself. He's a product of his upbringing, and he does seem to be trying to change.*

He studied the brochure. "Not particularly impressive from the outside," he said.

"Oh, it's nice enough, Karl. We won't stand outside all day looking at it. It's the inside that counts, and look at the location. Half a block from Half Moon Bay Beach, and an easy walk to the village. I can take the baby for walks to the shops or for picnics on the beach."

"Four bedrooms and two bathrooms. Where do we accommodate the live-in staff? We agreed we'd need a housekeeper/nanny to live in."

"We are only having one baby, Karl. And the house can easily be extended."

"There's only 918 square metres of land."

"Only! Karl, that's a good sized block. And it has accommodation for four cars. The garage could be converted later, to a studio unit, and a new garage built out front. That would make a lovely private suite for staff, detached from the house."

"I really had something a little more elegant in mind… more in keeping with our social status. Somewhere we can entertain in style. Look at the size of the dining room. It might accommodate eight people at a stretch, but—"

"I thought we were looking for a family home, Karl, not a status symbol. And since when do we have more than eight people for dinner?"

"When I'm a partner, darling, we'll have certain obligations. People will have expectations. I come from a well-known family with a history in this area. We should be looking for the kind of home I grew up in. A home suitable for entertaining upper class clients—"

"Something that requires an army to maintain and where we can get lost between the front door and the back. I'm trying to be practical, Karl. We're busy professionals. We aren't planning to spend a great deal of time at home. You've suggested having Hetty and Joe look after the place. They'd find a grand mansion quite intimidating, and far too much work to look after."

"Then we'll hire extra help. We can well afford it. And it's important to me to maintain an appropriate image."

Nata paused, sighed, and passed him the second brochure. "Maybe that one will be more appealing."

"Nice views," he remarked. "But the street presentation is rather ordinary."

"It has a private suite downstairs for the staff."

"It appears the master bedroom and studio share a downstairs bathroom. And there's no formal dining room at all. No, I'm afraid that's quite unsuitable."

"Well, I guess I'll just phone the agent and cancel the appointment, since you seem determined to be disagreeable."

"Ask her to find us something more suitable. No, I'll call her. I'll ask her to make a short list that we can drive by, and we'll take that drive you planned. I'm sure she'll be able to identify some suitable properties, and we can arrange inspection later in the week. Will that make you happy, my dear?"

She shrugged.

"Come now, Natalie. You know I don't like to disappoint you. But you really shouldn't have set your heart on something without... I mean... I would have thought you much more perceptive... much more aware of the requirements of my position."

"You're sounding like a snob now. Your position? Please. You're a lawyer in a renowned firm. Maybe about to become a partner. You're not royalty."

"The Albrecht name has always been associated with a certain level of class, Natalie. As my grandfather reminded me often, appearances matter." He tucked the newspaper under his arm and strode off to his study. She turned to clearing the kitchen and stacking the dishwasher. He returned, a half hour later, beaming. He spread the real estate section of the paper over the table and tapped a finger on one of the larger advertisements.

" 'Palatial five bedroom, five bathroom sandstone chateau. Two private suites downstairs, plus a large study. Entertainer's kitchen servicing a party-sized dining room and a huge cabana.' The agent describes it as one of the most distinguished homes in the district. And doesn't it look impressive in the photograph?" He moved his finger down the page to another sizable advertisement. "Or, this one. 'Five bed, three bath, five living rooms.' It's got a gym, private office, and home theatre. 'Feature stone facade. Well established. A Bayside icon.'"

"Meaning old, and therefore probably a maintenance nightmare," she mumbled, turning to gaze out the bay window behind the kitchen window seat.

"All right. If you want modern, how about this one?"

She turned back to follow his pointing finger and study a photograph. "Not particularly impressive from the outside," she said, imitating both his comment on her preference and the tone he had taken. "I suppose I'll have to reserve my opinion," she added, feeling a little guilty at not sharing his enthusiasm. "But I really don't want a huge mansion that's going to take an army to clean and require a search party to find my toddler when he or she decides to wander. I want a family home. Warm. Comfortable. Unpretentious."

"Why don't you wait until we see them? You might be pleasantly surprised."

"And if I'm not?"

"What are you asking?"

"Whether you will consider my preferences, or just buy a palace because you think Karl Albrecht should rate a crown."

He flared then, and stormed out, and she regretted her outburst. "Patience and tact, Nata," Hetty had advised, and it had been working. He'd conceded on some major issues. She'd handled this one badly.

She finished tidying the kitchen, and then she made him coffee and took it to him. "Peace offering?" she said, placing it in front of him. "I'm sorry, Karl. I should be more understanding. We grew up in different worlds, and that's created different priorities. But there's a house out there somewhere that we'll both love. I'm sure of it. We just need to be patient with each other until we find it."

She wrapped her arms around him then, and kissed the top of his head lightly, but his mood was spoiled. They drove by a few houses. He commented on the street presentation. She feigned enthusiasm about those he seemed to favour, but he was cool and distant, and nothing she said or did seemed to warm him.

#

Natalie manoeuvred the Porsche along the Esplanade. The river was alive with sailing boats and rowing boats and luxury cruisers. Cyclists and runners littered the paths that wound between vast stretches of grassed riverbank. The June sun's reflection danced across the water, making the tips of little ripples sparkle silver.

Hetty sank back into the plush leather seat as Nata dodged squealing brakes and honking horns. Hetty had never learned to drive. Joe neither. They'd never owned a car.

"So how is work?" she asked.

Nata replied without feeling. "I love my job, but it's stressful. Everyone has been wonderful, though, since we told them about the baby. They've all been fussing over me."

"As they should, my dear. As they absolutely should."

"Why? It's not such an extraordinary thing. Women have babies. Working women get pregnant every day."

"There was a time when they would give up working when a child was on the way."

"We keep having this discussion," Nata said in a tone of mild exasperation. "It's a different world, Mum. It's not like it was when you were young."

"No, but I think maybe it's not so good now. I think it was better then."

Nata shook her head. "Karl's mother gave up her career to raise him, and she was miserable. He has painful memories of her complaining of the sacrifice she had to make for him and how unhappy it made her."

"It's not like that for some," Hetty replied. "I loved the

life."

"And I love mine. You and Joe encouraged me to strive… to work hard. And I achieved all that Joe encouraged me to aspire to. I can't throw it all away now. I know I would be discontented."

Hetty turned to gaze out the window. "Seems to me you are often disgruntled, love. Always looking for something that's out of reach. Maybe motherhood will bring contentment?"

She turned back to pat her daughter's belly, smiling. "It's growing."

"I wish it would cease the football practice," Nata laughed. "It's tiring."

"It will get worse, love. You've a way to go yet."

"Thanks for the reminder," Nata said with a grimace. She turned into the parking station and stretched to press the button. She drew the card from the slot and dropped it into the centre console.

"Here we are, then. There's a baby boutique on the second floor, and, of course, baby sections in Myers and Harris Scarfe. Knock yourself out, Mum." She waited while Hetty flicked the mirror down and checked her hair, pushing a stray lock into place, then climbed out of the car and adjusted her skirt. She was always so fanatical about neatness.

"Let's get a coffee, shall we, before we start loading ourselves up with parcels?"

She chose a table near the entrance to the coffee shop and drew a chair out for her mother. They were miles from the mall in Footscray, but something about the decor recalled a treasured memory. "Strawberry milkshakes. Do you remember, Mum?" she laughed. "You were weighed down with bags of pretty dresses, and I looked so pretty, for the first time in my life I think."

"You remember?" Hetty replied, her eyes dancing.

"Of course. I was afraid of you and Joe, but you were so kind. But then there was that awful affair with the doll. I was sure Joe would beat me, or send me away. I was terrified."

"It took a long time for you to learn to trust him. It hurt him, because he adored you, right from that very first day. You weren't all that pretty back then. The looks came later, when your hair grew and your nose stopped running and the welt on your face healed. But to us, you were always beautiful."

"I worked hard for Joe's approval. I was always painfully conscious that my own parents rejected me and terribly afraid of doing something that might make you and Joe do likewise."

Hetty's eyes misted and her face twisted in a mask of pain. She lowered her face to stare at the floor and her fingers worked on the handle of her bag. She had reassured Nata, often, of their unconditional love. But she refused to talk of Nata's birth parents, and Nata knew that mention of them always caused her deep distress.

"And now I work hard for Karl's approval," Nata hastened to add. "But I seem to fail often."

The waitress came, just then, and took their order. Hetty kept her downward gaze, letting Nata order for her. When she looked up, her expression had brightened some, but worry lines creased her brow and her eyes bored into Nata, demanding truth.

"How is he, now, about the baby?"

"I don't know, Mum. I honestly don't. He said if it made me happy… but I don't want him just to accept it on account of me. I want him to want it. Sometimes it seems he does. But other times… We quarrelled again, yesterday, over the choice of a house to buy. I want a family home. He seems only concerned with image—a grand mansion. To use his words, 'something fitting for someone of our social standing.' I fear he'll want to mould our child into a… ummm… a prize to show off."

"We all do, love."

Shock waves jolted her. Her stare demanded explanation.

"We all want a child who is good looking, healthy and strong. We delight in our child's achievements, want them to do well. We tell ourselves it's for their own sake, and it is. Of course it is. We want them to grow up happy. But people flatter us when they praise our child. We dance and cheer when a daughter wins awards. It boosts our egos, makes us feel we are good at parenting. When our child misbehaves, or fails, we hurt. We punish them, not always for their own good, but sometimes because they remind us of our faults, make us fear failure. It's human nature, love. Parents aren't perfect."

"You and Joe came close," Nata said, her expression earnest as she gazed at Hetty.

Hetty laughed. "You complained often enough, about Joe especially."

The waitress came with juice and coffee then. Nata watched as Hetty ripped at the little sugar pack and stirred the grains in. She pulled back the tab on the milk vial and poured it in. White streams coiled about and gradually turned the black liquid creamy.

"He was hard on me," Nata said softly. "The other kids mocked me because my parents were old-fashioned."

She sipped her juice, then looked up at Hetty, and her look was intense. "I want for Karl and I to be the kind of parents you and Joe were, for our child to have what I had. But Karl is so high-handed and demanding sometimes. He wants to be head of the household, to make the big decisions."

"And so it should be."

"It's not like that in the modern world, Mum. But I wouldn't mind if he was like Joe. If he—"

"You didn't marry Joe, love."

"I love Karl, Mum. I do. But sometimes he's hard to understand. He comes from a very different world from the one I grew up in."

A small voice repeated, now, the explanation he had offered when she'd remarked that he was not close to his father; that he never called him or visited or spoke about his childhood.

No happy memories there, Nat. My childhood was not like yours. The only attention my father paid me was to arrange

*schooling or training in some field or other, or when he thought I
needed discipline, and there was plenty of that. His punishments
were harsh. I never felt he loved me. And my mother? She lived
in fear of my father's disapproval. And he disapproved fiercely
of her pampering me.*

"Karl has achieved a great deal," Hetty was saying,
obviously unaware that Nata's mind had wandered. "He's a
charming, well-respected gentleman. And he won your love. His
parents must have done something right, Nata. And when the time
comes, I'm sure he'll be as good at fathering as he is at lawyering.
The two tasks have much in common, you know? They both
require sound judgement and wise counsel."

Nata smiled at Hetty. "I hope that qualifies me well for
motherhood then." She paused a minute, staring out at the passing
crowds. "I just want Karl to love me and our child."

"He does, my dear," Hetty said. "I'm sure of it. And you
must love him, warts and all. Now come. I want to buy some
pretty things for my grandchild. And when we're done shopping,
we can search for a house that both you and Karl will be content
with; a home where you and Karl can be happy raising a child we
will all love dearly and who will make him as proud and happy
as you have made Joe and I."

Six

Karl braced himself for a confrontation and strode into the conference room. He shook hands with his opponent, Ian Johannsen, who acted for Rush and Munce, then took a seat directly across from him. He swung his El Casco calf-leather compendium onto the desk and opened it with a flourish, hoping Johannsen appreciated the quality and would guess at the price tag. He took his time arranging pens and papers. Taking a digital recorder from his pocket he laid it on the table. Then he placed the Patek Philippe pocket watch his grandfather had given him beside it. It was psychological warfare. Karl knew Rush's means, and that Johannsen lacked both pedigree and experience.

"I asked for a private meeting because I'm concerned that our respective clients might flare. There's a lot of heat between them, Ian."

"Understandably, on my client's part at least. There's a lot at stake, Karl. He paid over half a mil for the management rights of that building, and Knight wants to make him walk empty handed."

"For good cause, it would appear," Karl replied calmly.

"What cause? He's managing the building competently. The committee approve of him."

"The committee members are getting excellent rental

returns, but the vacancy rates are at a record high and a lot of the unit owners are doing it very tough, Ian. Seems units on the fourth floor generate good profits, and the balcony suites on the upper floors do well, but Max says bookings are way down because Rush has alienated foreign agents and abused guests."

Johannsen flushed. Deep violet eyes flamed with righteous indignation. "Rush says he's had to introduce disciplinary measures to stop kids trashing rooms and bringing uninvited guests in for wild parties, or to stay without paying. He's had issues with smoking in non-smoking areas, littering and excessive noise. He's dealing with teenagers, Karl. We all know they can be troublesome. And these are rich kids, accustomed to being over-indulged and allowed to do as they please."

"Rich doesn't necessarily mean over-indulged." Karl thought of his own childhood, and the rigorous discipline regime at the exclusive boarding school his father had sent him to. Plenty of rich kids there, and none of them allowed to do as they pleased. But Ian was self-made. Like Natalie, he'd grown up in a working class suburb with battler parents. Unlike Natalie, he had worked his way through school and university, and it had been a long, hard road. By his definition, any kid who was fed, clothed and educated and allowed to drive daddy's car on Saturday evening dates was over-indulged.

"It does in this case," Ian was saying. "Kids travelling the world unsupervised, using debit cards linked to daddy's bank account to stay in luxury accommodation."

Karl weighed his position, took a deep breath, and launched an untempered broadside. "Rush is running an illegal enterprise on the side, a rather sleazy enterprise, paying kids to provide entertainment. The kids are flush because they earn big dollars selling favours... selling their bodies, Ian."

Johannsen gave a strangled cough and gawked at Karl. "You can't seriously believe there's any truth to that rumour?"

Karl studied his opponent for a moment, then shrugged.

"I don't know. But I know Knight can't be persuaded to settle. He wants me to investigate his allegations, assemble evidence to substantiate his claims about Rush, and the committee members he thinks are covering for him and profiting handsomely for their co-operation."

Ian leaned back in his chair and pursed his lips. After a moment of tense silence, he leaned forward again and asked, "Are you sure you want to go down that road? Shawdforth was quite adamant that you should persuade Knight to settle."

"That we should negotiate a settlement, actually, though he did seem rather inclined to favour your client. So here's the deal, Ian. Rush walks. Knight is willing to give him a hundred and twenty days to find a buyer at the best price he can get. If he can't sell in that time, Knight will put a temporary manager in until a sale can be negotiated, and Rush will get the sale proceeds—in full. The committee resigns and none of them stand for re-election. Knight gets at least three of his picks on the new committee. No mischievous motions on agendas or inflammatory correspondence to owners. No stirring remarks at meetings by ex-committee or their henchmen.

"Knight gets to tell his foreign agents the establishment is under new management and send his marketing team on a promotional tour to win back the business he's lost. And he puts his own security team in to replace the uniforms Rush and the committee hired. That way, he can verify that nothing untoward is going on in his building. If there never was, it's business as usual and Rush is the only potential loser. If there's no unseemly connection, the committee shouldn't give a hoot for his losses. If Knight's suspicions are founded, a settlement buries the business quietly. No embarrassing exposures. No prosecutions. The committee members revert to getting fair rent but keep their illicit gains. Rush keeps the fat cash profits he's been enjoying to balance up any loss on sale of the business. Most likely, he comes out well in front."

Johannsen leaned back in his chair, shook his head vigorously and chuckled. "You can't seriously think I'm going to even try to sell that to my client?" he said. "If you do, you're not half as smart as I pegged you, old boy. In fact, I'd have to say you were thoroughly naïve. No deal, Albrecht. We put our cards on the table before the last hearing. The offer stands as it was then. Your client withdraws all allegations of impropriety and unequivocally apologizes for questioning my client's integrity. Rush retains his rights. The committee continues unopposed for its full term and all members have the right to stand again. Knight stops all interference. No more letters to owners. No more requests to buy proxies. No more mischievous motions on meeting agendas or inflammatory remarks at meetings. In return, my client undertakes to withdraw all claims for damages. Knight pays his member dues. Both sides pay their own costs."

Karl capped his sterling silver fountain pen and clipped it into his jacket pocket, closed his compendium, and stood up. "Guess we're done then," he said, extending his hand. "Thanks for your time."

"Wait! " There was a hint of alarm in Johannsen's voice, and his face was contorting.

His inexperience is showing, Karl told himself. *Hasn't yet mastered the poker face. Perhaps I should take pity on him and give him some lessons in the art?*

"Yes," Karl said, remaining on his feet with his compendium tucked firmly under his left arm.

"Shawdforth wants a settlement."

"Shawdforth isn't going to get what he wants this time, my friend. Not unless you can convince your client to give Knight a lot more than you're currently offering."

"So what happens next?"

"I would have thought that obvious, unless, of course, your client wants to withdraw or modify his complaint. Knight's counter claim stands. We seek thorough investigation to gather the evidence needed to substantiate his allegations, and we ask for relief."

"You can't seriously intend to pursue that investigation, Karl?"

"Why ever not?"

"Because… didn't Gil want this shut down?"

"It's my matter, Ian. Knight is my client. I decide how to run my cases. And I'm not at all worried by that little rodent-like Vance."

"Some of his friends are important people, Karl."

"Then they'll fall hard if Knight's suspicions are founded. Sad, but, people with reputations to protect should keep their pants zipped and their noses clean." Karl was doing a sterling job of faking a calmness he didn't feel. Gil had done more than hint that obliging Knight could mean trouble, and Karl had a great deal at stake right now. But he had a professional obligation and he intended to fulfil it. If Knight's allegations proved founded, he'd be doing a service to the community, and to Australia's foreign relations, by lifting the lid on crime and closing The Fourth Floor down. Surely Gil would see the merit in that and he'd be appropriately rewarded. Winning this case should absolutely secure his partnership and his reputation among the legal fraternity.

He shook Johannsen's hand, but he kept his expression solemn and resolute. He strutted out and closed the door firmly behind him.

"Leaving early, Renee," Karl said as he passed his secretary's desk. "And don't make any appointments for tomorrow. I'm meeting a client at his office and I'll be busy most of the day. Call Max Knight for me, will you please. Tell him I need to see him tomorrow at nine… coffee shop at Wanderers Mansions."

He needed a brandy. He licked his lips in anticipation and drove down to Henry's, where he sat at the bar weighing the likely risks of the course he had embarked on. A young girl on stilt heels teetered about in a tight, short-short skirt and low-cut see-through top. Her black-mesh-stockinged-legs went all the way up to her bum, and her boobs wobbled and bounced as she polished the tables. She looked a prime target for Rush and his madam, but she was paid a minimum wage and picked up a few modest tips for waiting on tables. Men enjoyed the view, but at Henry's, nobody touched. Henry was protective of his girls—mostly young students working to pay for their tuition: wholesome kids, who preferred to cover up; kids with decent young lads for boyfriends and mothers and fathers who looked out for them.

Who was looking out for the kids at Wanderers? Someone should. The task was not one Karl welcomed, but Maximillian Knight had made it Karl Albrecht's business. No matter who was caught with their pants around their knees—and no matter what price they paid for their indiscretions—he intended to finish what he had begun. Closing an operation frequented by VIPs was going to make his reputation. Uncover a judge's or politician's dirty indulgence and he could be sure his would be a name they wouldn't forget.

#

"I need some solid evidence, Max. Hearsay doesn't cut it in a courtroom. You know that."

Karl was seated at one of the smaller outside tables in Wanderers Connect. At nine in the morning, the coffee was fresh, there was a full selection of breakfast rolls in the display cabinet, and most of the guests had already breakfasted and headed off for their day of touring, work or play. Max had ordered three long blacks and had a waitress prepare a tray of croissants, scones and bagels.

"I'm a fitness freak, Levi," Karl protested as Levi pressed him to do justice to the generous spread. "Any more and I'll have to double the distance I run every day for the next week."

Max helped himself to a third bagel and summoned the waitress to refill his coffee cup. He had pursued a healthy eating and exercise regime for more than 60 years, and at 82 was still both mentally and physically agile. But there was ample evidence, around his waistline, of recent over-indulgence. His face was liberally lined with the age and worry creases, and his huge grey eyes were receding into depressed sockets. But he could pass for 60 most days and in his business dealings, he had the zeal of a 25-year-old on a mission to take over the universe.

Levi was breaking a croissant into bite sized pieces and nibbling like a deprived child determined to make a treat last. There was no risk of him running to flab any time soon. He was a six-foot-three bean pole with a long, narrow face, small nose, and overly prominent ears—quite the opposite of the stereotype Jew, including in his slow and deliberate manner of speaking. Karl wondered idly if he was, actually, of the Jewish religion. He had never inquired of the guy's physical or cultural heritage and he knew virtually nothing of Levi's background. Not that it was of any relevance, but lawyers had a tendency to be curious about where people came from and what made them tick. Such knowledge was useful when you needed to identify the right button to push.

"We told you there was very little solid evidence," Levi was replying.

"Perhaps I should gather some for you… first hand?" Max's eyes glittered with feral enjoyment. "I'm told the entertainment is of the highest quality. However much I disapprove of it being offered in my building, I don't mind admitting I'd enjoy a taste of the delicacies."

"Don't even think about it, Max," Karl said sternly. "Your enemies would like nothing more than to find you in a compromising pose, and to make a class-A scandal."

"Get caught in that playground and your reputation goes down the toilet," Levi warned him, "and quite possibly your marriage with it."

Karl recalled the accusations Max had so vehemently denied. He'd been convinced of Max's integrity, but now he was tempted to ask, again, for the truth of the incident four years earlier. He knew it would take more than a mild interrogation. He'd have to state and explain his suspicions—reveal his discomfort at Max's joviality this morning. Perhaps he'd take Levi aside later, and confide his concerns. Meantime, trust was a two-way street. He'd stressed to Max and Levi the importance of full and honest disclosure, and they were sufficiently experienced to know the potential risks of holding back. He would put Max's levity down to high spirits. He'd throw out some bait occasionally and watch Max's reactions. But if it transpired that he was the dirty old man he'd been painted, Karl's association with him and his business was certain to end badly. He needed a lot more from Maximillian Knight than the generous retainer he was paying. He needed to cross the finish line squeaky clean and hailed as a champion of law and morality.

Not that morals were the primary issue here. Protecting the young, the naïve, was virtuous. Helping small investors who were getting burned was noble. But men could have their pleasure, and he didn't want to bring men of importance down. The goal was to elevate Karl Albrecht. This case was his big chance. Do it right, and he would go from good to great. He would be revered, honoured, and feared. He'd rise to the top in both the firm and his profession: maybe Chief Justice, or even into politics. Attorney General Karl Albrecht. That sounded good.

He checked his watch, jotted some notes of facts Max and Levi had disclosed during their hour-and-a-half-long breakfast meeting, and then he excused himself to return to his office and plan for what was perhaps the most daring manoeuvre of his legal career.

#

"Are we going house-hunting this weekend, darling?" Nata asked over Friday night dinner. She had cooked for him and served him pre-dinner drinks. He had been enjoying her attention and quietly congratulating himself on shaping his domestic world to suit his preferences. A smart, beautiful associate who worked beside him all day and came home at night to tend to his personal needs. The evening had been perfect until now, but he felt heat rising in response to her pleading, and he flared at her.

"I told you I was working on a very challenging matter. I don't have time to flit around the suburbs comparing views and sizes of dining rooms. I told you my requirements. When you find a house that meets my criteria, tell me and I'll find an hour to look it over—after I've confirmed the price and terms are acceptable. I'll be working most of this weekend."

"But we're going to Joe and Hetty's for Sunday lunch, and I don't want to eat and run. We should spend some time with them. They enjoy our company, and they don't have many pleasures in their lives apart from our visits."

"You can go. I'll be too busy."

"And what about the scan tomorrow morning? It wasn't easy arranging it for a Saturday morning, but I did because I wanted you there."

His heavy sigh caused her neck to jerk upward and her eyes went wide with surprise. "God damn it, Natalie. I have absolutely no interest in watching some doctor smearing gel over my wife's bare belly and moving a sensor about to make cloudy images on a screen."

"That sensor produces a photograph of our child, Karl."

He noticed that her eyes glistened and her voice was brittle, but he couldn't help that. The fact was, she exasperated him with her silly notions.

"It's barely more than a grey blob, Nat. You can bring the photos home to show me, but I really don't see what all the fuss is about. I'll take an interest after the child is born and, more particularly, after it begins to grow into something resembling a real person."

She looked as desolate as a deserted child, but instead of eliciting empathy, her look sent a red mist of rage burning through him. His patience had expired with her first pathetic pleading question, and he was really quite fed up with her sudden obsession with babies and domesticity. She was his associate, and right now he needed her undivided attention to her work. But painful experience had taught him that pushing her too far had unpleasant consequences. And clearly she was on the edge now.

"Sorry," he said insincerely. "Nat, please understand. I'm under a lot of pressure right now. I need your support—both professional and personal. I appreciate your attention tonight. This is how it should be, but without the demands please. It would please me greatly if you would attend to clearing up and then come and assist with some correspondence I need handled."

"On a Friday night?" she said. The brittle tone had elevated to a grating shrillness.

"If we get some files out of the way, we can spend some time together later this evening," he said, proud of the concession he believed he was making and anticipating a gentle massage, and perhaps sex if he could soothe her annoyance. "What if I agree to go to lunch on Sunday, but we tell Joe and Hetty I have to be excused as soon as the meal is done, and you can stay on?"

"Don't bother," she snapped. "I'd much rather go alone. In fact, I'm beginning to think I'd rather live alone with my child than cohabit with a man who has so little interest in home and family and regards me as his personal servant rather than his life partner. You're my boss at work, Karl, and I can tolerate your brusqueness and presumption there—barely. But I won't tolerate effrontery in my home. I will not stand for you ordering me to work outside working hours, and I won't respond to orders to cook or clean. Clear up yourself—or leave it. I'm going to take a novel to bed."

"At 7 pm?" He suppressed an urge to bellow. A fire was burning blue in his belly.

"At 7 pm." she replied, sounding disturbingly calm and controlled. "I feel like reading, and I think I'll make an early night of it. Baby needs rest."

He watched her stride toward the bedroom. He waited, thinking to call her back when she'd had time to calm herself, but he decided instead to go to her and try to reason. Maybe swallow his pride and plead a little; tell her he understood that her hormones were in disarray, and she was not herself. Things would return to normal in a few months. He'd have his wife and his associate back, and the sooner the better. But if, meanwhile, he promised patience… endeavoured to be a little more indulgent…

He eased the bedroom door open and stepped in tentatively. His anger leached away at the sight of her. She was seated at her dresser dabbing her face with cleanser. She had let her hair down and brushed it, and it spilled in burnished russet waves over her shoulders. She had changed into a satin and lace nightgown with a plunging neckline that revealed firm creamy mounds. In the mirror, he could see the profiles of her nipples. Her face was set, but even pursed and tight, her lips were oh so kissable. He went to her and put out his hand and the touch of her hair was like silk against his palm. He felt that familiar tingling and stiffening, but she shrugged his hand away.

"Don't, Karl," she snapped. "Get out. Go do your work."

"Natalie… sweetheart," he said, his voice soft and honeyed. "I'm sorry. I'm stressed, I guess. Overworked. Please try…"

"You're not 'stressed', Karl. You're an overly ambitious workaholic obsessed with your image and the trappings of success—an extremely arrogant male chauvinist clinging to some warped and out-dated notion that a woman should be your obedient and respectful servant, catering to all your domestic requirements during the day and massaging your dick at night."

An electric jolt zapped through his veins. He had never

heard her speak so coarsely before. "Natalie! How—"

"I said, 'Get out', Karl. Go. I told you I would not clear your dishes or help with your correspondence, and I most certainly will not have sex with you. Take a cold shower. Find a prostitute. Pick up a desperado. I don't give a damn. Just keep your prod out of my panties and your hands off me."

He felt his shoulders sag to a defeated slouch. Weakness washed over him. He paused for a moment, half hoping she would regret her harshness, but he caught a glimpse in the mirror of her steely glare and he shuffled away to his bar and his brandy. He drank until the room began to tilt irrationally and the furniture swam, and then he staggered to the lounge to drop his swimming head on the lace cushion cover Hetty had crocheted and thrust his legs, with feet still shod, across the arm of the sofa.

Karl had never before succumbed to the temptation to get so drunk he could not undress. The very thought of sleeping fully attired, and without the nightly ritual of showering and polishing his teeth, was abhorrent. But he slept there until morning. He woke with shirt and trousers creased and a thundering hangover that confined him to the bathroom until almost ten, by which time he had thoroughly emptied his stomach and all but choked on his apology and swallowed pride.

He went with her to the scan that morning, and in the afternoon they drove to the Bayside to inspect three houses she said were appealing. But her heart wasn't in it. On Sunday, he was pleased she opted to go alone to dinner at the cottage, and he turned his focus to the Knight matter. But a persistent hammering in his head and a nagging echo demanding further atonement distracted him to the point where he again turned to brandy for comfort. When she returned, she found him strangely maudlin and petulant, but she offered no comfort.

During the months that followed, Karl slept in his study or the guest room. At work, he was reserved and professional, but he took pains to be polite. Nata worked on his less significant matters, mostly independently. Karl invested countless hours poring over records of the history of Wanderers, studying legal precedents, discussing possible strategies with Max and Levi, and drafting and redrafting a voluminous and explosive brief.

At home, he tried hard to be at least moderately attentive and considerate. He could suffer her coolness and distance, but he was determined to preserve their partnership, if only to avoid putting his professional partnership prospects in jeopardy. He accompanied her to scans. He went with her to Sunday dinners at Joe and Hetty's. He went with her on house inspections, substantially setting aside all but his most significant wants and avoiding negative comments on the dwellings she favoured.

And Karl Albrecht began visiting The Fourth Floor.

#

Karl spent three tiring weeks working mainly on Max Knight's matter. He spent his days in the office poring over precedents and notes, and most evenings in his office at home, writing a draft brief. On Saturday nights, he told Nata he was meeting friends at Henry's Bar, and indeed he went there for a brandy and to use the men's room to change. But nine o'clock saw him, dressed in a carefully contrived disguise, dodging security cameras at The Fourth Floor. There, he watched films, pretending pleasure. He bought drinks for young girls and went with them to their rooms. He quizzed staff and "hostesses" surreptitiously. He took note of who patronized the facility.

He spent countless hours with Max and Levi, pumping for information and discussing strategies. The more time he spent investigating, the more convinced he became that this case was the answer to his prayers. It could make his career. He was accumulating incriminating evidence against powerful people... people who would pay generously to have information suppressed. He was billing huge fees, and winning this case would make his name in the world of corporate law. But better than that, he would be positioned to ask favours of the state's power brokers and to smile graciously and whisper a gentle caution if they dared refuse him.

Karl responded to the knowledge he was acquiring with mixed feelings. On the one hand, he delighted in the power it gave him. On the other, it aroused some fear. Some of what he saw excited and thrilled him. He couldn't help but enjoy the attentions of beautiful young girls. The place was luxurious and patrons were pampered. Some of his conversations with other patrons were stimulating. But much of what he saw shocked and repulsed. He was neither naïve nor narrow-minded, but the exploitation of young people was not something he could condone. He had a strong sense of what was right and wrong, and while he was content to play in the grey when he deemed it justified, he found the games depraved men played abhorrent. The fact that they were men of position and title made it far more disgraceful. He believed upper-class men should exercise restraint.

Despite the long hours and some stomach-turning revelations about men he had thought worthy of admiration, Karl was enjoying his work more than ever before. He was aware that he was neglecting Natalie, but she had plenty of distractions. She had cut back her work hours and he had purposely kept her out of the Max Knight affair, assigning her to routine work so that he was free to focus. He was deeply annoyed when she announced that she needed a break and told Gil she was taking leave for a few weeks, but he bit back his protests and agreed that a break would be good for her.

It was only when work colleagues began pointing to silly errors in the work she'd been doing, and commenting on her lack of focus, that he recognized the signs that his wife was suffering severe stress. He promised to work less and take more interest in domestic matters, but he urged her to seek help, telling her he was working on a very important and challenging case and he needed his associate back. It didn't go down well. She wanted him as a husband and father to her child. She wanted him to be invested in making a family home and buying nursery furniture.

Karl was frustrated and impatient, but he could ill afford to have her sink further into the doldrums, so he tried to be more attentive. She firmly rejected any sexual advances, but she protested strongly when he went out at night. Thankfully, she accepted meekly when he gently rebuked her and told her he had pressing work at the office, and she settled for his promise to make it up to her when this important matter was completed.

He eased back on the little disciplinary measures he had relied on to control her. He even returned her favourite painting—a wedding gift from a friend—to the place where it had hung. He had removed it after catching her staring at it, distracted, while working one evening. She had asked him, several times, where it was. She had even commented that she worried he might remove her child from her if he perceived the child was a distraction from work. He had hidden his pleasure that she understood, so well, that he would not hesitate to withdraw pleasures and treasures if she failed in her obligations to him. But now, it seemed necessary to be much more tolerant—indulgent even—to preserve the relationship that was so critical to his image.

He bought her little gifts. He made a valiant effort to be gentle and kind, engaging extra household help so that he had no need to make demands or to complain about her inattentiveness to domestic chores. His efforts seemed to achieve little other than to make him often tired and irritable, but he forced himself to focus on the promise of a big win and a long-coveted reward. He told himself once Nat was wife of a partner, and a mother, her health would be restored and she would once again be the wife and associate he needed.

#

Gil summoned Karl on Wednesday afternoon. He asked him to tell Natalie he would be late home and invited him to have pre-dinner drinks with him. He had important business to discuss and wanted to go somewhere where they would not be disturbed.

Karl entered the club feeling buoyant. The office had been buzzing all afternoon. Staff were certain Gil had made his decision, and were speculating on whom he would name partner. Karl had been the favourite for some time, but lately the challenges his private life presented made it hard for him to focus. Gil noticed. He was sympathetic, but he was not the sort to let sympathy influence a business decision. Karl, however, remained cautiously confident. Tonight, Gil would confirm his decision. His invitation was either for a celebratory toast or to console Karl. Karl had assured himself a hundred times during the afternoon that it was the former. Tomorrow, he and Gil would sign a partnership agreement. Tomorrow, his name on a sign would finally prove his worth to his father and to the world.

The club was in a converted warehouse basement. Candle lighting, raw brick and dark polished timber walls gave it warmth and the duskiness ensured privacy. Karl ordered a drink and sank into a deep leather chair in a quiet corner to wait. He didn't have to wait long. Gil strode in looking pleased with himself and the world. He spotted Karl and made his way over. Karl stood to greet him, then raised a finger to summon a waitress. He ordered Gil's favourite drink and a refill of his own.

Gil shed his jacket, loosened his tie, and flung himself across a plush leather sofa. "Long day," he said. "That drink is going to hit the spot, but I might need another to loosen up properly." He smiled at Karl. "So, how are things with you?"

"Fine. Just fine."

Gil raised his eyebrows.

"At work, anyway."

"And at home?"

Karl shrugged and took a long sip of his drink. The waitress came and deposited two glasses and two small bottles on a small round table between them. Gil waited patiently until she was gone.

"Natalie is pregnant, Gil. You know, surely? Hormones running rampant, emotions all over the place. The baby brain is driving me crazy. I need my associate back."

Gil chuckled. "It will get worse before it improves. Wait until there's a persistently screaming and shitting little bundle of delight competing with you for her attention. Get used to playing second fiddle, Karl. And to staring at the back of her head in bed. But family life has its compensations. Trust me on that point."

Gil downed his drink and spent a few moments in silent contemplation. The waitress came with fresh bottles and clean glasses, hovering for a moment to ask if there was anything else they needed. "Not right now, thank you," Gil said in reply, and waited patiently until she was out of earshot before proceeding.

"Karl, you're a talented lawyer and a hard worker. You've proved a great asset to the firm, and your work of late has proved your ability to focus and be professional even when your personal life is challenging. I'd like to reward your dedication."

Here it comes. He said he'd like to, not that he intended to. Is he about to apologize? Or—

Karl set his now empty glass down and poured the contents of a small bottle into the clean glass. He picked it up, but didn't sip. He looked over the rim at Gil, waiting… trying desperately to look unflappable, but painfully aware that his anxiety was tangible.

"The office staff have you marked as front runner in the partnership stakes," Gil laughed. Karl maintained a poker face, eyes focused on his drink.

"I know how much you want it," Gil continued. "I also know you've been feeling reasonably confident. But there is another contender and he's worthy. Phillip Sharpley is a good man, and an excellent lawyer. He's bringing in some good revenue."

Karl felt his chest deflate and his stomach sink. Gil was

studying him closely, measuring his reaction.

"The thing is, Karl, there's a matter you're handling that's causing me grave concern." Gil was silent for a while, appearing to be deep in contemplation. When he spoke, it was slow and thoughtful. "I can't consider offering you the partnership unless we can agree on the handling of that matter."

Karl's head shot up and his eyebrows lifted. He cautioned himself to exercise restraint now. *Act professional. This is no time for emotion.* But Gil had never interfered in the way he handled his matters. As long as revenue flowed and the firm's reputation was maintained, associates made their own decisions.

"And that matter is?" he asked, and deliberately lowered his eyes to stare into his drink again.

"Max Knight's affair," Gil said. "We talked about it briefly before. I told you I was friendly with Shawdforth. I understand Max refused to settle?"

"He did. I asked for more time to consider where we want to go with it. It's not an easy one, Gil." *An understatement, Karl, old boy,* he thought, and wondered how much Gil knew about the grubby dealings in that building and the corruption that was covering it.

"Karl, you and I… we've been around the traps. We know how the world works. Laws are man-made, and they change often. What's legal one day isn't the next, and vice versa. We swore to uphold the law, and we are both honourable men. But even the most honourable men have to make tough decisions sometimes… decide what's worth fighting for and what's better left be." He sipped his drink and gazed at Karl thoughtfully for a moment before continuing. Karl was privately nursing resentment at Gil's interference in his matter. Criticism, even only mildly implied, raised Karl's hackles. But Gil was the boss and the stakes here were high. Karl had mastered the art, long ago, of affecting humility and deference.

"There are some well-connected people doing things you

and I wouldn't do, and don't approve of." Gil was saying, "But how others conduct their sex lives really isn't our affair, is it? I mean, prostitution is legal if certain conditions are complied with. Homosexuals now have legal rights. We are much more enlightened in our attitudes toward sex and the various ways some people like to get their pleasure than we were even just a few years ago. I'm a happily married man and I get my pleasure at home. But it's not my place to judge what's acceptable and what's not, or to determine who should or shouldn't be permitted to indulge in particular types of sexual activities."

"The laws are quite specific, though," Karl said. "We may not have a right to judge, but we do have an obligation to uphold the law."

"At what cost?" Gil said. "Karl, you know how the system works. The powerful play games. The system was designed to allow them to. It was designed to serve the requirements of those who can attain titles and those who will pay generously for protection. The people using Max's building are paying generously, Karl. Very generously, because they have a lot to lose if it gets out what they get up to in there in the evenings. It's not just the legal consequences that worry them. Public opinion. We all know politicians and senior bureaucrats live in a fish bowl. Journalists follow them everywhere, sniffing at their backsides, ravenous for the smell of faeces. And if they get a whiff, the whole world knows. Politicians, judges, titled officials… they get caught with their pants down or their fingers in the cookie jar just once and they can kiss goodbye to their career, their reputation, and often their family as well. And you and I both know that no law will protect the whistle-blowers when someone who's used to life at the top gets kicked downstairs. Max's enemies… we don't want them to be our enemies."

"But kids are being exploited, Gil. Kids the same age as your boys."

"Kids who should still be under parental supervision,

like my boys are, Karl. But these kids are travelling the world unescorted. And they aren't naïve desperados who either consent or starve. They're living in luxury accommodation and paying top dollar for it. They're well heeled. Most of them have grown up privileged, in well-to-do families. And many of them are over eighteen." Gil put strong emphasis on his last sentence.

Karl frowned. "But they're still kids. How would you feel if your kids were targeted by creeps like Vance and his mates?"

"I can be totally confident that they would reject any offer. One, they don't need the money. I provide enough for their needs. And two, they've self-respect and moral fibre. Celia and I have made sure of that."

He sipped his drink and continued.

"These kids make a choice, Karl. And if we cleaned up Max's establishment, they'd make the same choices somewhere else. They have abundant opportunities. They'll do what they want to do, and nothing we do will stop them."

"Doesn't make it okay for grown men to take advantage of them," Karl said cautiously, silently praying he wasn't taking his opposition too far.

"No. It doesn't. I never said I approve or condone."

There was a moment of uncomfortable silence.

"This isn't an easy thing for me to say, Karl. I'm an ethical man and I respect the law. I have a wife and children who respect the law. But it's because I have a wife and children that I have no choice in this matter. And neither do you. So you're going to shelve your file notes and any brief you've worked on that supports Max's complaint. You're going to tell Max that his best course is to accept a settlement offer and get on with his business, and if he won't take your advice on the matter you will have to withdraw from representation."

Gil raised his finger to summon the waitress. She wiggled across, tits bouncing and bum swaying provocatively. She refilled their glasses and shot Karl a predatory smile. His eyes followed her retreating backside and he felt his prod stiffen. He excused himself, claiming to need the men's room. What he needed was time to compose himself, and think. He entered one of the cubicles and latched the door firmly and sat down, his trousers still fastened, and he dropped his head into his hands.

Resentment simmered, as it had a thousand times during his youth when his authoritarian father issued a command. As he had done then, he weighed the cost of non-compliance.

This matter was going to make my career... establish my reputation. And now? Take a chance on greatness but give up the partner status that means so much? Throw away all you've worked for and invite trouble you don't need?

Karl had done things he wasn't proud of. He'd looked the other way when a company director told a lie to raise more capital for a distressed corporation. He'd supported a loan shark's debt claims despite knowing the loan terms were unconscionable and the victims had been deceived. He'd signed off on shady deals. He'd levied fees for sitting on his hands and pretending a negotiation was happening, when in fact the other side had caved in without putting up a fight. He was success-hungry. And when his ethics clashed with his need to win or to satisfy a well-heeled client, ethics generally lost. He could lie and cheat with the best and go home congratulating himself and toasting his win. But this?

Gil's a decent man. If he can live with his conscience, why can't you? Nobody need ever know.

Gil was asking him to turn a blind eye to prostitution, using foreign teenagers—grown men getting their kicks from vulnerable teenage boys who spoke little English. He was asking Karl to forget that he'd uncovered evidence that titled men—men held in high esteem by the Melbourne public—sat in The Fourth Floor lounge at night watching hard porn movies, starring Asian children—children found on the streets and lured into selling themselves for the entertainment of perverts. Children whose hunger and illiteracy denied them choices, and whose poverty-stricken parents were powerless to protect their infants from the evil beasts who exploited them.

So what will you do, Karl? Sacrifice your future at Adams Bryant? For what? Do you seriously think you'll stop what these people are doing? You might drive them further underground... to another location. You might invite a late night visit... put yourself and your family in danger. But stop them? Not likely.

No contest, Karl. You heard Gil. Cover it back over and forget you ever peeked. And enjoy your promotion and the admiration and nice fat profits that accompany it. Lawyering is a dirty business sometimes. Live with it.

He stood up, took a deep breath, and strode out into the bar. The leather sofa gave off a pffffttttt as he dropped into its softness. He lifted his glass and sipped. Gil was watching him thoughtfully. He raised his eyebrows now, in question.

Karl took a deep breath and ordered his stirring conscience to be silent. His father would tell him lines must be drawn. Playing in the grey is a requirement of the profession. Every successful lawyer does it. But human beings should be treated with respect, whatever their station or circumstances.

Yeah, that's what Dad would say. But Dad abused his wife in front of her child, after humiliating and tormenting the child until his spirit was nearly broken. Dad ridiculed and abased the woman he claimed to love. Who was he to moralize and preach? Gil, on the other hand, was a good man... a man who treated his family and employees with respect and courtesy... a man who was respected and admired by clients, colleagues, judges and opponents.

"I respect your judgement, Gil," Karl said, hoping he didn't sound too patronizing.

Gil smiled broadly and extended his shaking hand. "I knew you'd see sense. Now, one more for the road—on me?" He raised his finger again and the waitress sashayed over with her boobs bouncing and her nipples standing proud behind a skimpy film of lace. Again, Karl felt the familiar twinge, and he pondered how long it was since he and Natalie had… Sometimes it seemed she wanted him, but then she would scream and flail and bid him leave and never return, and he would slink away and seek relief in the shower and tell himself, again, to refrain from complaint while she felt so fragile.

He chastised himself for ogling and determined to go home and pamper his wife a little. If he was gentler with her, and more attentive, perhaps he could bring her out of her state of misery. If only she would open up and talk to him. Clearly, an old wound had opened. She had nightmares in which she screamed at "Papa" in fear. She adored Joe. Joe would never have made her afraid. He should ask Hetty, again, to tell him about her early childhood. He would tell Hetty about the nightmares. Perhaps if she knew Nat's state, she might reveal the family's secrets.

Perhaps if he spent less time on The Fourth Floor… Would he concede to Gil's demands? This case had promised him fame and fortune. And now?

SEVEN

Nata sat in the kitchen window seat sipping tea and gazing down at the traffic below. She was feeling lazy, but so wonderfully at peace. There was a hint of movement in her womb, and she reached down to stroke her belly and whisper words of love.

"It's going to be wonderful, little one. For a time, I was so deeply afraid, but it's all good now. We are going to find a lovely home near the seaside with a big garden for you to play in. Your daddy is going to adore you as he adores me. He was stressed out, that was all. Too many things were happening at once and he let the pressure get to him. But he's better now."

He had been more loving, lately. So different. He never wanted to be like his father, but she supposed it was hard not mimic the behaviour that was modelled to him in childhood. How was he supposed to know how to be a good, kind husband, when his father treated his mother so badly? From what he told her, his father must be an awful man. *Poor Karl.*

She smiled a little as her mind wandered: those difficult mid-teenage years. She had long since lost that silly fear of Joe and learned, according to Hetty, to "twist him around her little finger." He spoiled her, Hetty said. But she was a good girl and she deserved to be spoiled. At school, she was a star pupil. At home, she was obedient and polite. She followed the schedule

Joe had set for her, studying for long hours and working hard at the many chores he set her. She went to church and to confession, and she prayed and read the Bible with him every evening. But the other girls had so much more freedom, and she began to resent the restrictions. She wanted to wear makeup and go on dates like the other girls. So she had rebelled, begun sneaking out at night to go to parties. Of course it wasn't long before she was caught out, and Joe had set her a long list of extra chores to do—especially onerous chores. He allowed her no time at all for leisure, and he subjected her regularly to stern lectures and warnings of harsher punishment if she dared to defy him again.

The punishment had continued for six long weeks, and she had begun to think he would never forgive her. But then, one night at dinner, he had set his newspaper aside and smiled at her. "Nata, you haf done your work well. You haf behaved, these past weeks, as a young girl should. I want you to promise me that if I gif you more freedom, you will respect me and obey my rules. You haf learned your lesson, yes?"

"Yes, Dad," she had replied meekly. "I'll be good. I promise."

"You are goot," he had replied, emphasizing the "are." "I understant temptations, Nata. I know it is hart to be different from other girls. But it is for best. One day you understand why. It is to keep you safe and gif you best opportunities, so you can be all you aspire to when you are grown, so that you don't slave in factory, so that you can choose a goot man to love… a man who appreciate you and treat you well. Goot men want girls who are pure and clean… goot girls who will raise goot children."

"I don't want to marry," she had protested.

"You think so now, perhaps," he smiled. "But someday. And if not, you must be able to make your own way in the world. You must be well educated and capable, so you can take care of yourself and achieve your career goals, yes?"

She had achieved her career goals. But Joe was right.

Eventually she had fallen head over heels in love. She was a good girl and a good man loved her. And now she was carrying his child and they were planning a move to a family home. There would be more children. And she and Karl would work hard to be the best parents a child could wish for. Like Hetty and Joe: firm, challenging, but ever so loving and indulgent when the children behaved well.

Their children would want for nothing. They would go to the best schools. They would take music lessons… and dancing, perhaps. There would be private tutors if they struggled with learning. But they would learn the value of hard work. They would be polite and respectful and obedient, like she was. There would be strict rules. But they would never suffer the humiliation and abuse that Karl had endured.

She put down her cup and picked up the newspaper, turning to the Real Estate Guide. She had circled some properties to inquire about. She would phone the agent later, and then, perhaps, she would go shopping again with Hetty. There was more nursery furniture needed. She could choose and have it put aside for her. They would find the right house soon. Karl agreed they must be well settled in before the baby arrived.

There were flowers on the table. Karl had brought them home yesterday. Flowers, with a little love note attached. She read it again and smiled. Perhaps she would go to the markets and find something special to cook for his dinner. A romantic dinner at home, by candlelight. They seldom did that. She was always too busy. Sometimes she thought it would be nice to have time for domestic pleasures… to make muffins and scones and grow roses. She was enjoying the freedom, with her hours cut back, to go on leisurely shopping expeditions, sit in the sun and read novels, walk in the park and watch mothers playing with little children.

She should return to full time work. She was well now. The firm needed her. Karl needed her. But she was certain the stress of a busy legal office was not good for her child. The baby needed peace and calm. It needed a mother who was relaxed and happy and planning for its future. It needed a mother who strolled around the marketplace choosing healthy foods, and who came home to cook… parents who sat down together at night to a healthy meal over which they talked happily about their plans for their child. It needed parents who relaxed together in the evenings and retired at a sensible hour, and…

That was the only dark shadow in her life right now. Karl wanted her. He had changed. He had assured her of his undying love and that he would always be faithful. He had stopped ordering her about and making demands, and he had stopped criticizing her at every turn. He was back to the considerate, attentive man who had courted her. But somehow she could not bring herself to respond to him. He was patient and understanding, but she knew he was hurt and frustrated. She had to find a way to escape the demons that haunted her and make love to him.

She went into the hallway and phoned Hetty. *Baby shopping, yes. The markets. And then take Hetty home and go back and search the lingerie stores for something super-special. Silky. Flowing. A deep plunging neckline, but modestly gathered over her belly and reaching to the floor.*

She would let her hair down and brush it until it shone. Soft music. Candles. Flowers. Nata, looking serene and beautiful. She would seduce her husband. She would shower him with kisses and massage his weary shoulders, and then she would ask him to follow her to the bedroom and she would remove her gown and lie down and draw him to her. Tonight, she would make love to her husband. And in the morning, she would set a date to return to full time work. He was making such an effort. She must pull herself together and be the wife he deserved.

#

Flowing turquoise chiffon draped over her bulging belly, finishing in a zigzag hemline about her swollen calves. Despite the weight she carried, Natalie Albrecht was floating on air. Handsome, debonair husband gently guiding her, his hand cupped under her elbow, she waltzed from the agent's office and into the smog.

The evening was perfect. She and Karl met at the Melba and dined on roast lamb and cremè brûlée. He was unusually attentive—still uncertain, perhaps, if he'd been completely forgiven—unsure how deeply she resented his aloofness. But she loved him, and she understood him. He had worked hard, these past few weeks, to rebuild what they'd had. She wanted a life with him, and tonight he had reassured her, again, of his affection and his commitment. Elated, she had called the agent from the restaurant and begged a favour. It was late, but…

"Come… right now," Kerry had replied cheerily. "I'll have the papers ready."

Natalie had pranced into the office and they'd signed the contract of offer on their dream home. The house would be theirs. Karl had agreed, under surprisingly mild protest, to offer the full asking price. He wanted her to be happy. If motherhood and a family could chase her demons away and make her glow…

Horns blasted. Lights flashed in the thick, dirty air. A soft drizzle of rain wet the footpath at her feet. Karl opened the door to the silver Porsche and helped her in. She buckled the seat belt across her bulging belly, then stroked it lovingly, whispering words of love.

The past few weeks had slid by in a haze of intense happiness. Butterfly flutters had graduated to solid thuds against the wall of her belly. In the middle of a critical meeting, she would catch a client staring and become acutely conscious that a tiny foot or hand was hammering away quite visibly. The blood had rushed to her face so that it shone radiant pink in the lamplight… a maternal glow. Hetty had delighted in telling her over and over how it enhanced her beauty, but Joe merely said, "Achh! Our girl was always beautiful. Nothing can improve on perfection." Bless him! Even Karl appreciated the fresh sparkle in her eyes and her radiant smile.

She and Karl had spent weeks, after a cautious reconciliation, house hunting. A modern fifth-floor city apartment with expansive balcony was wonderful for two professionals but totally unsuitable as a home for a child. They needed a playroom and a back yard where Joe could indulge his passion for building swings and a slide and sand pit. They needed a nursery to hold the tiny white rocking cradle Joe was lovingly crafting and the rocking horse he listed as his next project.

They had arrived, exhausted, at Joe and Hetty's house one Sunday morning, convinced that finding the right house was an impossible mission. And then Nata looked properly—perhaps for the first time—at the humble little cottage she had called "home" throughout a blissfully happy childhood, and she felt ashamed. She had touched her swollen belly and shed a silent tear for Hetty. Such a humble woman, and so innately kind and good. Blissfully content with so little; rich in ways Natalie could not help but envy, and Karl would never truly understand. It was Hetty's complete unselfishness—her devotion to pleasing her man and her child, and her quiet acceptance of Joe's uncompromising manner—that had brought Hetty contentment and the family peace and happiness. If Nata could just be more tolerant… more understanding… more giving… And suddenly, her criteria for a dream home changed. All that mattered was finding a home that pleased Karl. She and her child would be happy wherever her man was content.

#

The engine kicked over and roared into life and the Porsche glided neatly into an opening in the snaking line of headlights. Natalie nestled back into the plush-red-suede seat cover, closed her eyes, and let her mind drift.

She was mistress of a mansion. Perched regally atop a sharp cliff that fell away to a hidden quarter-moon beach, its vast living areas opened through huge sliding doors to a massive column-lined, lace-balustraded veranda on which she pictured herself lounging—infant in her lap and the roar of the sea in her ears—on long lazy summer afternoons.

The upper floor featured a luxurious master suite, complete with his and hers wardrobes, love seat in a bay window overlooking the garden, and massive spa beneath a window that overlooked the sea. A sunny nursery—with papered walls on which elves and mythical animals danced—awaited the arrival of the child that kicked and squirmed in her belly. Four more bedrooms, each with large dormer windows, begged for further family growth to fill them. In time, she might oblige. Karl was resistant, but he would adjust to the idea of a family in time.

Downstairs, behind the vast living and dining rooms, shiny kitchen cabinets were topped with rich blood red granite, flecked with black and gold. A huge twin oven, seven-burner hotplate, and a generously shelved larder begged her to indulge a desire to entertain, and promised Karl a chef's heaven in which to rustle up weekend breakfasts for his wife. No expense had been spared and no detail overlooked in the construction of this magnificent palace. Hetty and Joe would be wide-eyed and open-mouthed in undisguised awe. Her friends would be overcome with admiration and suppressed envy.

Natalie Albrecht had arrived. The little girl from the poor side of town—the child who called a humble worker's cottage home; whose foster father worked twelve hour days and mortgaged all he had to afford a modest private school education and send his only daughter to finishing school and university—had finally achieved her parents' and her own sweet, wonderful dream. Now she could give a little back to the mother and father who had sacrificed so much for her. She would send them on a cruising holiday. She would buy Hetty beautiful dresses. She would indulge Joe's lifelong craving for driving lessons and a sleek new car, straight from the dealer's showroom, in the exact colour of his choice.

Hetty would take on the job of housekeeper. Nata would hire a cleaner too, so Hetty's workload remained light. Hetty could care for her infant while she worked. Joe could tend the rose gardens and trim the thick green hedges. They could take one of the upstairs rooms for their own. Hetty and Joe would be reluctant to leave their little cottage. They loved their life there. Nata had loved it too—a simple life in a modest little home that overflowed with love. But love would fill this mansion too. Hers and Karl's love: their mutual love for the tiny life inside her, for Hetty and Joe, for friends, and for the wonderful life they had been blessed with.

Natalie Albrecht now had it all, and the still fresh signatures on that contract sealed the deal. Two months from now, her belly would shrink and she and Karl would carry their tiny child up the stairs to tuck him into the carved rocking cradle Joe was making. Her perfect world would be complete.

A horn blast snapped her back to the moment and she sat bolt upright. A car was bearing down on them. Lights flashed.

"Shit… watch it, bastard!" Karl leaned forward, pulling hard at the steering wheel. Brakes squealed. Tyres skidded on the wet bitumen. A loud thud, then the fearsome sound of crunching metal as Nata was thrust forward. The seat belt held, tightening across her belly as the air-bag exploded, but something was pulling her sideways. Her neck seemed to snap. There was an explosion of stars. She plunged into oblivion.

#

Sirens screamed through the night and red lights flashed. There was a crushing sound… grating metal… banging… commanding voices and hushed, fearful whispers. A hand slid behind her back. She felt strong arms about her. She was being lifted, carried. A white trolley was pushed beneath her and they lay her on it. She was pushed up a ramp and into a cabin. The trolley was clamped to a side. Doors slammed. A man strapped himself into a seat beside her. A damp cloth mopped her brow.

There was blood. The raw metallic smell of it fought with the sharp odour of disinfectant. Great, savage waves of pain rose up and consumed her. Spears dug into her lower back, and then the monster gripped her belly and ripped and tore.

Not yet. Please God, not yet. It's too early. But the waves of pain went on.

She was on a stretcher. There were straps across her chest and high, round belly. Men in white were wheeling her down a ramp and through huge glass doors.

Moonbeams danced over her briefly, then the starlit blackness above changed to stark white, and she heard the swish of wheels on polished linoleum. Glaring lights blinded her. A red light was flashing. Metal doors glided apart and the stretcher was pushed in. A rising sensation. She moaned softly as a recorded voice announced the floors. "Going up!"

The motion stopped. Doors hissed open and now the stretcher was being wheeled again. Fear gripped her and she cried out.

"Shhh! It will be all right, darling." For a sweet breath of time, relief swept over her. Karl's warm softness covered her. And then, the pain came again. Her piercing screams drowned out the sounds of skirts rustling and heavy steps pounding and wheels sliding on the scrubbed rubber floor. They drowned the confident, commanding voices; drowned Karl's gentle urging.

Strong hands rolled her over. She felt a stinging prick in her buttock. She rolled back and stared at bright lights.

Someone grasped her arm. There was a tapping sensation on the back of her hand, then a needle prick. Bottles were hung overhead. Liquids dripped through tubes connected to her hand. The pain was easing. Her eyes closed and she was drifting… weary, cold. She was drugged, dazed, hovering between a fogged awareness of now and the sharp, fearful realness of before;

hurtling down a black, swirling time-tunnel to a forgotten place.

The pain bit into her again, engulfing and possessing her. It cascaded through her body in explosive waves that swept her back into the darkness and the fear. Back to then.

That's it. Good girl. Up and down. Up and down. Squeeze.

"No..o..o..oo. Go away."

Squeeze harder. Up and down. Good girl. You must learn to please men.

"No...o...ooo. Let me go."

"Shhhh! It's OK darling. I'm here. Hold my hand. Good girl."

"No..o...o..oo..." The weak cry faded as another wave washed over her and swept her back into oblivion. Blissful oblivion: dark, quiet, and alone.

EIGHT

Nata half-woke. There were bright lights above. The room was icy cold, and yet she was perspiring. A tray of shiny instruments rested beside her stretcher. Her legs were held in stirrups above her, wide apart.

Karl hovered nearby, grey with anxiety. He swept his fingers through thick black hair and he tried to force a smile, but his eyes were dull with worry and his forehead was creased.

Where am I? How did I get here?

There was a faint, teasing memory of squealing brakes and blasting horns… sirens… being pushed on a stretcher by men running… someone stabbing a needle into the back of her hand and fastening bottles above her. Dark red blood trickled down a tube beside her. She remembered swimming in a sea of panic and clutching at her belly, praying desperate prayers… pleading to a God she didn't believe in.

A sudden stabbing pain gripped her.

"Breathe!" said a commanding voice. "Pant, Natalie."

She tried valiantly to pant. She bit down on her tongue to silence the scream that formed in her throat. The pain consumed her. And then it eased and she relaxed with a deep sigh. And then, just seconds later, it came again… and again… and again. The intervals between grew shorter and the pains grew more intense, until she was so overcome with exhaustion that she was certain her life must be about to end.

"The head is crowning, Natalie. Almost here, dear." A thundering in her head eased a little at the sound of the midwife's excited pronouncement. Was her baby alive? She struggled to remember more: traffic lights; the squeal of brakes; a car bearing down on them; Karl screaming; a loud thud; blackness.

There were loud sirens and red flashing lights and crisp, calm, reassuring voices. Strong hands. How long ago?

"Push. Push. That's it. Push hard," the midwife commanded briskly—as if she had any choice but to respond to nature's urging.

The contraction subsided. Nata gave a loud sigh and let her arms flop heavily by her sides. "I… I can't .. do.. this," she muttered, tears trickling down her cheeks.

"Just relax now, dear. The next contraction might just do it."

"You're doing really well, darling," Karl said, squeezing her hand gently. She tried hard to smile, but she lacked the strength even to squeeze his hand in response. Another wave of pain gripped her body.

"Push hard," the midwife commanded briskly. "I can see the head coming down. Push… push… keep pushing… harder, Natalie, harder."

She gasped, and she felt as though her lungs would burst. Sweat poured from her face. She felt something icy cold—metallic—pushed up inside her. Then a sharp, stinging pain as the midwife snapped surgical scissors shut.

"Almost there," she said reassuringly. Just a little cut to make more room for baby's head. A few stitches, later, but you'll heal quickly."

Karl mopped her wet brow and whispered comforting words. His hand was cold on her forehead and his face was pale. *Was he frightened? Karl was never frightened. He was always so strong, so in control.*

The medical staff were calm, confident, briskly efficient as they went about their tasks.

They've done it all so many times before. Like this? Of course. They've dealt with every kind of emergency. Premature labour, induced by trauma, is nothing new to them. Oh, God, why? Why couldn't it have been the beautiful, relaxed birth we planned?

Another wave gripped her and she tensed.

"Almost there," the midwife said. "One more big push, Nata."

She snatched a breath and threw every ounce of remaining strength at the task.

"Aaaaaagggggggggggghhhhhhhhhhhhhhh!"

The pain cascaded through her body in explosive waves that swept her back into the darkness and fear. Her piercing screams drowned out the sounds of activity… shut out the bright lights.

Up…down…up…down…squeeze. The monster was back. His harsh command echoed in her head again. She fought to focus, ordering the voice in her head to be still, to let her forget. *He is dead. The nightmare ended long, long ago… gave way to a beautiful dream life. I have a wonderful lover. I'm bringing a child into the world. Hetty and Joe will be grandparents. Ah… how Joe will gloat!*

"I can see the forehead, the eyes, the nose…" Karl shouted. "Oh my God, Nat! It's coming. Our baby's coming."

"Now pant, Natalie. Quick little breaths. No more pushing. Don't push," the midwife instructed.

"What's wrong?" Karl's voice was thick with fear.

"Shhhh…" the midwife ordered.

"His face is purple," Karl said. Nata began to panic. She heard a slurping and hissing sound.

"The umbilical cord is wrapped around the baby's neck,"

a nurse explained calmly. "We need to cut it."

Out of the corner of her eye, Nata saw the nurse pass something shiny to the midwife. There was a loud click, and then another. Nata felt gentle downward pressure on her belly as another contraction gripped her. There was a sudden hot gush of fluid and now her upper legs and the sheet were soaked.

Blood? Perhaps not. She was too weak and tired to care. She closed her eyes and allowed her mind to drift, but the voice came again and she snapped back to consciousness and struggled to stay in present time.

"Get some oxygen," the midwife shouted. "He's not breathing."

There was a loud, slurping sound. Out of the corner of her eye, Nata saw a nurse carry a tiny body to a table in the corner of the room. A mask was over the midget face and a tube trailed from it. The little body was blue and lifeless.

Karl's face was ghostly white. He was trembling. Nata felt nauseous. An icy terror gripped her, but she was so tired… too tired to think…too tired even to be afraid.

Karl's anxious pleading rang in her ears. "Is he going to live? Is he going to be all right?"

A cold swab rotated over her left buttock… a stinging jab. A hand pressed down hard, but there was no more pain. The arms rolled her onto her back and the drugs dizzied her into blessed unconsciousness.

\#

Wet copper hair fanned over the pillow. A nurse came to sponge her wet cheeks and forehead. She stirred slightly as another wave lifted her up, then gentle after-ripples carried her out… far out into the dark depths. She stood and looked down.

Karl came to hold her and give her strength. The sea split apart and they rose above it. She was there, with him. They were floating. She felt better now.

"My baby. Why won't they bring my baby?" Her voice was weak, but urgent.

"Shhh! Everything's all right. They'll bring him to you in the morning. You must sleep now." A hand gripped her arm, but it didn't hurt like before. The covers were stripped away. Two strong arms rolled her over. A hand lifted her nightgown.

"Noo…oo..oo, Papa. Please, noo…oo..oo."

#

"Ah, welcome back! How are you feeling?" The crisp voice was officious, but kind. Natalie turned her head and forced a weak smile.

"How about some breakfast, eh? Build your strength, love."

"My baby…"

"Soon, dear. They'll bring him soon. First, try to eat something. You need your strength."

Hands slid under her armpits and lifted her. Another pair of hands pulled a metal backrest forward and plumped pillows behind her. She was half-sitting, now, still faint and dizzy, but the room was slowly coming into focus. Flowers. Balloons. Cards. Women in striped uniforms, bustling about checking monitors.

"You were in an accident, dear. It brought on premature labour. Don't worry. You're in good hands here. You're going to be just fine."

She struggled to remember: She hit her head. There were sirens. Her waters broke, and then there was blood… so much blood.

Someone pushed a trolley up close to her chest and deposited a tray. A nurse lifted the lid. The smell of bacon. Suddenly, she was ravenously hungry, but the meal was unappetizing. She sipped juice and nibbled toast. Her eyelids were heavy. She was swimming again. The rippling waves came to lift and rock her. She was back there now, eating Hetty's pancakes.

#

"Breakfast, Nata. Hurry along now. You don't want to be late for school."

A serving platter was stacked high with pancakes. There was bacon sizzling in the pan, and Milo: thick, rich steaming-hot Milo with loads of chocolate lumps on top, just the way Nata liked it. Her schoolbooks rested in a neat pile on the end of the table. There was a lunch box on top, filled with treats: dainty sandwiches filled with her favourite cold cuts; fruit, muffins or fruit slices, three chocolate mints. Always three chocolate mints. Three after lunch and three after the evening meal and a small bar of chocolate or a chocolate ice cream on Saturdays. There was always cake in the afternoon, too, when she came in from school, cake and a giant hug.

Nata was silent through breakfast. She enjoyed it. When she was done, she carried her plate and cup to the sink and said, "Thank you. That was delicious." She ran to fetch her brush and ribbons and Hetty plaited her gorgeous copper hair for her. Hetty said she looked smart in her school uniform. After four months with the Dreyers, she was filling out. The dullness was gone from her eyes. There was a hint of sparkle in them, and her cheeks were rosy.

She still trembled and cowered sometimes, when she thought she might have done something to displease. But Hetty reassured her that no-one would ever hurt her again… that she was safe and loved in this house. She wanted to trust them, but there was no certainty in her life. Joe terrified her. Hetty told her he was a kind and gentle man, but still, he was a man. She pulled away whenever he approached. She took pains to be obedient and polite whenever he was near. She would not give him cause to want to punish her. But Hetty was there to protect her. Hetty assured her she would never let anyone harm her.

Nata collected her schoolbooks and strode off down the hallway. Hetty followed her to the door and watched her skipping up the street. The school was just a block away and Hetty watched her until she reached the gate. Friends ran to greet her. She liked school. She was a good student. Her teachers liked her. Everything was good in her life now, except that she was afraid of Joe. He tried so hard to win her affection. She didn't know why she feared him so. He'd never given her cause.

She had run away, months later, when Hetty left her with him one day. Joe was enjoying a public holiday and Hetty had some "women's business" to attend to in the city.

"I have to go into the city today, sweetheart," she told Natalya.

"I can come with you," Nata replied eagerly.

Hetty shook her head. "I'm sorry, little one. But this time, you must stay at home with Joe. He'll take good care of you. I've left some pie in the refrigerator for your lunch. I'll be back late this afternoon and I'll bring you something—a little reward for being a good girl while I'm gone. You will be a good girl for Joe, won't you?"

Nata frowned and hung her head.

"Please, Natalya," Hetty implored. "Why do you resent Joe so? He loves you, little one. Has he ever been unkind to you?"

She shook her head.

"Well, then?"

Silence hung heavily between them. Nata was sullen. Joe watched and listened quietly. He looked sad.

At last, Hetty shrugged and reached for her coat.

"There's nothing else for it, then. You will just have to get along with Joe for a few hours. It will be good for you, for both of you. It's time you learned to be friends. It's time we began behaving like a real family. Joe is your father now, and it's time you started to treat him like a little girl should treat her daddy. He's a good man, Natalya. He's a wonderful father. You couldn't wish for better."

Hetty left then. Natalya watched her walk to the bus stop

on the corner, then she went to her room to play. She kept the door tightly closed. At lunchtime, Joe called to Natalya. She gave no response. He called again. She ignored him. He went to her door and tapped lightly. Then he opened the door and entered. She cowered in a corner, hugging herself and trembling like she always did when he approached her. He told her she must come and eat. She buried her face in her shoulder and pushed closer to the wall.

Joe moved toward her, cautiously. Suddenly, she leapt up and pushed past him. She ran to the front door, tugged it open and charged through, slamming it behind her. By the time he got to the door, she was already out the gate and running. He chased her, but she was lightning-fast on her feet, and he was aging and unfit. He was no match for her. He had to let her go.

#

"Natalya?"

She remained still. She had been there for hours, huddled under the bus stop seat. Hetty had dismounted the bus and was about to start for home, but then she saw her there.

"Oh dear Lord in heaven! What on earth? Natalya, love, come out of there. Come!"

Natalya remained motionless, sobbing softly.

"What happened, my little one? Whatever is the matter? You'll be catching your death of cold huddled there in the night air after a sunny day. Come on out now. Whatever it is, I'll take care of it. It will be all right, I promise."

Nata remained motionless, and Hetty put down her bags with a heavy sigh. She seemed to think for a while, perhaps pondering how she might manoeuvre her generous form under the seat to draw Natalya out. She scrounged in one of the bags and extracted a small package. "Look, little one! I brought you something special. You must come out, though. I won't pass it to you in there."

Nata replied with a soft whimper, and remained still.

"Oh, Natalya, please! Please come out!" Hetty's frustration showed in her tone. She sighed deeply and shifted her weight. At last, she gathered her bags and started for home, leaving Natalya behind.

Natalya did not follow. She wanted to, but fear gripped her. She was afraid of staying under that seat all night too, but that fear was less than her fear of Joe. He would be angry with her for running away. He might punish her, like Papa used to. Joe never had, but she'd never run away before.

Dark was descending when Hetty came back. Deep down, Natalya had known she would, but she feared Joe would be with her. He wasn't. She came alone. She was carrying a little bag. She sat on the bus seat and opened it, drew out a banana, and started to eat.

"Would you like some of my banana, Natalya?" she asked. "Or perhaps you'd rather some cake? I brought chocolate cake. I know it's your favourite."

Natalya hesitated for a moment, then extended her hand, reaching up to touch Hetty's knee.

"Oh, no. You have to come out to eat," Hetty said. "You can go back when you've finished, if you want to. But you must come out and sit beside me if you want food."

Natalya hesitated a while, but eventually she crept out and perched beside Hetty. Hetty gave her cake, and a banana. She ate it quietly. When she was almost done, Hetty rose and gathered her belongings. "There's a nice cosy bed at home for you, and I brought you a present, just like I promised. But you will have to come home with me and apologize to Joe, then promise never to run off like that again." Hetty's tone was kind, but firm. Natalya sat in glowering silence, staring directly ahead, lips pursed, cheeks puffed in a pout.

"I know it's asking a lot, Natalya," Hetty said. "But you gave us such a fright. Joe is dreadfully upset. He loves you,

you know. He couldn't bear for anything bad to happen to you. Neither could I... Oh, Natalya, darling, we just want to love you and care for you. Won't you please let us? If you're frightened or upset, talk to us. Let us help you."

Natalya sat a moment longer, still silent. Hetty sighed and started to walk toward home.

"Well, I have to go home and fix supper for Joe. If you stay, I'll come back in the morning with some food for your breakfast. Will you be all right here alone? You won't be frightened of the dark? I would be. And it might get cold too. Perhaps I should leave you my coat?"

She had gone about half a block when Natalya decided to follow. She walked slowly at first—hesitant, unsure if she wanted to stay or go. But then she broke into a run, and Hetty turned and held her arms out and caught her. She fell against Hetty's skirt, sobbing. Hetty held her tightly for a time, then she gently eased her away, turned her around, grasped her hand, and they headed for home.

Joe was in the living room when they arrived home. Hetty took Natalya to the kitchen and fixed soup and sandwiches for their supper. She called Joe to come and eat with them. Natalya quailed when he sat across from her. His expression was solemn, but he said nothing. When the meal was done, she went to the living room to read. Hetty came with her knitting. Then, after a while, Joe came in carrying a little sack. Opening it, he pulled a package from it and turned it over twice in his hands.

"A little something I found for you," he said, depositing it on the table near the sofa.

Hetty smiled at him. "Yet another gift? Another book, I'm guessing. You spoil her, Joe."

"The Magic Pudding," Joe said, grinning broadly. "Man in book store say all children her age love it."

"Thank you very much, Mr. Dreyer," Nata said, without raising her eyes from the package. "You are very kind to me."

He watched as she tore open the package and struggled to conceal her delight. Joe reached across the table to touch her hand, but Hetty shook her head and he pulled away. Natalya recoiled, pressing her back against the chair and her hands into her lap.

"I could read it with you if you'd let me," Joe said hopefully.

"I can read," Nata said, clutching the book to her chest.

Hetty went out for a moment, then returned to place a cup of cocoa before Natalya. She gently removed the book from her clutches, placing it on the sideboard. Joe's expression, when he glanced up at his wife as she placed his coffee cup before him, was sad. He sipped his coffee in silence.

Natalya finished her drink, then picked up the book and went to her room. Hetty went in, later, to tuck the covers about her and say good night. She was hugging her large panda tightly. Hetty kissed her cheek. When Joe tiptoed to the doorway, Nata smiled and extended her arms toward him. His shoulders lifted and his face flooded with joy. He came and sat beside her, and she touched his arm hesitantly. He stroked her hair and kissed the top of her head. She sat up and laid her head against him, and he held her gently.

"I luff you, my little one," he whispered into her copper curls. "Please don't be afrait of me. I wout never hurt you."

"I love you too, Mr.... um...," she swallowed hard. "Joe," she said. "I'm sorry I ran away. We can read together tomorrow if you want."

He hugged her hard. He rose and stood gazing at her for a moment, and under his bushy eyebrows his eyes were filled with mixed relief and rapture. Then he and Hetty tiptoed away, gently pulling the door closed behind them.

#

Natalie woke in a hospital bed, confused. Karl was there. He woke her from her dreaming with a kiss. Why was she here? She struggled to remember, but the past was a fog. She only knew she was hurting… down there.

Perhaps Joe hurt me? Punished me for running away. Or for smashing Hetty's doll?

She had been so afraid of Joe. She had taken care to be ever so polite and proper and obedient when he was near. But Joe would never hurt her. Joe loved her.

Perhaps Papa came back, and they told him, and he punished me. His punishments were always harsh. Papa warned her to be good. He'd said he'd come back for her, and that Joe would tell him if she had misbehaved.

But Karl is here now. Karl would not have let Papa hurt me.

Suddenly, she was hurtling down a time tunnel. Her memory returned. She gazed up at Karl. Her smile was radiant. Her eyes danced and her face glowed.

"We have a son, Karl," she whispered.

Her words drifted, hanging in the air. He patted her arm and forced a smile, but there was something in his eyes: something sinister and fearful. All the pleasure drained out of her as though it was her blood. In its place was a cold, icy feeling of deathly despair. He stroked her gently and she drifted away again.

When she opened her eyes again, he was leaving. He left the door ajar. Fear came in and took his place beside her.

NINE

Her doctor prescribed tranquillizers. The hallucinatory episodes ceased.

As she lay there, hour upon hour, her arms aching and her heart thumping against her ribs, an implacable commanding voice in her head screamed, "Bring me my child; let me hold my baby." But they would not. They would tell her only that he was "progressing" and that she needed to build her strength. A dark, numbing bleakness washed over her, and a snaking coil of icy fear filled her belly.

They brought a meal, but she pushed it away. "You need your strength, Natalie," they chided her and passed her a menu and a pencil, urging her to choose something that appealed. She left the menu blank, turned over, and pretended sleep.

Hetty brought her a food treat to tempt her, and she sat with her, uttering words of comfort, trying to distract her with trivial conversation. She was grateful for Hetty's company, but she rejected the food and she begged her not to talk. She pleaded with her to appeal to the doctors to bring her child, but the doctors said the baby could not be moved and Natalie needed to gain more strength.

The Neonatal Intensive Care Unit (NICU) was two floors above. When—on the second day—the doctors judged her strong enough, an orderly wheeled her bed to the elevator and she and Hetty rode up together. They pushed her bed down a long corridor. Room after room was lined with little plastic crates in which lay tiny babies—some smaller than a can of soda—connected to arrays of wires and tubes, with beeping monitors above them flashing graphs and statistics. Nurses bustled about, pouring milk into feeding tubes, adjusting valves and wiping tiny eyes and mouths with cotton balls.

The walls were decorated with dated photographs of infants—some still with tubes attached and funny little caps on their heads—sprawled across the chest of a smiling, hospital-gowned mother, with a beaming father standing behind. Stuffed toys and mobiles hung over some of the cradles. Gowned visitors sat beside the little crates gazing in—worried, frightened, happy, bland. The mixture of expressions encompassed every emotion.

They pushed her bed into a room and up beside a crate labelled, "Albrecht, Sean. Mother: Natalie. Father: Karl. DOB: 11/7/09."

He had weighed, at birth, just under a kilogram, and the sight of him alarmed her. He was barely as long as her outstretched hand. A machine breathed for him. Sensors taped to his tiny, bare chest connected him, via wires, to beeping monitors and flashing screens. A bandage stretched across his belly. His tiny arm appeared to be in some kind of splint, and a light was taped to one foot. She turned away from him in horror, but Hetty made her turn back and calm herself. A nurse opened a tiny trapdoor and, at Hetty's urging, Natalie reached in and laid her hand on the tiny child's belly. It was warm and soft to touch. She remained there for ten minutes, and then the orderly came to take her back to her room.

Each morning, after that, she was taken up in a wheelchair and allowed to stay an hour. On the eighth day, Hetty supported her as she eased herself up from her bed and practised a slow and hesitant walk in the hallway. On the tenth day, she walked with

Hetty to the elevator and they rode up together. She scrubbed her hands and arms at the sink near the nursery entrance, and she donned the shapeless green-linen robe they handed her. She spent the morning beside Sean's crib, sometimes whispering to him but mostly staring silently, consumed with worry for him... aching with love.

Each day, from that day on, she watched the sleeping baby, hour after hour... day after day. Now and then, she would open the little round trapdoor and put her hand in and rest a finger on the boy's tiny abdomen.

Hetty sat beside her, knitting—needles clicking in time with the monitor's beeping. She knitted booties and tiny jackets and little caps. When Nata protested that Sean might never wear them, Hetty replied calmly that there were plenty of babies in need, but she wasn't giving up on Sean and neither should Natalie. Maybe she might pray? But Natalie's faith had left her long ago, and seeing her baby so gravely ill did nothing to revive it.

Hetty took her for walks down the hallway to the NICU visitors' kitchen. The walls were lined with photographs and letters of thanks from grateful parents. Photos of healthy toddlers were captioned with notations of gestation weeks, birth weights, and time in NICU. Here and there, a photo was captioned with a death notice and a thank you to dedicated staff for trying so hard to save a life. But these were few, and Hetty urged Nata past them and on to a report of another happy outcome.

"Michelle, age 3. Born 29 weeks gestation, 815 grams. Forty-nine days in NICU. Now a healthy, happy toddler with no disabilities or ongoing health issues. Thank you NICU staff. Love, Kevin and Anna."

"Damien (712g) and Jason (695g). Identical twins. Born 30 weeks and 2 days gestation. Thirty-seven days in NICU. Pictured celebrating their second birthday. Weak eyesight, but otherwise perfectly healthy. Sincere thanks to all the doctors and nurses who cared for them. Jeff and Patricia."

"Catherine Eliza. Born 890 grams at 32 weeks gestation. Eighty-two days in NICU. Now a healthy four-year-old. Our gratitude defies words. Thank you NICU staff for your dedication, your skill, and your compassion. Ian and Jennifer."

The posters numbered in the hundreds. Babies as tiny as 480 grams and as early as 22 weeks gestation had survived, most with relatively few ongoing problems. NICU was a place of miracles. The stories gave Natalie momentary glimmers of hope, but they could not sustain her. Back in her bed each day, Nata wept silently, and Hetty stroked her hair to give her comfort.

Karl came each evening. He sat with her, mostly in awkward silence. When he talked, he spoke about the weather, or relayed information about the progress of some trivial matter. She had no interest, and she was relieved that he had the good sense not to stress her by mentioning the more challenging cases. Once or twice, she tried to talk about the baby's progress. She was learning to interpret the graphs and numbers. She knew the ideal temperature in the humidicrib and the optimum blood pressure, heart rate and breathing pattern. He showed no interest.

He did not go to the nursery. When she spoke of the child, he sought to change the subject. If she persisted, he told her, coldly, that he thought it best she not think about the baby—not let herself form an attachment. "It might not survive, Natalie," he said. "Best we don't grow any hopes that might be dashed."

But Natalie had grown hope. After the first week, she compelled herself to eat three balanced meals each day, for Sean. Six times a day, she attached a pump to her breast and watched in frustration as the watery milk trickled slowly into a bottle. She measured the quantity, and she wept when there was insufficient for the tiny infant's needs. A fragile bubble of joy erupted inside her when she saw them take the carefully labelled bottle and fill a vial atop a tube into his abdomen. At least she was able to give him sustenance.

On the twenty-ninth day, they told her the child needed

her touch. "Skin to skin," the nurse explained. "We know, from research, that a mother's touch does much to help a baby thrive." They arranged the oxygen tubes and adjusted the cords and wires. They sat her in a vinyl recliner chair and flicked the lever to raise her legs. They plumped pillows and arranged them behind her.

"Comfortable, Nata?" the nurse asked, smiling.

"Very, thank you."

"Undo your gown and bra," she instructed.

They laid the naked child on her bare breast and covered them both with a blanket. Her heart leapt with joy. She sat stroking him and talking to him for twenty minutes, and then they lifted him carefully into the crib, adjusted all the paraphernalia again, and sent her off to the lounge to take a cup of tea with Hetty.

"They want you to hold him too, Karl," she told him that evening. "It's an incredible feeling. There are no words to describe the magic. You must come tomorrow, during the day. Arrange it with the nurse on duty."

"I prefer not to, Natalie," he said tonelessly, his cold expression filling her with a dark, numbing bleakness.

She asked the doctors and nurses, daily, for assurances that her child would survive. They told her he was in no imminent danger. She begged for more information. They told her they could give no guarantees. His low tone and inability to breath unaided gave cause for concern, but it was too early for a diagnosis.

"We just have to wait and see, Mrs. Albrecht," the doctor told her again and again. "Just wait and see."

"He was very premature, Mrs. Albrecht," the nurse told her. "They'll run some tests soon. But he needs time to grow and gather strength."

"But will there be lasting damage," she asked over and over.

"We can't tell. We have some concerns. We are usually able to wean them off the oxygen sooner—get them breathing independently. But he's growing and gaining weight. We'll know more when they run tests. For now, we just have to be patient."

Natalie was anything but patient. She wanted answers, and she wanted them now. But her persistent badgering of the staff produced no more than cautious remarks that his progress was causing concern, but only time would tell.

#

Weeks flew by. Natalie went home. Sean stayed. Doctors tried to be reassuring, but they had warned that Sean's seizures, breathing difficulties, and abnormal temperament suggested possible brain injury.

Karl had arranged for their belongings to be moved to their new home. He talked happily of the amenities the new home offered, and of the status he believed its presentation conveyed. Nata could garner no enthusiasm.

They wheeled her to the hospital doors, and dispatched Karl to bring the car so that she needn't walk far. Her legs were still weak and she tired easily.

While she waited at the door, a new mother emerged on her husband's arm. Her husband carried the child in a carrier. It was just days old. The mother held a bunch of pink balloons, printed with the words, "It's a girl." Behind her, an older woman carried a navy-blue overnight bag and a huge bunch of pale pink lilies. An elderly man drove up in a slick silver Camry, alighted, and opened the rear door of the car with a flourish. Nata watched as the younger man carefully transferred the baby from carrier to car seat, wrestling with the safety straps. The older woman helped the young mother around the car and into a seat beside her child. She reached across and stroked her baby's head.

It should be like that for me. Karl should be strapping Sean into his car seat. I should be taking my baby home to lie in the little crib Joe made for him. I should be waking to his cry at two in the morning and hastening to comfort him. I should be putting him to my breast six times a day and bathing him in the morning, and changing him, and reading to him and stroking him, and taking him for walks—pushing his pram along the streets and through the parks. I should be taking him to visit Joe and Hetty and welcoming friends to admire him.

The wait seemed to go on forever. The baby was safely settled in its seat now and the husband checked the straps again, then rounded the car to slide into the back seat next to his wife. The older woman folded herself into the front seat and the older gentleman took the wheel. They waved as they departed, and tapped the horn lightly. Smiles split their faces almost from ear to ear. Their eyes were alight with joy. The balloons pressed against the window, broadcasting their happy news to all the world. Bystanders smiled and waved and shouted their congratulations, but Nata could not force a smile. Jealousy ripped at her heart and black desolation and despair washed over her. She turned away, fighting to hold back tears.

When Karl came, at last, he found her with her head in her hands, weeping silently but inconsolably. He drove a sparkling new white E250 Mercedes.

"A gift for you, my love," he said, opening the passenger side door. "The Porsche was a write off, of course. I thought this might help console you."

"A car, Karl? A car instead of a baby to take home? Do you honestly think I give a damn about a motor car?"

He lifted her from the chair and supported her for the few short steps to the car, and he helped her in. He checked that she was comfortable, then closed the door and left her there while he pushed the wheelchair back inside. And then he came to sit beside her and gaze at her a moment, thinking.

"Nat," he said softly, "What has happened is a terrible tragedy. It will take a long time to forget the pain. But we mustn't let this break us. We have to be strong, and go on. We can try again… have a healthy child. Maybe two or three."

She turned to him, eyes blazing. "And what about Sean, Karl? What happens to him while we are playing happy families with his healthy siblings?"

"Sean?" he said. "Must we call him that?"

"It's his name. And…" Natalie wasn't sure where the words came from, but she found herself saying, "he's our gift. From…God."

"But when we chose it, we didn't know… gift from God, Nat? Hardly! For a time, it seemed unlikely he'd survive. I dared to hope. But he seems, now, to be getting stronger. He'll be here for some time yet, though, and when he leaves here—if he leaves—he will go to a home where they care for cripples. And we can get on with our lives. Apart from the expense, he will not be our responsibility. We can put him out of our minds, and get on with living."

"They haven't even given us a firm diagnosis yet, let alone predictions for his future, but already you're planning to discard him like a piece of rotten fruit. He's imperfect. Cast him out. Find a replacement that meets your quality standards. Even change his name to something that reflects your dislike. You are just like your father. Everything in your world must pass your quality control test.

"You're a cruel, heartless, unfeeling bastard, Karl Albrecht… and I despise you."

"Shhh! You're distraught my darling. It's understandable. You've been through a great deal. It will take time, but the pain will ease. And when you're ready…"

"When I'm ready for what, Karl? To have your designer baby… the perfect child you craved… one you can accept, because your friends will admire it and it will grow to fulfil your ambitions for it? One you can dress up in fancy clothes and be sure he won't walk with a hobble or lean to one side and drag a limp arm along behind it?"

"Surely you want to raise a healthy child, Nat? Surely you

want a normal infant to love?"

"I love Sean."

"But loving him will bring you nothing but heartache. We must learn to disconnect, my love. It's the only way to get through this. And we must go on living, Natalie. We can't let this be the end of our dream of family life."

"What dream was that, Karl? I seem to recall you bullying me to have an abortion… telling me fatherhood didn't figure in your life plan."

"And how I wish you had, my darling. Oh, how I wish you had."

#

The clock had struck seven. The city was lighting up for the night. She was preparing to leave the hospital, and she was bothered that Karl would be angry… again. He saw no need for her to linger in the NICU nursery after dark.

"There are nurses to care for the boy," he had chided her. "You should be home making dinner, and you need your rest."

He was a capable cook, but he protested that his work was pressing and he hadn't time for domestic chores. With her at home, not working, he saw no reason why she shouldn't perform her "wifely" duties. He had claimed to despise his father, but it seemed he had no qualms about mimicking his chauvinistic attitude.

"You're turning into your father," she had said one evening.

"Nonsense," he had replied. "I could never be like my father. But I am a man, and most men expect their wives to pay a little attention to domestic needs. And most wives recognize an obligation to pay appropriate attention to their husbands. In future, you will tidy the house before leaving for the hospital, and you will return by five and prepare our dinner."

His stentorian tone set her blood boiling, but for the next few days she had complied. And now he would be raging mad because she had not.

"Mrs. Albrecht?" A nurse approached her as she neared the door. "The medical team want to arrange an appointment with you and your husband. Tomorrow, at ten, if that's all right?"

She nodded, and thanked the nurse, mechanically, hoping it wasn't too apparent the advice left her awash with fear. She found herself gripping the wheel, white knuckled, as she drove home. She sat a while in the car, searching for composure. Then she braced herself for Karl's rebuke.

"You're late again," he said as she entered the kitchen. His tone was taut and his look accusing. "I made my own dinner. There's left-overs in the fridge if you're hungry. I've got work to do." He started toward the study.

"The doctors have asked us to meet with them tomorrow," she said, "Can you make a 10 am appointment, or should I ask them to arrange another time?"

"Do I need to be there?" His voice resonated irritation.

"Of course you need to be there, Karl. It's about our son."

"I'm quite sure you are capable of answering any questions they have and relaying to me any information they provide. I've got clients to attend to, Nat. The firm has one associate out of action, and I have a partnership offer pending, in case you've forgotten. I have professional obligations and they take priority over domestic matters. They *should* take priority over preparing meals, given that I currently have a stay-at-home wife. But she seems incapable of arranging her busy schedule to accommodate her husband's needs."

"Karl," she said, struggling to sound calm, "I can deal with your chauvinistic arrogance and your absurd and out-dated misconceptions about marital responsibilities. I can even admire your diligence and ambition when it comes to work. But I cannot and will not tolerate you putting aside your obligations to our child. You will be at the hospital tomorrow at 10. And as of right now, you will discontinue behaving like your selfish asshole of a father, or I will start divorce proceedings and you can kiss your precious career aspirations goodbye. I won't hesitate to air all our dirty laundry publicly, and I'll make damned sure Gil knows exactly what kind of narcissistic prick you really are. He might admire your dedication to your work, Karl, but he's also a devoted family man with morals and a conscience."

She was conscious that her voice had risen to the shrill tones of a fishwife, but she also noted that Karl had paled. He was staring at her in shocked silence. She turned to fill the kettle and set it to boil, spooned coffee grains into a cup and turned back to glare at him questioningly.

"I'll have Renee rearrange my appointments," he said, his voice low and tremulous.

"I'll see you there at 10," she said. "And I'd appreciate it if you'd sleep in the guest room tonight, since you'll be working late. As you rightly pointed out, I need my rest. I don't want to be woken when you decide to retire."

He stood there a while, looking distressed and uncertain. She ignored him, and went about preparing coffee and a snack. Finally, he shrugged his shoulders and went to his study, but he didn't walk with his usual confident stride. His shoulders slumped and his head hung low.

#

On August 28th, six weeks and six days after Sean's dramatic entry into the world, Natalie went in early to the NICU. She helped them bathe Sean, and she fed him. She gazed at him a while, and then she went to the visitors lounge and made coffee. At precisely 10 am, she sat, white faced and trembling, in a small meeting room facing a team of medical professionals and a hospital social worker. Karl arrived late and flustered.

"I've asked our social worker to join us," the specialist explained, "because your response to Sean's diagnosis, and the effect of it on your relationship, is every bit as important as the treatment program we elect to follow."

Karl gave an exasperated sigh. "Can we please just get on with it? My time is limited. I need to get back to the office."

The doctor paused a moment and shot Karl a disapproving glance, but he let the comment pass. Nata glared, but bit her tongue. This was no time for a marital dispute.

"We've talked before of the worrying signs of possible brain injury. The accident you were involved in brought on premature labour. Natalie's due date was September 11. She gave birth at twenty-nine weeks and one day, depriving little Sean of nine weeks of growing in utero.

"Babies are generally said to be 'term babies' if the pregnancy lasts past thirty-seven weeks. We are finding that babies born twenty-four weeks plus have a good chance of surviving. But birth at anything less than thirty-two weeks implies a range of potential health problems and developmental difficulties, some of which may imply permanent disabilities.

"In Sean's case, we have the added problem of trauma resulting from a motor vehicle accident injuring the mother, and inducing traumatic pre-term delivery. The child endured enormous stress."

Karl scowled and began tapping his foot. The doctor ignored him and continued, seemingly unflustered. No doubt he'd done this many times before, and he would have witnessed all kinds of reactions.

"Accurate diagnosis and prognosis is difficult at this early stage. We need to run tests... some of which either can't be administered or won't yield reliable data until Sean is two or three years of age. We will continue treatment programs, of course, but until we have a definite diagnosis, I can't give you any reliable indication of what we can expect. What I can tell you is that medical science has come a long way in recent years, particularly in the treatment of premature infants. Miracles happen."

Karl stopped tapping and leaned forward, suddenly

involved... optimistic, even. "Money is no object, doctor. He must have the very best care. The most skilled specialists —"

"We give every baby the best care available, Mr. Albrecht. But care isn't always enough. Sean may have quite serious disabilities. We've seen some disturbing symptoms, and we've seen some worrying indicators in test results. We know that Sean suffered Perinatal Asphyxia. Perinatal Asphyxia results when too little blood flows to the foetus or when there is too little oxygen in the blood. It results in the newborn appearing pale and lifeless, having a slow heart rate, and breathing weakly. In Sean's case, it has resulted in seizures.

"Survivors of this kind of trauma can suffer permanent neurological damage, ranging from mild to quite severe. It can affect brain function... hearing, speech, sight, mental capacity. And it can result in physical disabilities."

He paused a minute, and his expression was grim.

The colour drained from Karl's face. Everything he'd said, for weeks, declared he'd given up on the child. But for an instant it seemed he'd seen a glimmer of hope. And now it was dashed. Natalie felt herself crumbling. Whatever faint hope she'd been clinging to was gone. The blood in her veins had turned to ice, and she was shivering. A nurse solicitously remarked that it was cold in the room and offered to get her a blanket, but Natalie shook her head.

"We'll need to monitor Sean's progress over a period of a few years, at least. And of course we'll administer treatments as appropriate, even before we confirm a diagnosis. What matters now is that you, as his parents, understand the challenges ahead and have access to the support you are going to need to cope. I wanted you to meet the social worker and have an opportunity to talk to her about the services her team can offer."

He passed Natalie a collection of leaflets.

"I've included some information on cerebral palsy. It's a possibility that we can't rule out, but neither can we confirm.

It's rarely diagnosed before a child's second birthday. Even if we rule it out, there's a strong possibility that Sean will suffer many of the typical symptoms of CP, at least in his early years, so I thought some knowledge of it may assist. It's a relatively common disease that affects about one in a hundred babies. It implies loss of movement or nerve function, but the implications vary enormously from one sufferer to the next. The symptoms can be quite mild. In some cases, the disease implies only physical disability. In other cases, cognitive functions are affected. It can affect body movement, muscle control, muscle coordination, muscle tone, reflex, posture and balance. Sufferers may also have visual, learning, hearing and speech impairments, epilepsy and other intellectual impairments. Whether he has CP or not, we think it likely that Sean will suffer these sort of impairments. CP is incurable, but if he doesn't have CP, the impairments may be temporary.

"Developmental delays are a certainty," he continued in a detached tone, "and we expect that delays will be significant. We also anticipate that Sean might display mild to quite severe mental retardation, but there is no way to be certain of his mental capacity. That won't be clear for some time yet. I'm always cautious about making predictions, because babies are surprisingly strong and resilient. Medical research is constantly delivering new and exciting treatments. But while not wanting to cause undue alarm or distress, I have an obligation to be frank with you. Brain injury is irreversible. Large portions of the human brain are substantially inactive. Therapies can train normally unused brain cells to do the work of damaged cells, but there are limits to what even the most intensive therapies can achieve."

Natalie stared at him, nearly hypnotized. Her mind refused to process the information and her memory refused to retain it. Karl had to half-carry her back to the visitors' lounge, where she met the waiting Joe and Hetty. Hetty plied her with tea while Karl repeated the doctor's advice. Nata shivered. Her face was the colour of pastry and her eyes glazed. Karl's voice seemed to rattle on and on, and she fought an illogical yet implacable urge to throw her tea in his face to silence him.

Joe went to her, took her in his arms, and pleaded with her to cry on his shoulder. "Let it out, love," he whispered. "It will help."

Karl waited until Joe and Hetty had gone to propose his solutions. They would sue, of course. Medical negligence must have been a factor. There must have been more they could have done. He had already lodged an insurance claim, and police had charged the other driver. The payout would be significant. But now he would inform the insurers of the full extent of the damage caused—

"How can you think about money, Karl," Natalie screeched. "Money won't fix our child."

"We'll need money to pay for his care, Nat. We need to be practical now. We'll want to find a quality home for crippled children... somewhere that he will receive the very best attention. It will be costly."

"I will care for him. I will give him the very best attention. And if necessary, we'll sell assets to pay for the best medical treatments available."

"You need to return to work, Nat," he said. His tone was matter-of-fact... unfeeling. "The child needs full time specialist care. There are places for kids like him. We can go on with our lives. This doesn't have to destroy our future."

"You can't mean that, Karl? How can you— " Her tone quivered with anger.

"I'm not saying it won't be hard sometimes. I have feelings, Nat. But it's the only sensible solution. Surely you must see that?"

"Karl, he's our child. Our flesh and blood. I carried him inside me... loved him." She was conscious of her pleading tone and berated herself for her weakness.

"And now?"

She dissolved into a flood of tears. "I don't know. How can I know?"

"That's precisely it, Nat. You're too close to it. Too emotional. When you regain your strength… have time to think clearly…"

"Get out!" she screamed. "Just go, you bastard. Leave me. I never want to see your face again."

And again the grief consumed her.

#

Natalya had known grief and pain. In her infancy, it had been her constant companion. For decades, she had struggled to fight the memories down. And she had won. She had won Joe's adoration and approval. She had won Karl's affection. Life with Karl and Sean promised such jubilation… such ecstasy. But now the lights had gone out. Her world was again a dark and soulless place. A persistent dull pulsing behind her temples and a bruised, hurting heart drained her energy and left her spent and worn.

She couldn't return to work. They had moved into their new home, but it gave her no pleasure, and she had refused to even involve herself in unpacking, let alone in planning renovations or improvements. She had let Joe and Hetty put the baby's things in the nursery, and then she ordered them to close the door firmly and not to open it again. She could not bear to look at the tiny crib that Sean might never sleep in.

Long, arduous days were defined by repeated trips to the hospital to hold Sean and feed him and endless hours with doctors, listening to long-winded progress reports, read out in a language she didn't understand; discussing treatment options; struggling to accept an increasingly grim prognosis.

She wanted to love Sean. She wanted to hold him, stroke his cheek with her finger, let him suckle at her breasts and grip her finger in his tiny fist. Yet when she went to him, she was filled with bitter resentment. She nurtured a sense of having been cruelly betrayed. A part of her wanted to lash out and hurt him… destroy him… end the trauma. In his death, there would be closure. She would grieve and friends would comfort. She would take a little quiet time to heal, and then she would return to her life. Things would be normal again. No endless treks to specialist surgeries and staring vacantly at walls while she waited for results. No tortuous twisting of her gut as she struggled to understand yet another uncertain diagnosis. No fragile hopes. No crushing disappointments.

Karl repeated his advice, over and over. "Surrender him, Nat. Hand him over to the care of those who commit their lives to the care of infants like these… to people trained and skilled and equipped with all the necessary aids. Let him grow up with others like him, in a place where he will not feel out of place. Set yourself free. Set me free. Give us back what we had and let us go on with our lives and our careers."

Her responses ranged from stressed gibberish, to blank astonished stares, to unmitigated, murderous rage. She turned purple with anger and bade him leave and never show his face again. And then she fell into his arms and sobbed like a baby, promising to do whatever would bind him to her and give them peace. When she lay silently sobbing in the false dawn, he rolled over and wiped her eyes gently. He kissed her, took her in his arms and assured her of his undying love. He promised the pain would heal. They both knew what was best for all of them. It would be hard at first, but work would distract her and fulfil her. The memories would fade.

She yielded to him, but when he sought to penetrate her, she screamed and kicked and flailed him and the fierce burning hatred flared up inside her. He took on Papa's features. She smelled Papa's stinking breath and felt sticky fluid erupting over her fingers. The bile rose in her throat and her stomach churned.

Up and down. Up and down. Squeeze.

"Don't touch me," she screamed. "Get out of my bed."

When he left her—slinking away silently like a beaten dog—she curled up in a ball and rocked back and forward until she heard the front door close behind him. Then she staggered to the kitchen to make tea that burned her throat. She sat at the table planning: *A pillow over Sean's face; drop him while bathing him; let his slippery little body slide from my grip. They say drowning is a painless, peaceful death. Who would know? A tragic accident. Sean would be at peace. Karl and I could go on.*

She dressed, then, and drove to the hospital. She marched, stone-faced, to the NICU nursery. She sat beside his crib and stared at the tiny, helpless form.

Fruit of my womb. My flesh and blood. My child.

The nurse lifted him gently from his crib and placed him in her arms, and the stinging tears welled and the love pain swelled to fill her chest. Her head pounded and her heart ached.

#

Again and again, Karl pleaded with her to place the child in an institution and free them to go on with their lives.

"Sean needs love. Other parents find ways to care for children like him."

"But we're not like them, Nat," Karl protested. "We're educated... rich. We have careers. We can afford expert care for the boy... but we need to..."

"The boy? His name is Sean, Karl, and he's our son."

"I know, but it's not like we planned it, Nat, is it? I mean..."

"I know exactly what you mean, Karl. You mean you wanted Sean... the perfect son... good-looking, smart, athletic... the designer baby. But it doesn't work like that. Couples get pregnant; they take a risk. You get what you get. Sometimes it works out as you prayed, and sometimes you are blessed with a special child. Who knows why? I don't know how God chooses parents for the..."

"Oh for pity's sake, Nat. Special? Parents chosen by God?

Get real. Children like that boy are an unfortunate accident of nature. In a less technologically advanced world, they wouldn't survive the trauma of birth. No merciful God would curse any parent with…"

"Stop, Karl. Shut up!" she screamed, throwing her still partly filled cereal bowl at him. It hit to the left of his head and milk trickled down the wall in grubby streaks, forming a tiny puddle around the little pile of wheat flakes, dried fruit and shards of broken china that clung to the skirting board.

"Get out, you bastard! Just get out!" she sobbed, dropping to her knees and burying her head in her hands.

"Nat…" He started toward her, a hand outstretched, but she shrank away. He shrugged, turned, collected his brief case, and strode out, closing the door firmly behind him.

Natalie coiled against the sideboard and let the grief possess her. Violent sobs racked her body, echoing back from the hallway as though in answer. Rivers of tears etched angry red scald marks over her cheeks. Sour breast milk leaked from swollen, throbbing breasts, turning the front of her soft cream pyjama shirt a dirty, dark yellow-brown. *Why had she persisted with regular expressing, desperately hoping Sean might, one day, suck? Why had they encouraged her to hope?*

Over the ocean, the sun was breaking soft pink. Far out to sea, a golden orb reflected off silken-blue, still water. A soft light played at the windows, but the heavy drapes let only the smallest sliver of light penetrate where the fabric panels met. The room was grey. Her world was black. She would leave the drapes closed. She might never let the light in again.

She hugged her breast. A dull, achy pain wrapped about her heart, creeping down into her churning belly. It tiptoed down her limbs and weighed them down until they felt like lead, and even her fingers and toes hurt. Her head was as mushy as a melon and her eyes were sorry slits under swollen lids. She was quite sure she would never see the light or feel the warmth of the sun again.

She didn't know how long she huddled there, sobbing violently... moaning... and now and again cursing God and nature and Karl and life; wishing she could will away her life— just end it. Let them lay her out in a satin-lined box and bury her under six feet of soft, warm earth. Let her sleep forever, free from heartache, free from worry and stress, free from the heavy weight of obligation to care. But then guilt entered. It knocked at her heart and hammered in her head. Sean needed her. He needed her love and care.

Do I have any love to give? Can I learn to care? I don't know. I only know how much it hurts to even think his name.

She dissolved in yet another round of burning tears and wrenching sobs. The sun rose higher and the clock ticked on, and she knew she should pull herself up and shower and dress and go him. And yet she felt she could never bear to look at him again, and she prayed he wouldn't survive another day.

I hate myself. I hate Karl. I hate Sean. I hate the cruel, vengeful God who cursed us with this burden.

And again, she wondered if this was her penance for hating Papa. For although she knew her thoughts were evil, she never forgot, and she never stopped praying for his demise. She wished for him an ugly, painful, tortured death, with a teasing voice reminding him—with every wave of pain—of the wages of sin, and of the grave and monstrous sins he had committed.

Perhaps this was her and Karl's penance for not wanting a child... for contemplating abortion. Abortion is a cardinal sin, and she did contemplate it. She even told Hetty she planned to. For a while, Karl was adamant.

Did he ever really want Sean? Did I?

Once the reality of Sean sank in, I wanted him with all my heart. I could never have aborted. I loved him from the moment he first moved inside me.... no, before that even. I loved him from the moment I saw that pink stripe on the test strip. I let Karl, and my wish for a life I thought I wanted, confuse me for a little while.

But I have grown. Sean made me grow. Sean taught me how to love. And then, a vengeful God betrayed me, and now I wonder can I ever love again?

She went to the kitchen. The sun had risen high, lighting the room, polishing the cabinet doors to a glistening shine and dancing over the blood-red granite counter tops. It willed her to eat and face the day. How long had she been up there, huddled, sobbing, screaming angry curses at God and Karl and Sean and Papa, and the world? Her cheeks were swollen and scalded and her burning eyes were reduced to tiny slits that squinted at the light.

How did I come to this? Natalie Dreyer, Summa Cum Laude, Master of Law, successful corporate lawyer in a prestigious legal firm, wife of a soon to be partner, and... mother of.... Oh God, why?

And she dissolved again. Her body racked with sobbing.

She heard the key in the door. Milley, the cleaner, had come. She shrivelled against the counter and wondered how long she might hide, but after a minute, she pulled herself up and gathered her thoughts. She smoothed the damp front of her pyjama shirt and stumbled to the door. She watched until Milley disappeared into the laundry, and then she hastened to the stairs and ran up them, two at a time, desperate to seclude herself in her locked room while Milley cleaned downstairs... desperate to avoid facing her.

And what will I do when she moves to the upper level and seeks to change my linen and dust my dresser? By then, I'll have showered and dressed and repaired my face some, and I'll go to him. I'll go and look at him and hold him and weep over him and wish him dead, and love him... a deep, protective, hurting love that will tear out my heart and make me hate myself for wishing him gone. And yet I can't help but resent him for what my life has become because of him.

Sean! Tiny, helpless, malformed, blue and crimson body.

Object of my deepest bitter hatred. Object of the most awesome, overpowering, maternal love.

Ten

Gil had asked Karl to meet him, again, in Henry's bar. The invitation sent a spine-tingling thrill through Karl and made his face glow. The partnership offer? He was certain. The office had been buzzing with the news that Gil had made his decision. Karl was front runner. Everyone said so. The staff were certain he had been chosen. Despite his pain and struggle over the past months, he had managed to keep his clients happy and his billing high. Gil had complimented him, more than once, on his diligence and stamina.

Karl almost waltzed into Henry's, jacket slung over his shoulder, oozing exuberance. He took his usual place on a leather lounge in a dim corner and summoned a waitress to bring him a drink. The other end of the sofa still bore an imprint, and a half-drunk brandy rested on a coaster on the table in front.

"Mr. Bryant will be back in a moment," the waitress said, and he thanked her with a broad smile.

Karl didn't notice the grey envelope bearing his name until the waitress plopped a coaster on top of it and set his drink down. He hesitated to open it, wondering if he should wait for Gil's return, and perhaps for his boss to hand it to him. Impatient for the expected confirmation, he extracted the envelope and opened it carefully, letting the contents spill onto his lap. But what spilled out sent an eerie sense of danger washing over him. It left him muddled by suspicion and sudden dread: a photo of his mangled Porsche, and a gruesome image of his bloodied wife lying on a stretcher. Across the image of the car, the words, "Cause of accident(?): failed brakes??" were printed in a hand he didn't recognize.

The words snapped his mind into fragments of fear. He stumbled back to the bathroom and into a cubicle and bolted the door. He leaned against the wall and swallowed hard and ordered his knotted belly to relax and be still, but it defied him. He sat on the closed toilet seat and bent over in a huddle of helplessness, reliving the dread. The memory of her cry addled his brain and madness overcame him, but he forced his lawyer mind into gear and ordered it to focus on the facts.

He didn't recognize the writing over the photo. There was no evidence that Gil had placed it there. And yet it sat right beside his drink. He could not have failed to see it. Perhaps he had come across the photo and passed it on to Karl to prompt him to seek investigation? There was no reason to suspect Gil was in any way involved, or even had knowledge of... what? Cause of accident? Or was it, perhaps, not an accident?

Powerful people... late night visit... because I have a wife and children, I have no choice in the matter...

It was an accident, Karl: a terrible, tragic accident. The roads were wet and slippery. Your brakes were sluggish. In heavy rain and darkness, the other guy's vision was poor.

Afterwards, he couldn't say how long he stayed there, see-sawing between terror and attempted reason. But as he exited the bathroom, he saw a familiar rat-like face in a dark corner. Vance nodded to him and raised a finger. He smiled an evil, twisted smile that sent fire and ice surging through Karl's veins. Karl forced a poker face and nodded in return. Somehow he kept his calm until he was well away and back on the sofa, swallowing burning gulps of brandy.

As Gil approached, Karl shrugged off his disquiet. There would be a simple explanation. Gil was not involved. Gil was his friend, and a good man. Sure, he'd insisted Karl turn a blind eye to evil, but for sound reason. It was as much for his own and Nata's protection as it was for the good of the firm and the benefit of people they were required to please. He reprimanded himself silently for suspecting Gil of involvement in causing him hurt. *How could he, anyway? He'd been out of town that night.* He would show the photo to the police, but he wouldn't tell them where he'd found it. He trusted Gil. When the time was right, he'd ask him, and he would accept Gil's reply. Perhaps he might confide in Phillip. His colleague was trustworthy. He'd ask his advice. He'd let him make inquiries for him. If the crash was not an accident, Phillip would quickly get to the bottom of it.

But it was an accident. How could it be anything else?

He'd conceded to Gil's request. He'd told Max Knight to settle, and when he refused, he'd politely dumped him; told him he could help him no further. He'd sorted the file carefully, taking all incriminating evidence and his own brief home, where it rested under a huge pile of papers on the desk in his home office. He'd passed over, to Max only, a copy of the revised brief that indicated that his investigations had found nothing to suggest The Fourth Floor was anything more than a clean and perfectly legal entertainment business. He'd billed Max a hefty sum, which was paid, albeit with protest, and the matter was closed. He had followed proceedings, of course. Max had found another lawyer and asked for yet another stay. Shawdforth was reportedly getting very impatient, but happier to grant postponements than risk the truth being exposed in his courtroom. The whole affair would be making him extremely nervous. Unlike Karl, Shawdforth couldn't safely step back from it, not without certainty of the intentions of his replacement.

Max and Levi were, of course, still frustrated and angry, and more determined than ever to expose the crime. But it was as Vance had said. They had just signed a fourth lawyer to represent them, and they weren't happy with him either. They were spending a fortune and getting no value.

Karl was secretly delighted that his replacement was unlikely to achieve the notoriety that he had sought by taking that case on. He was not at all pleased that the criminals were still protected and the crime was continuing.

#

Gil took his seat beside Karl, smiling broadly.

"Karl, my friend! I trust you are well and your family situation is improving. How is your beautiful wife? Did Celia's visit cheer her?"

Karl forced a smile and nodded. "Thank you, " he said. "It was kind of her to go." He refrained from confessing that Natalie had complained of the woman's self-righteous interference and that his wife's mood had deteriorated considerably as a result. Celia meant well. Nothing seemed to please Natalie lately.

"How is Celia?" he asked.

"Fine."

"And the boys?"

"Teenagers!"

Karl chuckled. They sat silently, side by side on a vast leather sofa, while the waitress attended them. When she had gone, Gil asked after Natalie and the child. Karl's face clouded.

"Talk to me, Karl," Gil urged. "I know what you are going through is horrific. I honestly don't know how you can continue with work, but I admire your stamina. But keeping it all in and just forging on isn't healthy. It's okay to lean on your friends sometimes."

"Nat's depression seems to have worsened," Karl replied. "And there is no change in the child. The prognosis is still uncertain, but… Gil, I wish I knew how to break through that wall of pain… how to make her see reason. I've tried to be patient and understanding. But I see only one solution to the problem. It's not ideal. Nothing ever can be. But Sean needs expert care, and she needs to resume her life."

Gil appeared deep in thought. At last, he said softly and with slight hesitation, "Karl, maybe it's time to stop being patient and understanding and take a firm hand. Perhaps what she really needs now is for you to be strong and in control. It's easy to wallow in self-pity while the world sympathizes and indulges. Sometimes we need incentive to pull ourselves up and get on with business."

An incentive, Gil? Is that what it was? Wasn't advice enough? Or did you arrange the "incentive" long before you spoke your mind?

Karl chastised himself silently, shrugging off his disquiet and assuring himself that the photo didn't in any way evidence that Gil was involved in the accident. It didn't even indicate that it wasn't an accident. Lawyers were supposed to retain their objectivity, and he must retain his. Investigate, but assume nothing until the investigation is complete.

He weighed his boss's advice in relation to Nat. Gil was a wise man. He'd had his fair share of heartache. His first wife had died of cancer after a long and tiring battle. Before her diagnosis, she had suffered four miscarriages and been treated several times for acute depression. Gil had first-hand knowledge of dealing with a wife ravaged by the black dog. Maybe....

"And how are you coping under the strain?"

Not well since I opened that envelope.

"Oh, I manage. I learned a long time ago to leave my home troubles at home and focus. And right now, being able to focus on work is keeping me sane." He looked up at Gil and his expression was earnest. "I have always worked hard to be an asset to Adams Bryant and Co. I intend to ensure my contribution to the business continues to impress, and my fee revenue continues to increase. I'm ambitious, Gil. I was trained to be an achiever. I am not going to let a tragedy in my private life destroy what I've worked so hard for."

Karl had been trained to achieve. His father had no patience with anyone who let emotion get in the way of work. Both his father and his grandfather were staunch believers in the value of harsh discipline. Displays of affection reflected weakness and spoiled children. Leisure—even a young child's play—was a sinful waste of resources and an education in idleness and waste. Praise had no place in a training regime.

Karl's father responded to his failures with punishments and ridicule, and to his successes by declaring the goal too accessible, the challenge too easy. Nothing pleased. Karl was branded weak—unworthy of his heritage and undeserving of privilege. But he had achieved. And he was intent, now, on taking his achievements to the next level—on earning a title that might, at last, earn him his father's respect and his grandfather's admiration.

"And the Knight case?"

Karl gave an involuntary shudder and prayed it went unnoticed.

"Investigation closed. Found nothing to substantiate Knight's fantastic allegations about activities on The Fourth Floor, and everything to support a recommendation that he take Shawdforth's advice and close the case down. I submitted a five page brief suggesting a compromise that I told Knight was the best he could hope for while I'm his adviser. He didn't like it, of course, so I raised a hefty bill of costs and politely resigned from the matter. I understand he's engaged Russell Page, and Russell's asked for yet another stay. He's the fourth lawyer to enter Shawdforth's courtroom representing Max, and Max has spent a small fortune for zero results."

Gil nodded gravely, then lifted his head and grinned broadly. He extended his shaking hand and his eyes glittered.

"Karl, your dedication to your work and your contribution

to the growth of my company hasn't gone unnoticed. You know I've been considering who might replace Ewan Adams as a partner, and I know you fully expected I would choose you. I've deliberated long enough. With the Knight affair closed, there's no reason to delay a decision any longer. I would like to offer you a full partnership in Adams Bryant and Company. Congratulations, my friend."

Karl's heart refused to dance as he'd expected it should. The hand he extended was limp and cold, but Gil shook it enthusiastically.

"A celebratory drink is in order, I think," Gil said. "Let me pay for this one, partner."

"Thank you, Gil," Karl said, gathering himself now, playing the role that he had so long wished for. "I don't have to tell you how much this means to me. I've wanted my name on the partner list since the day I joined the firm. You can rely on me completely to do whatever is required to advance the interests of Adams Bryant and Company."

"Keep Shawdforth happy, Karl," Gil said with a smile. "He's got friends in high places. And he's a smart fellow."

Karl nodded and forced a smile, but pain ripped and tore at him, unbearable and unending. His face drained of blood and a cold faintness spread out from the pit of his stomach. He looked at the boss he had so respected and admired and he saw vile darkness about him, a dangerous and evil intent.

They drank, and Gil indulged in small talk while Karl forced away the fear; forced focus on constructive endeavours. He silently considered the potential merits of a change in his approach to Natalie. The strong hand hadn't worked well before. He had been forced into a humiliating back-down, and he'd battled to find a way to return to her good graces. She had made it clear she would never be the subservient wife he'd sought. But she was strong and healthy then. She was in control of herself. And the issue was one she was passionate about. Now, she was overcome with grief and fear and confusion. She had no answers for herself. She was incapable of making a choice, and she flip-flopped back and forth by the day, and sometimes by the hour. Perhaps what she needed was his courage and strength, if, indeed, he could muster any.

Yes, he decided. *My wife needs me to be a man. And I need my woman.* He would resume his rightful place as head of his household. Tonight. He would put aside his own silly fears and suspicions. He would tell her, firmly, what was to be. And then he would take her in his arms and console her, and he would insist that she acknowledge his conjugal rights. He would assert his authority as her husband. He would take his pleasure. And his strength and certainty would release her from her prison of indecision and remind her of the life they had, and the life they would return to. It would set them both free.

"You're a good man, Karl, " Gil was saying. "And now, I think it's time I went home to my good wife and you went home to yours. Give Natalie my regards. Tell her if there's anything at all I can do—. Tell her we want her back... soon."

Karl shook Gil's hand again, firmly this time. And then they said their goodbyes. Minutes later, Karl was steering his Ferrari through the evening traffic and planning his announcement to Natalie. He was a partner in Melbourne's top law firm. Now if she would just see sense in this matter of Sean, and if he could put his fears about that accident to rest, they could get back to the perfect lives they had dreamed of and he had worked so hard for.

He felt a familiar twinge and rubbed his penis hard. Surely, tonight was a night for celebration? Maybe he could distract her from her troubles and remind her how life should be... how it could be again if she would just see reason. There could be other babies, even. Tonight was a new beginning. He was going home to make love to his wife, and when she lay in his arms after, he would persuade her. He would persist firmly... promising rewards... until she did as he had done. She must recognize that life deals us blows, but sometimes we have to just roll with the punches and get on with it; do what needs to be done to go forward and live our dreams. He would persist with his arguments until she conceded and did what a dutiful wife should do… put her husband's needs ahead of her own… recognize his authority and, in accordance with the vows she took on their wedding day, obey his commands.

#

It had taken him two hours to reach home. An accident had caused traffic to back up and, after being stalled for over an hour, he had inched forward, ever so slowly, for five kilometres before turning off into flowing traffic close to home. By the time he reached the house, both his delight and his courage had deserted him. He was tired. The contents of that envelope haunted him. He needed food, several strong brandies, and sleep. He had wanted sex, but the thought of having to plead or argue or command had killed his desire.

In the end, he went quietly into the house, pecked Natalie's cheek and told her, quite casually, that Gil had made him a partner. She congratulated him without enthusiasm, told him there was a meal in the fridge, and went to bed.

He ate alone, downed three glasses of brandy, and went, again, to the guest bed to sleep. In the morning, he left her sleeping, aware that she rarely slept and relieved that she had finally managed to shut the world out for a time. He took care not to disturb her, and he left, again, without saying goodbye. The title he had craved so desperately and worked so hard for no longer mattered.

ELEVEN

Natalie had decided that forcing herself to attend to overdue domestic chores might take her mind off her misery. Joe had always said physical work was therapeutic. Hetty always scrubbed and polished when she was upset.

She hadn't meant to pry, but Karl didn't allow the cleaner in his office and the dust was building up under the piles of papers on his carved blackwood desk. When she'd lifted the stack of folders resting on the far end, the brief had fallen out. She picked it up, and it was impossible not to notice the yellow sticky note clipped to the top right corner. "Destroy" was written in large red letters. Under it, there was an envelope addressed to Karl.

With shaking hands and guilty heart thumping, she opened the envelope. A bundle of photographs fell out: Gil and Karl shaking hands; Karl holding the partnership agreement he'd signed a few days earlier; Karl's office door displaying the new brass plaque that now adorned it, engraved with his name, and the word "Partner" beneath. There were several photos of lithe young girls in seductive attire lounging on satin-covered settees with their heads on the laps of naked men; young boys kneeling in front of much older naked men, their heads pressed against the men's loins; naked men kneeling next to settees on which naked girls lounged with breasts cupped in men's palms or with men's lips pursed around a nipple. Folded and clipped above one of the photos were three credit card receipts from The Fourth Floor. In small letters under the business name, they displayed the words "Discreetly indulging discerning gentlemen." The charge on each was two hundred and fifty dollars. The slightly shaky signature below was unmistakably Karl's.

Wrapped around the photos was a note. It bore the words: "Congratulations on a wise decision, Karl!" The scrawly hand was unfamiliar and the grubby, tattered note was unsigned. "Always remember that partnerships—and marriages—can be dissolved. We wouldn't want to disrupt either relationship, would we? You keep my friends' secrets safe, my friend, and I'll keep yours."

The clock declared it only minutes that she stood there, nauseated and trembling, but it seemed an eternity. At last, she folded the pictures and receipt back inside the note and placed them in the envelope, and she clipped the envelope back in place. She carried the file to the kitchen, made herself tea, and settled on the window seat to read. An hour later, she rose to return the file to its rightful place, but she swayed on her feet like a drunk after a binge. Giant purple-bellied thunderclouds filled the sky, and storm clouds in her throbbing head fogged her vision. She fought down the grating echo, but there was no escaping the awful, perfect understanding.

Karl had composed a detailed response to a legal complaint against Max Knight. He had done his homework and uncovered the depravity. He had named names: esteemed political leaders, senior bureaucrats, judges, barristers, lawyers, executives and directors of major public companies, foreign dignitaries… even movie stars. He had documented the evidence, eighty pages of it. It was a masterful work, and her lawyer brain could not help but admire his thoroughness and clarity. But her woman brain execrated the depravity, and her wife brain screamed and howled at his apparent betrayal of her trust.

The Fourth Floor was obviously a section of Wanderers' Mansions—Max Knight's upmarket backpacker hostel—that had been converted to a haven for perverts. She knew of the hostel. The building was tall, elegant, and prominent against the Melbourne skyline. It had been in the news more than once— notably, a few years back when Max Knight was publicly accused of sexual harassment of young female guests. Youngsters— travelling foreigners—stayed rent free in the luxury suites, and, according to Karl's brief, went on their way with their pockets loaded. Dignitaries and VIPs got their sexual gratification from the young hostel guests, or from watching the pornographic movies screened in the private lounge.

Members of the building's management committee owned luxury suites that were rented at hourly rates to the building manager, who, Knight claimed, moonlighted as a pimp. He let the remainder of the suites in the building to well-heeled young tourists, but the fourth floor suites were converted and reserved, and netted premium yields. The fourth floor lounge, a gymnasium, and an indoor heated swimming pool were all fitted with key-card readers and patrolled by security guards. Cleaners and laundry maids working night shifts kept suites and common areas spotless and bounteously endowed with creature comforts, and were apparently well rewarded for their diligence and circumspection. Holidaying residents served as hosts and hostesses, dispensing alcoholic beverages, cigars, and a variety of aphrodisiacs, uppers, downers, trippers, memory-blockers and hallucinogens. Anything, it seemed, that produced a costly but illegal thrill was on offer to those with means and inclination to indulge their deviant cravings.

One of the building lifts had been designated "Private— management use only" and was used to convey patrons from a private entrance near the management parking area to floor four. The manager's office was located near enough to the lift that the pimp could keep close watch and approve every entrant. No effort had been spared to ensure the protection of patrons' privacy.

But Max Knight had unveiled the debauchery. He had sought to have the manager's contract terminated and had lobbied the unit owners to replace the management committee. Vote manipulation, bribery and blackmail had been employed to thwart him, and a bogus lawsuit was initiated in an effort to silence him. Their claims were transparently frivolous and the judges reviewing them surely knew it. But Karl's notes reported court schedules being rearranged and court rules ignored. His handwritten margin notes referenced repeated long delays, grave breaches of procedure, and demands for settlement on terms no judge could deem fair. He had postulated that brown paper bags were changing hands regularly, and threats had been made to silence judges and investigative journalists who rejected generous offers of payment for their silence.

Following the eighty pages of exposé, an unsigned five-page brief confirmed Max Knight's reluctant consent to a settlement proposal. It confirmed his agreement that the manager and management committee should remain empowered and continue, as they allegedly always had, their efficient and highly professional management of the facility. It noted that any and all allegations of impropriety and/or illegality either relating to use or management of the facility or to the conduct of legal disputes were acknowledged baseless, and unequivocally withdrawn with profound apology. It recorded Max Knight's agreement to withdraw from any form of lobbying voters and from framing "vexatious or suggestive motions" and making "defamatory or inflammatory statements" in meetings or in communications with lot owners. It acknowledged a claimed mutual agreement that both sides should meet their own costs, and that the terms of their agreement would remain strictly confidential. It was unsigned and undated, clearly never filed. If Max had even sighted Karl's revised draft, he had rejected the proposal.

Natalie's world tipped and spun. She knew Karl's faults.

He was vain and self-seeking. He was arrogant, presumptuous and overbearing. But he was ethical and decent. He respected the law. She believed him faithful. He had abandoned his religion, but not Christian morality. And yet, it appeared he had traded his honour for the position he had craved. And he had indulged his sexual fantasies in a house of ill-repute. While she carried their child, and struggled with repressed memories and overpowering fears, he had paid girls young enough to be his daughters to satisfy his physical desires.

She staggered to the bathroom and heaved violently. She heaved again, and again, and when there was nothing left to expel, she retched until her throat locked on a ball of fire and hot coals burned in her belly. She laid the brief on the kitchen table, and she took a highlight pen and formed a great pink question mark over the sticky note on its cover. And then she retired to her bed and lay staring at the ceiling, waiting for his homecoming, and the eruption that she knew would follow.

#

She heard his footsteps in the lobby and his key turn in the lock. She pictured him depositing his briefcase, hanging his jacket and shuffling through the mail on the hall table. Always the same. Next, he would go to the kitchen and make coffee. And then he would sit at the table to drink it and contemplate the day and his plans for the evening. Then he would see it, and he would know what she had done… what she knew. She waited, her muscles tense and her brain echoing warnings and recriminations. Time spun out, minutes seeming to take hours to pass.

At last, she heard the heavy footsteps. The door flung open and he was standing there, face ablaze, waving the papers.

"What the hell were you doing reading my files?" he thundered. "Do I have no privacy in my own home? I ban the cleaner from my office, but I should be able to trust my wife."

She took a deep breath, crossed her fingers tightly, and

prayed silently for control.

"What the hell have you done?" she asked, her voice low and taut. "Bought your precious promotion? Condoned and excused crime... the worst kind of crime. Condoned it for personal financial reward. Took a bribe, Karl! You took a bribe to turn your back on... not just crime... filth and depravity of the worst kind."

"That's not how it was."

"No. Really? It all looked pretty clear to me."

"It's none of your business, Natalie," he snapped. "It's between lawyer and client. It's confidential." He thrust the papers on the dresser.

"None of my business? ...None of my business?" she was screeching now, despite her promise to keep calm. She reminded herself that she was righteous and the righteous didn't need to get angry. But a raging fire burned inside her and boiled the blood in her veins.

"I'm your wife, Karl. I have a right to know what price you decide to pay for advancement. I have a right to know when you suddenly decided to place yourself above the law... to discard all your principles. I married a man of integrity. I thought I did. I have a right to know if I was mistaken. And I have a right to know who you sleep with while I'm carrying our child, or while my body is healing after delivering your son."

"Natalie, " he said, his stentorian voice fading now as his confidence evaporated, "You don't know the whole story. It wasn't an easy decision, but— "

"Wasn't an easy decision? Which? To sleep with whores, or to turn a blind eye to crime and corruption? To excuse paedophilia and pornography? How can it not be an easy decision, Karl? You made a commitment to uphold the law. And this goes way beyond a question of law. This is a question of basic human decency. Have you no scruples at all? Who the hell is this man I'm married to?"

He crumpled then, collapsing to sit at the end of the bed, despairing, with his head in his hands. His breath was coming out in strangled little sobs, and he was trembling.

"I've been vomiting all afternoon, Karl. I vomited until there was nothing more there, and then I retched until my throat was on fire. The very thought that you could excuse this kind of filth… that you might be as vile and depraved and disgusting as these animals you protect. I knew money and position mattered a great deal to you… far more than I think healthy… but to stoop to this for — "

"I had no choice, Nat. These men… they will kill to protect their reputations if they have to. Look at the names. They are powerful. I ventured into dangerous territory. I should have heeded the warnings. I wish I'd stayed ignorant. For the rest of my life, I will struggle to live with my conscience… and to stay silent. But what else could I do? It wasn't just the partnership. It was my life… and yours. You know I'm right. To these people, it's all a game. They have no conscience. There is no limit to what this kind of vile degenerate will stoop to. They pay judges to keep their secrets. They blackmail. They would murder without a moment's hesitation to preserve their standing and their claimed right to their perverted pleasure."

He was weeping now. She had never seen him like this. He was always so confident and assertive. But she could feel no compassion. She was too consumed by her own horror and despair. Was there no end to the trials? Would there never be light again in her world? What evil had she done to deserve such suffering?

"He will by no means leave the guilty unpunished, visiting the iniquity of fathers on the children and on the grandchildren to the third and fourth generations."

Was she being punished for Sergei's sins? Or maybe for leaving the church? For contemplating abortion? For wishing her baby dead? So many sins. So many grave and dreadful sins. But

hadn't she been taught God forgives? If she went to confession…
But how could she have faith in a God who made her suffer so?

Karl had lifted his head from his hands and was staring at
her now. His face was a mask of pain.

"It's no good, Natalie, is it? It hasn't been good for a long
time. Not since we quarrelled over the abortion issue. And now…
you despise me. You think me selfish and evil and depraved. But
I only wanted the good life we planned together."

*The good life we planned together? The dream life I
thought would make me happy? Career, money, admiration…
Joe and Hetty have always been happy, and they have none of
that. And I have never really been content.*

"At what price?" she asked, more to herself than to him.
"How much of our souls do we have to sell for that dream? And
where does our son fit in all this, Karl? What kind of example
will you set for him? What morals will you teach him? Oh, that's
right. You want to put him away and forget he exists. Leave it to
someone else to care for him. Your brand of ethics and morality
condones depravity, apparently. Why should I be surprised that
you reject the responsibility of raising your child."

"It's probably not even my child."

"What? Karl, I don't believe… how can you even think
something like that?"

"Your mother was some kind of whore, wasn't she? I did
some investigating, Nata. Two half-brothers you've never met.…
thrown out before you were born… half-sister somewhere,
thrown out as a teenager. And you palmed off on foster parents.
Unwanted. Mother must've been a whore to let that happen."

"You're disgusting."

"I should have listened to my father. Beauty, brains and
breeding, he said. I got the beauty and brains part, but I thought I
could overlook the breeding given your upbringing. But blood's
thicker than water, they say. You've still got your birth parents'
genes."

Nata slapped his cheek then, hard. Her hand burned, and there was a bright red imprint on his face. Shocked, and afraid he would retaliate, she stepped back. Her hand flew to cover her gaping mouth, but the shock passed quickly and she hastened into the dressing room and snatched a small suitcase. She laid it on the floor and began carelessly tossing things in. It was so unlike her not to fold garments neatly, but she could sort them at home.

Home... Why did she still always think of Hetty's little cottage as "home"? She had "made it" in the world... lived in luxury... earned enough to buy nearly anything she desired... and yet she yearned for the simple warmth and safety of the cottage and the love of people she could trust... people who loved her unconditionally, without caring where she came from or whose genes she might have inherited... people who could love her son unconditionally... people who would not try to force her to...

God, why? What sin have I committed that you punish me this way?

She paused for a moment to reflect, and the answer came, then, that she'd rejected religion. She'd long ago stopped believing... stopped going to church... stopped going to confession. But she had done no evil. She tried to live a good life and be kind to others.

Supporting wrongful legal claims by the rich. Permitting clients to lie... just a little... to avoid having to pay fair compensation to past employees or victims of their company's dirty dealings... Helping the rich evade tax obligations.... Helping clients word investment offers to mislead ...just a little...

And now ignoring her moral obligation to report Karl's client's crime. She should not have confronted him at all. She should have gone straight to.... who? Gil? Could he be trusted? Did he know about this business? The Attorney General's Office, perhaps? Or were the politicians in it up to their eyeballs? Police? Who could be trusted in this filthy, corrupt, greedy world?

I chose to play in the vipers' pit. How could I think I

wouldn't be bitten?

She resumed her careless packing. There was no sound from the bedroom. Was Karl still there, nursing his burning cheek and his wounded pride? She ventured a peek and saw him seated on the foot of the bed. He would be seething. He would be plotting revenge. She must get past him and out of the house quickly, and to the cottage. She would be safe at the cottage. Joe would not let Karl hurt her.

When, finally, she closed the suitcase and timidly stepped with it into the bedroom, there was no anger in his gaze. Her hand-print still blazed red across his cheek, but his eyes were filled with deep sorrow.

"Perhaps it's best you leave. I don't think it can ever be good between us again," he said sadly.

She wanted to argue. She wanted to assure him of her love. She wanted to want him... to beg him to hold her and comfort her and make everything right again. But he was right, and she knew it. And she wasn't sure she could ever bear to look at him again, let alone to have him touch her. What he had done... it was beyond unforgivable.

"You're saying we should separate."

"I'm going to file for divorce, Nat. You can have the house. I'll provide generously for you and Sean."

He went to her then and touched her shoulder tenderly, but she pushed his hand away. "I'm sorry, Natalie. I wish it could have turned out differently. I will always have feelings for you... deep feelings. And whatever else you think of me, you must know that I was never unfaithful. You may not want to believe it now, but I swear it on my mother's grave. I went to The Fourth Floor to ask questions... to uncover evidence. Nothing more. I sat with those lovely girls and my heart bled for them. We talked. We shared a drink. I stroked their hair and pretended desire. But they kept their panties on and I kept my trousers zipped, and if you believe nothing else of me, you must believe that. And also that I love you. I may not know much about how to love, but you have always been the love of my life and I doubt that will ever change, whatever may pass between us.

"I'll go to Phillip's for a while. I'll try to make this as painless for you as possible."

She flung herself face down on the bed then and let the blackness consume her, and a part of her hoped she would sleep... and never awaken again.

#

She went to Joe and Hetty's. She went carrying a great burden. There were great dark circles of weariness under her eyes and her cheeks seemed to have caved in. But she'd had time to think and rationalize a little, and her anger with Karl had lessened.

When Hetty asked her how she was, she gave the obligatory answer. She spoke lightly, as if it was of no consequence.

Hetty glanced inquiringly at the suitcase. She said she needed to be closer to the hospital, and she needed Joe and Hetty's wisdom and comfort while she struggled to come to terms with Sean's condition.

"I need company. Karl works such long hours. When we're together, he pressures me rather than comforting."

She spoke as she would to an inquirer she knew didn't really care to hear. And yet she knew Hetty cared greatly.

Joe asked after Karl. Nata said he was busy with a challenging case. Hetty asked if he was still pressing her to return to work. She just nodded and turned her attention to laying out the table.

They ate. They made small talk about the weather and the food. Nata picked at her meal.... said sorry, that she had no appetite today. No reason. Just how it is sometimes. Hetty remarked that she had grown gaunt and haggard. She looked seriously unwell.

After they had cleared away, Nata took a seat across from

Joe.

"Can we talk, Dad," she asked. Her tone was earnest. He folded his paper and gazed at her with avid curiosity. She floundered a little, unsure how to begin.

"Karl took a bribe," she blurted suddenly.

Joe paled. His shoulders slumped. Under his bushy silvered brows, the whites of his eyes widened until the pupils were all but lost. She paused for a moment, struggling to find the right words to explain.

"It's not what you're thinking. I shouldn't have put it quite that way. He traded his integrity for the partnership he wanted so badly, but he didn't have a choice. It was that, or sacrifice his livelihood—forego everything he's worked for."

"Always there's choice—" Joe began, his voice tight with indignation. But she shook her head and motioned him to silence.

"Karl uncovered crime. Serious crime. The worst... the most abhorrent kind. There were threats, Dad... against Sean and me as well. He took a bribe to stay silent."

Joe's chair crashed to the floor as he leapt from it and stormed out onto the veranda. Hetty paled. The clock counted off pregnant seconds, then minutes, before a thunderous crash set both women running. But Joe was already returning, nursing his right fist and cursing under his breath. Behind him, a new sheet of timber had a ragged hole right through it.

"He put you in danger? You, and the child?" he whispered. "I will kill him for that."

Nata's gut was somersaulting. She had never seen Joe rage like this before. It had worried her, sometimes, that he always appeared so controlled. She fought for the right words to make him understand.

"You don't understand, Dad. It was the kind of crime men don't hesitate to kill to cover up—especially men with titles and position. He tried to do what was right... what we are told a lawyer must do. But it's a dirty world out there. Judges... politicians...

the power brokers in our world… too many of them are evil. And they wield such power. To oppose them… Sometimes, when a client takes you into that dark, evil world, there's no way back. Not without sacrificing yourself and everyone you care for.

"For evil men, it's all a game… a game that entitles those who rise high enough to do as they please, and to stamp on anyone who tries to stop them."

Joe pondered a while, and finally nodded. He was a good man, but he was not naïve. He knew how the world was. He had expressed fear for her, often. But not for Karl. Never for Karl. He had always thought Karl so strong… so… always in control.

For hours, now, she had been fighting the still small voice. She had weighed her principles against her understanding of the system, and she was forced to admit to the ugliness in her world. She could not excuse what Karl had done, but she was beginning to understand.

"Karl chose to turn the other cheek," she said. "He chose silence for self-protection. I can't blame him. But I'm not sure I can do the same. The whole affair has me wondering if I really want to do what I do."

Joe's face was working in an uneasy contortion of fear, distress and disapproval.

"I loved my job, because I thought we lawyers… we put what was wrong in the world right. We stand up for truth and fairness. I believed that, but it isn't true.

"I thought of handing in my notice. But after you worked so hard to help me achieve… after all you encouraged me to do… how could I throw it all away?"

"I strive to gif you choices only, Nata. To open doors for you. I never mean to make you sink you got to go srough them. Or you can't turn back when you want to. And now, you have goot reasons to consider another way of life. Which way you go… it is for you alone to choose."

"There's something else."

His brows knotted. Her breath was coming in little puffs, now, and she felt washed with a bleak sense of guilt and despair.

"Karl and I…. we've parted. He's filing for divorce."

Silence hung then, heavy and awkward. Hetty's plump, ruddy face had deflated and her eyes were misty. Worry lines sliced Joe's forehead and pulled at the corners of his eyes.

"Now you are disappointed in me," she said, her eyes downcast. "You taught me marriage was sacred. The church says divorce is a sin… that Christian marriage is indissoluble."

When she dared to glance up, his gaze was warm with compassion.

"Not my place to judge you, Nata."

"But you've always been so passionate about commitment and responsibility."

"Maybe too passionate about many sings," he replied, his voice filled with sorrow. "I want for you to haff what I want and can't get: not just a job to make a living. I want for you to haff money enough to live well and enjoy goot things that Hetty and I haff to go without. I also want you to believe in what we believe in; do what we sink right. But now I see that haffing what I want for you to have does not make you happy. Now I ask myself how do I know what is right?"

"How can you ask that? You and Mum… you are such good people. You always do what is right."

"Not always. We did sings we are not proud of. We haff our secrets, Nata. And now, I see maybe I not the fader I should be."

"You are a wonderful father. The best."

"I was… how you say… too much the rules. Not understanding. I push you to be what I want you to be. You strive always to please me, Nata. But you do not please yourself."

He was silent for a moment, and he seemed deeply disturbed over something. He had the look of a man who was drowning in regret and remorse, and it alarmed her. Joe had always been so self-assured… so certain and controlled. His way was right, and her compliance with his demands had never been negotiable. There was no scope for question or debate. But she admired him, and he rewarded her compliance generously. As long as he loved her, she would do whatever was required to win his approval.

"With discipline, I help you built a moral code, " he said. His tone was thoughtful and apologetic. "My rules… the small punishments when you disobeyed… it was to keep you safe until you wise enough to make your own choices. My values serve until you decide yours. But now, you grown up, you should set de rules. Right and wrong… what do I know? It is for you to decite."

He reached across and laid his hand over hers. "You got to pursue your own happiness, Nata. How you lif your life now… it is between you and your conscience. My luff for you…. it comes widout strings. My wish is only for you to be content with your life."

She lifted her face to him, and it was illuminated, now, with blessed relief.

"Karl insists Sean must go into care. If I agree, maybe we can… but I have a duty to… Oh, I'm so confused. What should I do, Dad?"

"What your own heart tell you," he said. "Reach deep inside and find what brings you happiness and peace."

She pondered this advice for a moment, then summoned courage to make another announcement.

"I want to find my birth mother," she said.

#

Joe had returned to his carpentry, perhaps looking for distraction. Hetty took his afternoon tea out to him and came back to sit opposite her daughter at the lace-covered table. A dozen fresh-baked scones were arranged on her best china platter, and she had spooned jam and cream into little crystal bowls, but Nata had no appetite. She sipped at her tea and struggled to read Hetty's thoughts; to measure the level of distress her last statement had caused. Today, it seemed, was a day for announcements that rocked her parents' world. But wanting to find Mama... after all these years... after Hetty had given her all—for more than two decades—to being "Mum".

"Are you sure?" Hetty asked, her face a mask of shocked confusion.

"No," she said softly. "Not at all. But I'm desperate for answers, Hetty. I just thought... maybe..."

She gazed about the little cottage that had been her childhood home. It was a place of warmth and comfort. In Joe and Hetty's home, she had always felt safe and loved. She struggled, now, to recall her first home. She had suppressed the memories for so long. On the rare occasions she allowed the memories to surface, she remembered pain and misery and fear. She recalled a mother she had loved... a mother she had been sure had loved her. But Mama had abandoned her. She had never written. Never phoned. Never visited. There was not a word from her to suggest that she even remembered her little girl had ever existed.

"Mama gave me away, Hetty. She gave me away and she never came back for me. She got on with her life and forgot me. It's what Karl wants me to do with Sean. What I might have to do, I suppose. Maybe she can tell me how."

The colour rose up Hetty's neck and flooded her cheeks. Her eyes were a mist of tears and her hands shook. In a trembling voice, she whispered, "She came back for you, Nata."

Silence fell, heavy and awkward. For an instant, Natalie wanted to reach across and wrap her hands about the woman's neck. She wanted to squeeze the life out of her, while demanding explanation. But a thousand treasured memories flooded her brain—memories of being loved and wanted, cared for and protected.

Hetty was rattling now, talking as fast as her lips would move, unburdening herself. Her words drifted in a confused stew and Natalie struggled to take the message in. *Mama came back? When? Why didn't they tell me?*

"You were ten. We'd had you for two wonderful years and we'd fallen hopelessly in love with you. You were the daughter we had yearned for... the child we craved so desperately. Your laughter filled our home and our hearts and we adored you." She paused a moment. She was staring at the floor, her face a mask of guilt and sorrow.

"Do you remember what your life was like with your Mama and Papa, Nata?"

Nata stared at her thoughtfully for a moment. Dare she remember? "I loved Mama, but Papa was a beast. His punishments, when I displeased him, were cruel, but Mama copped the most. He punched her stomach and face. He pulled her hair out and he thumped her head against the walls and the table. He kicked her sometimes, too. Once, he beat her so savagely that an ambulance came to take her away to hospital. Not long after that, they brought me to your house. They promised to come back for me, but they didn't, and I'm glad."

Hetty swiped at a tear. "Your Papa owed money," she said. "Gambling debts. Joe loaned him money and he left you with us to secure the debt."

A wave of nausea flooded over Nata. She had been traded, like a piece of real estate or a precious work of art. She was nothing more than a commodity. The thought sent a dark mist burning through her that made her want to lash out at Joe; made her want to choke Hetty into silence.

"Two years later... your Mama came back for you. Your Papa was dead."

Hetty paused while Nata processed the shocking announcement. For an instant, a fragile bubble of joy had formed in Natalie's heart. Her Papa was gone, and her Mama wanted her back. Her Mama loved her. But why didn't Hetty tell her? The joy dissolved. She glared at Hetty with accusing jury eyes. A raging fire began to burn in her belly. Hetty just rattled on, her voice quavering. "She offered to buy you back, but I pleaded with her to leave you here where you were safe and happy. I asked her what she had to offer you. In the end, she agreed. We made a pact. She promised to stay out of your life as long as I wrote her regularly."

Hetty sucked a gulp of air. Nata rose and teetered for a few minutes on unsteady legs, afraid they wouldn't carry her. The nausea overcame her and she ran to the toilet and stood there retching for what seemed an eternity. A memory hammered at her forehead.

She was sixteen. It was during a brief period of teenage rebellion. She had gone to a wild party she'd been forbidden to attend. Joe had punished her unusually harshly for disobeying him, lying and breaking curfew. She thought it unfair, since he wouldn't have known about her breaking curfew had she not suffered guilt pains and confessed. She had railed at him and told him she was fed up with all his strict rules, sick of going to church and confession, and tired of the endless hours of study he made her do.

"When you adult, you can do what you want," he had replied calmly. "While you are a chilt, you got no choice. You do as I say."

"Not if I run away," she'd countered. "What would you do then? You're not even my father."

"By law, Hetty and I are your parents," he'd said. "Your mother and father... they sign papers. They gift you away to us because they cannot care for you proper. We are your legal guardians, and until you considered adult under law, you under our control. You do what I tell you. If you run away, police bring you back and you have even less freedom than now." He had patted her shoulder then, and his tone had softened. "I only want to protect you, my little one, because you are precious to me. Sometimes, I got to make you a little discomfort to help you understand. Your choices put you in danger. You not yet wise enough to make goot choices. I got to impose my way until you learn more. Someday, you thank me, I think…. I hope so."

It was a lie. Joe had lied to her. Honest, solid, dependable Joe, who always kept his word; the father whose promises… and threats… could always be relied upon completely. He had taught her the importance of honesty. He had punished her for lying, and she had known it pained him. He delighted in pampering and spoiling her. He lived for her hugs and smiles. He would do almost anything to make her happy. But he had lied to her… about something of such critical importance. There were no signed papers. Her mama loved her. She had come for her… just as she promised.

She sank to the floor, weeping.

Joe lied. Joe bought me from my father and then he and Hetty kept me from the mother who loved me. The words replayed in her head, over and over. *Joe lied. Joe bought me. Joe lied.*

At last, she wiped her lips and flushed the bowl, then stumbled to the bathroom to wash her mouth. Hetty came up behind her.

"Nata?" she said, her tone pleading and fearful. "Natalya, please let me—"

Nata shook her head.

"I need to— " Hetty began. Natalie could hear the silent tears… hear the awful anxiety. Her fear was palpable.

"Let me go," Nata said. "I have to leave now."

"When will you come back?" Hetty sobbed.

"I don't know, Hetty, " Natalie said, and stumbled to the kitchen to collect her handbag, then half ran up the hallway, out the door, through the gate, and, blinded by tears, down the street. She picked up pace as the blocks fell away and she ran, seemingly without direction. Twice she stopped to empty more of her stomach contents into the gutter. Several times, she halted to wipe away tears that obscured her vision and to wait for walk signals at busy corners. Part of her wanted to charge out into the traffic. Let it run her down. Let it put an end to the awful agony.

How much more, God? How much more suffering must I endure? Will you take from me everything that matters? I lost my mama. I've lost my husband. You have given me a crippled son. And now you have destroyed my trust in the only people who ever really loved me... the mother and father I thought I could trust implicitly... rely on always to care for me and keep me safe.

She was in front of the church now. Had she gone there purposely? She had no awareness of consciously deciding a direction. But there it stood, like a safe haven, beckoning, promising peace. Could she trust that promise?

It was a long time since she had found peace there; a long time since she had believed the doctrine. Joe and Hetty believed the doctrine. They had taken her there with them twice each week throughout all the years of her childhood. They had insisted she go there every Friday to make her confession. Joe had demanded she continue that practice throughout her years at university.

"I pay for your tuition, young lady," he said sternly. "You will respect my wishes and continue to honour Got and obey church law. You will live as we haf taught you. And sat includes attending church each Sunday and making a weekly confession."

She had done as he commanded. Except for a few small instances of teenage rebellion, she had always done as he commanded. And on those few occasions when she defied him, she suffered greatly, knowing he was displeased with her. She had searched desperately for ways to make amends. She revered him. Joe and Hetty had represented all that was good and pure in the world.

She stumbled into the church and sat at the end of a pew near the door. She stared, for a moment, at the stained glass window above the altar. And then she sank to her knees and dropped her face into her hands and cried... and cried... and cried. She cried for what seemed an eternity, but time had stood still. The world had stopped turning. She wanted never to move from there… never to stop the flood of tears that burned her cheeks or the strangled sobs that choked her.

A warm hand touched the back of her neck. A soft, kind voice… a familiar voice… asked, "Can I help, my child?" She shook her head.

"Something is troubling you terribly, my dear. And talking to God seems not yet to be delivering comfort. That bothers me."

"God can't fix what is wrong in my world," she sobbed. "I don't know why I'm here. God has betrayed me."

"I wish you would talk to me, my child," he said. "Perhaps you would feel more comfortable in the Confessional?"

She turned her face to him. "It is not me who should be confessing," she said, and her tone was acrid.

"You believe someone has wronged you?" he asked gently.

"Good Catholics. Church-going saints, preaching God's law and pretending virtue. Demanding I join them in worship. Making me come, every Friday, to confession, to ask penance for my sins. But what of theirs?"

The priest was studying her tortured expression closely. His eyes were filled with concern and his voice with deep compassion. He moved his hand from her neck, now, to cradle her chin. With the forefinger of the other hand, he gently wiped away a tear.

"They betrayed my trust, Father. They lied to me… the most dreadful, awful, hurtful lie. How could they do that? How could they—" And she dissolved again into violent, gut-wrenching sobs.

He stroked her back. He muttered syllables she couldn't understand. And then he prayed, aloud. He begged for mercy for sinners and comfort for those they sinned against. He begged the Lord to give her strength to forgive, but she railed at him. "How can I forgive them? They lectured me about the importance of honesty. They punished me when I told a little lie about where I had spent an evening. They sent me to confession to beg God's forgiveness and to pray for understanding of right and wrong…

so that I would not commit such sin again. And you… you gave me penance." She made a hissing sound that spoke of hatred and contempt.

"I have not seen you in church for some time. How long is it since your last confession?" he asked.

"I may not ever pray again," she replied. "How can I believe in and trust a God who betrays me? Who takes from me all that I hold dear? Who makes a mockery of all that I believe in?"

"God did not betray you, Natalie," he said.

"He destroyed everything that matters to me," she retorted, her tone filled with malice.

"What is it that has hurt you so," he asked. "Please tell me."

She raised her eyes truculently in anger and distress, but she shook her head and her lips tightened. She may despise them now, but she could never betray them… never condemn them to a man who respected and admired them. She could not speak to him of their sin. He waited a while, and when she seemed to calm, he left her, and it was then that she silently mouthed the words that haunted her.

"Joe and Hetty… They bought me. They traded me like a commodity… paid my vile beast of a father to give them his child. And then they lied and let me believe my Mama had no love for me… that she gave me to them and never came back. But they paid for me. They bought me, and when she wanted to repay them and take back the child she loved, they refused her. And they kept us apart. And they let me believe she did not care."

The answer came back from somewhere deep inside her hurting heart.

They must have wanted you desperately… to pay money for you and then to make so much sacrifice to give you a good life. They must have loved you very much indeed. They paid for you, not because they regarded you as something to be bought and sold, but because an evil man required them to make payment in order to be allowed to save you from him. They kept you from your mama because they feared she would take you back into the evil world into which she had brought you... a world of pain they sought to rescue you from. They loved you. They wanted you. They needed to keep you safe.

The sun had long since drowned in the blackness of a moonless night when, at last, she bowed to the altar, signed the cross, and strode purposefully out into the drizzling rain. Her scalded cheeks were dry now. Her stomach had calmed. Her heart ached, but it was the dull ache of a heart that was mending. Her mind shuffled memories and reviewed them... rich, wonderful memories. One by one, she took them out, dusted them off, and replayed them.

Joe, sitting on her bed at night listening to her talk of her day, giving her advice, comforting her when she was sad; Joe, reading to her; Joe, reviewing her homework; Joe, strutting into the cottage after an interview with her teacher, waving a report card, shirt buttons straining, his smug smile lighting up the room and his booming voice asking what reward she wanted this time, while Hetty hugged her and told her how the teacher had praised her. She had basked in a glory that was not hers, for without Joe's patient guidance and firm insistence that she apply herself to study—without the books he bought her and the tutoring he paid for but could ill afford—she could never have won accolades.

And there was Hetty... gentle, kind, protective. Cooking her favourite foods night after night; filling her lunch box with little treats; sewing pretty dresses for her; taking her hand and walking with her to school each morning and waiting patiently at the gate in the afternoon to walk her safely home; doctoring her little wounds; nursing her when she was ill.

She drew a card from far down in the pack. She was twelve, and in the sixth grade. At the start of that year, Joe had gravely informed her that some things were about to change. It was time for her to learn about responsibility and the value of hard work. He had assigned chores she must do daily, and drawn a schedule fixing time for study and for music practice.

She had come in from play one afternoon, hot and flustered, and apologising, and there was Hetty—calm, unruffled, unassuming Hetty—vigorously polishing the cabinets and the pine dining table; smiling gently at Nata and whispering, "We won't tell Joe. I know you meant to be home on time to do your chores and study, didn't you?" she said, "And in future you must my dear, yes? But just this once..."

Nata had hugged her and thanked her profusely and promised not to fail in her duties again. But later, she had suffered pangs of guilt and confessed, and Joe had punished her, but mildly. He had lectured her about fulfilling her obligations... being responsible... and about the value of work. Hetty had stood shaking her head and looking puzzled. Nata had kissed and hugged her and told her she loved her, but that they had taught her honesty and to accept responsibility, and she could not deceive Joe. And Hetty nodded and told her how proud she made them both.

Hetty would have lied for her, to save her from suffering Joe's little punishment... to save her the agony she always suffered when she incurred Joe's displeasure. Hetty knew how her heart ached whenever she disappointed her father, and she would do anything to protect Nata from even the smallest hurt. She did, often. "Little white lies," she called them. "To protect those we love from pain or suffering," she said. "We must always take care not to take it too far. But sometimes..."

How many times had Nata lied to save them from worry? Small lies... lies that, despite the conscience Joe's discipline and Hetty's fine example had given her, she could excuse because they were lies for their protection. She would have lied to Joe had she gone ahead with the abortion; lied by omission, just as Hetty had done.

Where do you draw the lines, Nata? They lied to protect you. Some lies are okay.

Natalie felt her anger leaching away, and a warm glow washing over her. "I forgive you both," she muttered under her breath, and then she started to run. She ran the rest of the way back to the cottage and she flung open the door and she charged in, arms outstretched, fresh tears trickling. She fell into Hetty's arms and dropped her face into Hetty's shoulder and they hugged. She heard Hetty's great heaving sigh and she felt her shoulders lift, and she heard the quivering voice… filled with remorse and contrition. She clung to Hetty for the longest time, and then Hetty made tea again. They drank and ate, and Hetty told her of her meeting with Lidiya, and how two women had fought for the little girl they both loved.

#

Hetty went out of the room for a moment. Nata heard the heavy footsteps down the hallway. There were sounds of drawers sliding, and papers shuffling, then a long, deafening silence.

Hetty reappeared, at last, clutching a bulging folder. Hands shaking, she passed it to Nata. Then she buried her face in her hands to hide her shame. Nata turned back the cover and her blood rushed to her feet. There were letters… dozens of letters. They were written in a somewhat untidy longhand. Most bore a prison letterhead. All were signed in a style she remembered from notes she'd carried in her school bag… long, long ago.

"My dear Hetty," the letters began, and they closed, "In love and gratitude, Lidiya."

Nata stared at the pages, shocked and reeling. Her fingers tiptoed over the return address: Dame Phyllis Frost Correctional Centre. She looked up, inquiring. Hetty had regained her composure now, and was watching Nata intently.

"Your mother killed your father, Nata. Self-defence, I'm guessing, though the verdict was premeditated murder."

She paused while Nata processed the revelation.

"She was arrested not long after she visited me. I followed the trial on television and in the papers. I struggled to keep it from you. Thankfully, it was brief. Nobody knew your former name and anyone who might have had an inkling who you were was sensible or compassionate enough to stay silent."

Black moths swarmed in Nata's belly. Hot, denying tears seared her cheeks and a hammer pounded against her temples.

"Now I really have to see her, Hetty," she said urgently. "This changes everything."

"Would you like me to go with you?"

Nata thought for a moment. The warmth in Hetty's offer sent a flood of compassion washing over her... compelling her to forgive. "I'd love to have you to lean on, but no. This is something I have to do alone. Thank you."

Hetty sighed and wiped a stray tear from her cheek.

"It won't change things, Mum," Nata said softly, reaching for her hand. "Between us, I mean. You will always be Mum. I will always love you, and I'll be eternally grateful for what you and Joe did for me."

"We lied to you, Nata. We let you think your Mama didn't care for you."

"You did what you thought you needed to do to protect me. You did it out of love."

TWELVE

Hetty handed Nata a letter dated April, 1986.

> *Dear Hetty and Joe,*
> *It has taken much longer than I had hoped, but at last my circumstances have changed for the better. I am now in a position to put things right with you and to be a mother to my daughter. I shall come on Wednesday morning at 9 o'clock. Please have her and her things ready.*
> *Thank you for caring for her all this time. I will be eternally grateful.*
> *Lidiya Popovich.*

"The day I received that was one of the worst days of my life," Hetty whispered. "There are no words to describe the horror and fear. I thought I was about to lose you, Nata, and I don't think I could have lived with the pain."

Tears welled as the memories came flooding back.

#

She re-read the letter for the tenth time, or was it more than that? Her head was spinning and her eyes watered. She could hardly recall what she had done five minutes ago, let alone when the note had come or how many times her eyes had scanned it, desperately hoping that re-reading it would somehow change the content. She looked at the clock again. At least three hours to go before Joe would come home. She wished she could run to him now, cry on his shoulder, lean on his strength. No matter how bad things were, he always seemed to stay strong enough to comfort and reassure her.

Unable to face the hours alone, she called on her neighbour for support, but would Martha's company help, or would solitude, perhaps, be preferable? Was it fair to make Martha party to deceit? Could she trust her to conspire to lie, if that is what her heart said she must do?

School would finish soon. Nata would be waiting for her at the gate. Somehow, she had to hide her pain and terror from the child. She could not let her know. *But if the woman came for her? Could she stop her reclaiming what was hers?* She reached for a handkerchief and dabbed at her cheeks.

"No! It can't happen. She's been gone so long. She wouldn't take her back now, would she?" She fingered the note and stared across the table at Martha.

"But you said it was always a temporary arrangement?" Martha said.

She stared at the words again. No mention of Sergei.

"I can't send Nata back to that place, Martha."

"I don't see that you have much choice in the matter, Hetty."

"But they have shirked their responsibilities for two years… while we have loved her and cared for her and provided for her. Given her a good home and everything a child could need."

"Yes. You've done wonders with her. I remember the little girl she was. I've watched her grow and blossom. I've seen the school reports. And if I had the power to make an order, I wouldn't hesitate to say she should stay with you, where she is safe and loved. I would say the parents had forfeited their claim to her. But it's not how the law works, Hetty. You haven't made a formal application for custody… haven't reported the parents and had them investigated for neglect… have you?"

"Of course not. I wouldn't want authorities to interfere, and I certainly wouldn't want to risk Nata knowing how she came to us. No child deserves to feel unwanted by the parents who brought her into the world. That we love and want her would never be enough to erase the pain that knowledge would cause."

"But she must know anyway. They've made no contact before? She couldn't help but feel they had abandoned her."

"Lidiya has phoned a few times. She asked how Nata was; asked me to pass on messages… to tell her she loved her and would come back for her soon."

"And did you…. tell her?"

Hetty shook her head. "I tried to once or twice, but the words wouldn't come. I couldn't bear seeing the pain on her little face at the mention of her Mama. There was enough sadness in those first months, until she began to forget."

"Does she ever ask about her parents?"

"Not now. She did, at first. Asked if they were coming back for her. She never seemed to want them to, really. Though I got the feeling that she loved her mother… would have liked to be close to her. She seemed terrified of Sergei. He was a beast. He told Joe to beat the child often. And he all but confessed to beating the mother too."

Martha gave a little shudder. "Poor child…. Poor woman! But could she take her child back to that? Surely she has found a way to put an end to it? She did say her circumstances had changed for the better." Martha rose and quietly refilled Hetty's teacup, then her own. "But she is coming now. So what will you do, Hetty?"

"What choice do I have, Martha. If I refuse to surrender

her… they might go to the police. We could be charged with kidnapping."

"Somehow I doubt they would go to the police, Hetty… or the child welfare authorities. I suspect they wouldn't want the authorities to know they had ignored their child for two years… let someone else care for her… failed to contribute to her keep, or even to keep check to ensure she was safe and looked after. You and Joe are not in a good position, here, but I'll warrant it's a better position than theirs. You've done nothing wrong. Just cared for a friend's child… at their request… when they couldn't."

"I'd hardly call them friends. I don't even know the woman, and Joe dislikes Sergei intensely." Hetty paused to blow her nose. "So what do we do, Martha? What would you do?"

"Ah, Hetty dear! Please don't ask me to give you advice. I have no idea what I'd do in your position. I only know that it's a dreadful position to be in. I feel for you… deeply. I know how much you love that girl, and what you've given her. And I know she needs you. But I also know that girls need their mother; that there can be no substitute, no matter how kind and caring. It's never quite the same."

Hetty lurched forward, almost choking on a mouthful of tea.

"I'm sorry, dear. I know how that sounds. But Lidiya brought her into the world. Surely you must see…"

"And she left her to… maybe starve, be abused, be used as a slave. How would she know that the girl would be loved and cared for?"

"Hetty… dear! One meeting with you or Joe and anyone could be confident you would never harm a child; that you'd be good to the girl. Lidiya came to your home. She met you and Joe. She ate lunch with you. She saw how you warmed to Nata."

"And now she wants to take her from us."

"She wants her daughter back. She's a mother, Hetty. Nothing could be more natural than to want to be close to your child."

"So now she is a mother, after two years of not being a mother!" Hetty felt heat rising in her neck and was ashamed to realize she had been shouting. She opened her mouth to apologize, but all that came out was a broken sobbing sound. Martha rose and rounded the table to wrap her arms around her.

"Go ahead and cry, Hetty. Let the emotion out. Then, when Joe comes, you need to think it through carefully and figure out how to reply to Lidiya. Maybe there are choices… other than just handing the child over. Maybe you need to tell the girl. She's growing up, Het. You might be surprised at how maturely she copes."

"And I might not. Telling her might undo two years of hard work. It might destroy her." Hettty's head dropped and she began sobbing again.

"Then you have to figure out what you can and can't do about it."

"I can keep her. That's what. I can send her to school on Wednesday, just like usual. And I can talk to Lidiya.... convince her that what she's doing is wrong... tell her how happy the child is with us and that she wants to stay; that she has no desire to go back home. In fact, I don't think I'll wait until Wednesday. I'll call on her. Yes, that's what I'll do. I'll go to her. That way, I'll see what sort of home she proposes Nata should live in. See if she can convince me that she'll be better fed and cared for than she was before she came to us. I'll go tomorrow, as soon as Nata has left for school. But now, I must walk to the school to meet Nata and walk her safely home."

Martha reached across and squeezed her hand. "God be with you, Hetty," she whispered. "God give you strength."

#

"I didn't feel strong, walking to the school gate that day, Nata. But you were my child, and I was determined to fight for you. I swore to fight for you as your birth mother didn't… to keep you, no matter what the cost."

"I went to see her. She was slow to answer my knock. I sensed her eye peering through the peep hole… looking me up and down and desperately trying to process the image and recall where she had seen me before. Finally, the door opened a crack. I pushed on it and stepped into a dimly lit hallway.

"I remember thinking how painfully thin she was, and that her eyes still had that fearful, haunted look. But her face was in far better repair. There were no shiners."

Hetty fell silent as her mind drifted again.

#

"I'm Hetty Dreyer. You wrote me."

Lidiya looked confused.

"I've been caring for your daughter these past two years. Yes, Mrs. Popovich, that's how long it's been. And you've made no effort to see her, to write her or send gifts. You've taken no interest at all. And now you want to take her back. Well, I'll not be handing her over to a woman who cares so little for her. I've come to tell you to stay away."

"I phoned," Lidiya protested weakly.

"Ha! Asked me to tell her you would be coming for her soon. Good thing I didn't. How many disappointments do you think a child that age can deal with, Mrs. Popovich?"

"But I…"

"No need for you to take her now. She has forgotten you exist, I'll warrant. Joe and I are her parents now, and she loves us. She is happy with us. Look…" Hetty drew a photograph of the child from her handbag and handed it to the woman. "See how well she looks. I've fed her well and she's filled out. She plays sport. She excels at school. We bought her a violin and sent her to music lessons. She has everything, now, that a little girl should have. We love her like our own, Mrs. Popovich. We've made her our own…

"She took some time to settle… to recover from whatever misery and trauma she suffered here. Her papa… he treated her badly, didn't he? She was terrified of Joe for the longest time. But now… he's her papa, and she adores him. I'll not be returning her to the life she had before she came to us.

"I'm sorry, Mrs. Popovich, but if you have any love at all for your little girl, you will let her stay where she is safe and loved and happy."

Lidiya stood in the open doorway, staring at Hetty. Hetty had pushed past her and hovered in the middle of a long, dark hallway. Silence hung like a thick blanket of cloud. Lidiya looked desperate and deflated. Hetty suddenly regretted her outburst… felt sorry for the poor, frightened woman.

I should have been gentler… taken it a little more slowly. But what I said had to be said, and there was no easy way to say it.

"But I'm her mother," Lidiya whispered at last. She fell back against the wall and the tears came. "I have missed her so much. I wanted to see her… wanted to… You don't understand… you… I… "

She began to slide down the wall. Hetty reached out and caught her; lifted her and put her hand under her elbow.

"Come," she said, her tone gentle and compassionate now. "You need to sit. I'll make us some tea."

An hour later, Lidiya was smiling sadly over the photographs Hetty had brought: Natalya in her school uniform. "She is smiling, Hetty. Her face fairly glows with happiness."

Natalya at the breakfast table, eating pancakes. "No wonder she has filled out so well. Look at the size of that stack! I fear you spoil her."

Natalya practising on her violin; playing on stage at a recital. "I could never afford to give her music lessons. I wish I could hear her play."

Natalya receiving an award at school speech night; accepting a trophy at a sports carnival; Natalya, sitting on Joe's lap; hugging Joe; sitting on the mat in her room placing jigsaw puzzle pieces; dressing a doll; peering into her wardrobe to choose a dress to wear. "So many dresses! You do spoil her, Hetty."

There was a photo of Joe holding a shiny new bicycle with a huge ribbon tied in a bow on the handlebar. Natalya was on the bike, laughing. Joe was holding the back firmly; his face ruddy and sweat dripping from his forehead. He'd been running behind her to make sure she didn't fall.

There were photos of her room too: a collection of dolls and stuffed toys on the bed; more on the dresser; a bookcase bulging with books, and a little red transistor radio on top with two tall stacks of tapes beside it. A desk was piled high with schoolbooks; merit certificates pinned to a bulletin board above. There was doll's pram in one corner, and an enormous doll's house in another—a stunningly beautiful doll's house with balconies trimmed with miniature Victorian lace panels. Tiny wooden beds and chairs and kitchen cabinets, quilted mats and lace curtains filled the rooms. There was even a battery-operated lighting system. Joe had made it for her ninth birthday. He made most of the furniture, too. Hetty had sewn the curtains and mats and upholstered the settees. They had spent a hundred late night hours on it, suffering sleep deprivation, but it was a labour of love. In the wee small hours of the mornings, they had carried it to the back shed and covered it with blankets. And at night, they would check carefully that Nata was sound asleep, and then retrieve it and place it on an old sheet in the living room, and set to work.

"You have spoiled her terribly. I could never give her what you have given her," Lidiya mumbled, her eyes misting. "But I am her mama. And I do love her. You could never understand, I know. You have a good man, Hetty. Sergei… he made life hard. Too hard. He… I couldn't…"

"And you want her to return to that life?" Hetty said, struggling to hide impatience. She must try to show compassion for the woman, but all she felt was anger and contempt.

"Sergei is gone," she said softly. "It would just be the two of us. I have very little money, but we'd manage, and I'd shower her with love… I do love her, Hetty. You must believe that."

Hetty's heart pounded against the wall of her chest. Although the room was cold, beads of perspiration glittered on her forehead. A feeling of panic locked her throat, so that no matter how she tried to speak, the sounds would not come. Lidiya's forehead pleated over a pale face and sunken cheeks, but there was a faint sparkle of hope in her eyes.

"You could visit. I'd want you to. You could take her some place nice sometimes, on the weekends. We could spend Christmas together. I'd like that, Hetty. Natalya would too; I know she would."

Hetty's voice came thin and strained. "Natalie would like to stay right where she is… where she feels safe and loved and she has everything a child needs to grow up well-adjusted and capable. You may be her birth mother, Lidiya, but I am her mama now, and Joe is her papa. That's how she sees it. And you have forfeited your claim to her."

She gazed at the woman, struggling for a calm she didn't feel. Anxious butterflies were dancing in her stomach and a wave of goose bumps erupted over her skin. "Mrs. Popovich… I can't pretend to know how you are feeling right now… what it is to be a mother parted from your child. But surely any mother wants what is best for the child? And surely you can see that Natalie is better off with us?"

Lidiya sucked in a breath and flicked at a tear trickling down her cheek. Hetty gazed about the room. Her eyes fell on a photograph: Lidiya, with two girls clutching at her skirts, uncannily alike. Natalya at maybe six or seven? The other, older, wearing a school uniform. Thirteen or fourteen, perhaps? She stifled a surprised gasp and struggled to gather her thoughts.

"You have two daughters, Mrs. Popovich?" she said, and studied the woman's reaction closely. Lidiya's eyes followed hers to the photograph.

"Two daughters and two sons," Lidiya replied, a tide of crimson flooding her face. "My boys were placed in care... by court order. Elena is in care now too. The boys are not Sergei's. Elena neither. Only Natalya is his child."

Lidiya's fingers closed so tightly over a tissue that her knuckles turned white. "He wasn't always like that... Sergei. At first, he was good to us. I was a widow, you see. He claimed he loved my kids and wanted to give all of us a good home; free me to be a proper mother. I was working in a bar at night... not a nice place either. The bar girls... they took their clothes off....

"You are shocked, I can see. I understand that. But I had little choice. With three kids, it was the only way to make a living after I lost my dear husband."

A flood of pity set Hetty stomach churning. She reached out and touched Lidiya's hand gently. "You poor dear. Go on," she said gently. "It's not my place to judge you."

"Sergei swept me off my feet. He could charm when it suited. He was always harsh when displeased, but I worked hard to make him happy. I cooked and cleaned and washed for him and satisfied his physical needs, and he provided for us well.

"As the boys grew older, they went wild... out of control. He tried to discipline them, but he was cruel and they rebelled against him. They started getting into trouble with the law—petty crimes, shoplifting, vandalism. Sergei told the court they were bad boys and needed locking up... asked for them to be sent to a reform school. Made me sign a statement surrendering them to institutional care. I was stricken with grief, but he gave me no choice. They'd have been locked up soon enough, anyways, if they'd stayed under our roof. They were way too deep into mischief and nothing we tried would stop them."

Hetty studied the woman's knotted face and tried to feel empathy, but her heart was cold with contempt now. She could not condone any mother giving up on her children.

"Sergei said we could have a child together. It would distract me... make up for losing my boys. Natalya came along, and for a while things were good. He adored her, and doted on her. And he was pleased with me for giving him a baby girl, so for a time he treated me well. But when he lost his job and couldn't find another, he resorted to the drink to console himself. When he drank, he was vile. As time went on, he stopped looking for work. Our savings ran out. He blamed me for our poverty. He said I'd spent all his money on my brats of kids.

"By then, Elena was growing up... and wanting a life that Sergei wouldn't permit. I tried to make him understand that she was growing up in a different world... that women in this country weren't merely servants to their men folk. It wasn't working. And then, he decided I was no longer attractive to him, but my daughter... He started to... ''

Her hands crept to her throat. "Eventually, I sent her away to a girls' home... for her own protection."

There was a moment of pregnant silence. When Hetty spoke, she fought to sound controlled. "So you have surrendered three children into care, and given one to a stranger to look after and had no contact for two years. Mrs. Popovich, if we applied for a custody order—"

The woman's face turned as pale as wax and her thin, shrill voice gave off a sound like an expiring mouse. Hetty waited silently for her to compose herself. Her thoughts were tumbling about, now... swimming in a pool of relief.

"We'd rather not, you understand?" she said in a voice now iced with condescension. "It would be much better for you to just voluntarily give up your parental rights; let the child grow up in a home where she is happy and has all the comforts and privileges you admit you are unable to provide for her."

Lidiya gave her a mournful stare. All signs of hope had melted away. Her eyes dulled behind a prism of tears.

"Would you let me visit?" Her tone was that of one resigned to loss. She expected her request to be declined.

"I think it would be better not. I think it best to let things go on as they have been. Avoid disruption and confusion."

"Then at least promise me you will write often. Send photographs... tape recordings of her violin recitals. Would you do that much, at least, for a sad, old woman whose life is empty now, without children to love?"

A pang of guilt stabbed Hetty like a sword as the sad memory of loss flooded over her, and she relived the misery and hopelessness that had overwhelmed her at the start of every monthly. She tried to imagine a young widow, alone in a cruel world of uncaring people, struggling to feed her babies.

But she gave up on her children. Surely there were other ways?

Hetty struggled for composure. She could not let Lidiya see weakness.

"I will write often," she promised. She could see no harm in that, and it was surely the least she could do for a woman who had given her and Joe so much. "I will tell you everything that is happening in her life. I will send you tapes and photographs. And when Joe and I think the time is right, we will remind her that she had a mama who loved her deeply, and we will bring her to see you. But you must leave it to our judgement to decide when the time is right."

Lidiya rose and followed her to the door. She wore the look of a woman utterly defeated and devoid of all hope... a woman whose spirit had departed; a woman in whom the light of life had long since been extinguished and who now waited patiently for death to end her suffering.

#

Hetty finished her story with tears filling her eyes and trickling slowly down her cheeks. "She loved you, Nata," she said softly. "You have hated her for all these years, but out of love for you, she endured the greatest pain that can ever be inflicted on a woman.

"I wrote to your mama. Every month… just as I promised. I rented a post box to receive her replies. I kept them all. I hid them. I didn't even show them to Joe."

Thirteen

Nata spent a week at the cottage, and then she returned home. After three nights at Phillip's, Karl had moved to a hotel. He had bought the home to please Nata, and as a status symbol, but he'd said it carried no status if he lived there alone. It was too far from the office and too far from the bars and restaurants he liked to frequent. For a bachelor, a hotel room in the city was infinitely more convenient.

Nata struggled to believe Karl's promise to give her the house. Yet it suited her, for now, to move back from the cramped little bedroom in the cottage to the home in which she had planned to raise their son. The home she had wanted to fill with children and love and laughter was now an empty, soulless place. The nursery door remained firmly locked. She had no heart to think of redecorating the living room or putting her personal stamp on their bedroom. She had no interest in restoring the garden to its former glory, nor in planning where the sandpit, swing and slide should go. They may never be wanted. But she loathed the thought of letting the lovely mansion stand empty, for that meant an end to hope... the end of a marriage, and the end of a dream. She was, as yet, in far too much pain to face the reality that their love had died and their partnership was done.

She sat at her desk in the corner of the bedroom. The study

belonged to Karl, and, like the nursery, its door remained closed and bolted.

Drawing a sheet of scented paper from her drawer, Nata took up her favourite fountain pen and began to write in an elegant hand.

Dear Mrs. Popovich... Mama,

It has been so long. I have missed you, but I have been well cared for and loved.

I know that Hetty has written. You would know that I am a lawyer now, married, and a mother. And I expect you know, by now, that Hetty has finally unburdened herself. She has told me that you came back for me. She has told me of your incarceration, and why.

The news alarmed me. I cannot grieve for Papa. He deserved his fate. But I am shocked and pained that you suffer so.

I must see you, Mama. Would you add me to your visitor list, please? If you will permit it, I would like to come next Wednesday afternoon. The details you need to provide to the Prison Manager are printed below.

Your loving daughter,

Natalya
(Natalie Albrecht)

Her head and heart ached as she printed the name 'Natalie Albrecht'. Would she keep that name? Perhaps it would be best for Sean, but she hated it now. She was Nata Dreyer. Dreyer was a name she could wear with pride. Nata Dreyer was a girl who was deeply loved.

She folded the paper and slipped it into an embossed envelope and carefully penned her mother's name and prisoner number and the prison address. She fixed a stamp in the corner, placed a silver return address sticker on the back, and slipped into a pair of flat-heeled shoes to walk to the post box.

#

Nata telephoned Karl. She had weighed the arguments for and against. She had cried a river and smashed things and slammed doors and kicked furniture. She had tossed and turned at night in that monstrous lonely bed. Sometimes, in the dark of night, she would wake to a terrible wailing sound that she knew came from herself.

In the early mornings, she had staggered, exhausted already, from the parking station to Sean's hospital bedside. She had wept in despair as she gazed down at him. When she looked at her child, her vision was obscured by a wall of fear. At times, she loved him beyond measure, but at other times, the hatred filled her and she would lurch into the bathroom to vomit, overcome with sickening guilt and wallowing in black despair. She tended competently to his feeding and changing, but she nursed a silent sense of utter helplessness and incompetence. The future stretched out before her like a dark, cold corridor to nowhere.

She tried to nap during the day, but in the little visitor's room, interruptions were constant.

Hetty came to the house some evenings, to cook for her. She was living on snack foods and the weight was falling away. A gaunt, hollow-cheeked, whey-faced stranger looked back from the mirror. Her clothes sagged on her. Despair was written in every line of her.

It was all too hard. Karl was right. She didn't belong in this life. She could admire women who had the stamina to do this, but Sean was too heavy a burden and she would buckle under the weight. When she talked to his doctors, her pretend calm cracked and her anxiety showed through. Her shoulders drooped and a gush of air rushed out. When his doctor told her he had an infection and he could not go home yet, she could not hide her relief.

"It gets easier, Nata," he said in a voice rich with empathy and understanding. "The first few months are always the hardest. He'll come off the oxygen, and gradually he'll start to move and make sounds, and then we can give you a more accurate prognosis. But meanwhile, you need to do something about your own health. You can't go on like this.

"Karl?" he asked gently.

"He left me," she mumbled, raising her guilt-ridden eyes to meet his. "It was all too hard for him to deal with."

He touched her shoulder gently. "And for you, too," he said.

"I'm stronger than I look."

"You're not," he said with vehemence. "Find a good counsellor, Natalie. Hire help if you need to. Start eating healthy meals, and get some sleep. Whether Sean goes home or not, you have to find a way to mend."

Her defensiveness died away at his sincerity, and she felt her strength creeping slowly back. Karl had been right, after all. She needed the stimulation of her job. She needed her work friends. She needed the satisfaction of achievement, the thrill of winning. And she needed her husband. He was overbearing and arrogant and selfish. He was intolerably pompous and pretentious and egotistical at times. But she loved him. She had made a commitment to him, before God, and she wanted to find a way to make her marriage work. She had never wanted a partner, but now she felt unable to face life alone. They had been happy before Sean was conceived. Maybe they could find a way to go back to what they'd had?

"Can we talk please, Karl," she had begged him.

"Of course," came the enthusiastic reply. "I'll come now."

"Tomorrow," she said. "After work. I'll make dinner for you. I have somewhere I need to go today."

"Tomorrow evening will be good. And dinner would be

nice. Thank you."

#

A gate closed behind her with an ominous clang, but when she glanced about, it was not at a dark and dismal place that filled her heart with pain and fear. The atmosphere was oddly inviting. Clad in blue prison tracksuits, women strolled about freely in the grounds and chatted amicably with fellow inmates. A few shot her curious glances. Some smiled.

She passed through the reception area, submitting to the usual entry procedures of evidencing her identity and having her picture taken, and handing over the package of gifts she carried, then she stepped through to the Visitors Centre.

Weary sentinels—thickset women in dark uniforms—leaned against the walls, rings of keys dangling from their belts. One stood by the entrance, her face as hard as tempered steel, with watchful eyes that burned through you. The place might be less forbidding than expected, but the staff were typical prison wardens.

In an airy, brightly lit room furnished with a scattering of small tables and simple stackable plastic chairs, the atmosphere was cheerful. She strained to make sense of the muffled drone of conversation—a meaningless stew of human voices, sentences punctuated now and then by light chuckles; high, tinkling laughs; or the occasional guttural curse. She scanned one blurred image after another in the sea of faces, searching.

From the rear corner, a pale, haggard face stared up at her with an expression of wretched surprise. An icy chill tiptoed up her spine. The blood drained from her face and her knees began to give way. It was the same face that she saw daily in the mirror, only old... ever so old and worn, with eyes that reflected the serenity that comes with acceptance of an unjust fate, and the loss of any hope of redemption.

She teetered a little, then gathered herself together and

strode resolutely across the room, passing a dozen or more women in blue trackies, all seated at tables and engaged in animated conversations with their visitors. Only the old woman sat alone. A withered, bony hand crept to her throat and her face paled to the shade of old parchment as she watched the visitor approach.

Nata was not entirely a stranger to the prison environment. In her work as a corporate lawyer, she had, on rare occasions, had to visit a client behind bars. Mostly, they were temporarily incarcerated in holding cells, in buildings far less modern and attractive than the one she had entered today. She had been inside jails, too—most far more ominous settings than this one. But she was not here to visit a client. She was here to visit a woman she had, for almost two decades, wished dead. She was here—God forgive her—to ask the woman's help. She had come to seek counsel from a woman she'd despised and cursed; a woman who, it was now apparent, could not help herself, let alone be of any use to a visiting stranger.

Forcing a composure she didn't feel, she flicked at a wave straying across her forehead, smoothed her skirt, and tried hard to smile as she took her seat opposite the woman. "Lidiya?" she said softly. And then she could hold it back no longer. The tears flowed freely and the words that followed were punctuated with sobs.

The old woman's eyes misted as she reached for the visitor's hand and stroked it gently. "Natalya! At last, you have come."

"Hello, Mama," she said softly.

They made small talk for a minute, and then there was a tense, eerie silence. They heard the other prisoners and their visitors chattering.

"You have a grandson, Mama. His name is Sean."

"Hetty wrote me and sent pictures," Lidiya replied. "She tells me everything. She told me you'd come... and why."

She ought to have asked about her mother's health and how she was coping; how she spent her time; who she was friends with. But suddenly, Nata was pouring it all out, unburdening herself to a stranger, begging advice from a woman she had hated and condemned and believed incapable of ever knowing what was right. How could Lidiya advise her? And yet, somehow, she had to find the answers.

"What should I do, Mama? Karl says I must put him away. I'm sure he's right. It's the only sensible thing to do. And yet… Please tell me. How does a mother go on living after giving up her child?"

Lidiya stared at her for a long time before replying. At last, she answered with a question.

"What do you remember from before you went to live with the Dreyers, Natalya?"

Nata hesitated for a moment. She had blocked it out for so long. She didn't want to remember. An urge consumed her… an urge to rise and run. The walls seemed to close in on her and the guard's presence threatened. She began to tremble. And then it came again… that coarse voice urging her. Those awful haunting words echoing in her head.

Up, down… squeeze. That's it. Good girl. Make Papa happy. Show Papa you love him. Harder now. Squeeze harder. Up and down. Up and down. Girls must work hard to please men. That's their job… to keep their man happy. Practice hard and you will be a good wife someday. Papa must train you. Good girl.

He had been on the grog again; that hot, sour breath panting over her; his stinking sweat; that ugly, bulging, wrinkled gut; the red, plump, pock-marked face, evil smile, and hot feral gleam in his eyes. Natalya felt sick. She hated touching Papa this way, but she did her best to please. If she tried really hard to appease him…

Mama? Where was Mama? Cowering at the door again? Listening, but afraid to enter? Or on her bedroom floor, too battered and sore to get up?

Nata swallowed back bile and worked her hands harder.

Please… please let it be enough.

"Ah, good girl. Someday, you make good vife. Not like you Mama. She lazy. She not try hard enough to please Papa. You must not be lazy, Natalya. Never be lazy. Men not want lazy vife."

Mama wasn't lazy. She was tired. He had worn her out with his endless demands and cruel treatment. Even as a tiny child, Natalya had understood that. She had come to understand, quite early in life, that her Papa was a bully and a brute.

Up and down. Squeeze. Up and down. Up and down.

Her hands ached, but she kept at it. His contented sigh and lecherous grin suggested he was satisfied at last. He rose and pulled on his trousers. He reached for his belt. Natalya made for the door, but he reached out and caught her. A flock of anxious butterflies made her heart pump. Her clammy skin erupted.

"You stay!" He spun her round to face him and waved a finger at her. His green eyes glittered with menace.

"You need lesson, leettle girl. You hit Papa. You shout at Papa. Got to learn respect. Papa got to teach you respect… for Papa. For men. You not find good husban' if you not respect men."

Her stomach dropped out. Her blood raced so hard she could hear it pounding in her ears. An iron hand gripped her upper arm so hard the blood flow stopped and she feared her limb would fall off. He took the belt in his other hand and it whistled as he raised it high.

When he was done, her buttocks were on fire and an intense, throbbing ache worked its way up her back. Her eyes were burning pools of pain. She fought valiantly to stifle the cries of agony she knew gave him such perverse pleasure.

"You learn respect, leettle girl. Da!" His voice was thick with menace and contempt. He thrust her roughly to the floor and gave a satisfied grunt as he strode away.

#

"He did it to me again later," Nata whispered. "He made me watch him beat you, and then he beat me. Then he made me do it. Said he had to teach me, but I must show him that I understood and I still loved him anyway."

Lidiya's face was streaked with tears now. "I so desperately wanted to protect you," she sobbed. And then the opportunity came. He had gambling debts. The men he owed money to threatened to expose his part in a crime. He had to pay to escape arrest and jail. He offered you to Joe and Hetty in return for a loan to pay his debts. I agreed, because I knew they'd love you and care for you. I knew you'd be safe there… safe from your brute of a father… safe from the poverty… safe from watching your mama suffer his beatings. I loved you so much, Natalya. I never stopped loving you. But I had to let you go."

She paused to wipe tear-streaked cheeks and blow her nose loudly.

"Sergei wasn't always a monster, Nata. He was handsome, and a charmer…that's for sure. For a while, before you was born, and even for little while after, life with him was good. He was a good provider and good fun. I can see him, still, dancing in the kitchen, singing and handing your sister pennies to buy sweets. Bringing me gifts on pay day.

"Then he lost his job. After that, there were few treats, but still we never went hungry. Sergei had always worked hard, and saved. We had a decent house to live in. I had a little money to buy clothes for meself and me babies. Your papa bought you toys.

"It was the grog, Nata. He always drank too much, but when he had no work, he spent all his days in the pub. Drink turned him into a monster."

"And back then, there was no help for abused women with children to protect," Nata said, her anger melting into pity.

"I thought it better to put up with what he did than risk starving me kids."

Silence reigned for a moment, then Lidiya resumed her

story.

"And then there was that awful day, just before your fifth birthday, when you seen him fondling Elena."

Nata reached across and closed her hand over her mother's as the memories came flooding back. She took up the story.

"Elena was whimpering and trying to push him away. His trousers were across the chair back and his belt lay across the seat. I took it and began thrashing him. I shouted at him to stop hurting my sister. He laughed and snatched the belt from my grip.

"You sent Elena away the next day, so Papa had only you and me to vent his rage on."

"He was harsh with you when you angered him," Lidiya said, swiping at the scald tracks her salty tears had made. "His punishments were cruel, but not frequent. I believed he loved you. Some of the time, he was good to you. I never knew of him doing nothing indecent with you again. I'd made him promise he wouldn't. I told him how dreadfully wrong it was. He promised me, and I believed him.

"Just after your eighth birthday, you asked for money for a school excursion. I had none to give you, so I took some from his wallet while he slept."

"I remember the excursion," Nata chimed in. "We rode Puffin Billy, the steam train, through the Yarra Valley."

Lidiya ventured a weak smile. "When he found the money missing, he beat me. I tried to keep it from him what I took it for, but you came home dancing and singing about your wonderful day. He beat you for being selfish and greedy, taking money that we needed for food. He'd have spent it on grog or gambling if I'd left it for him, but he would never admit to that.

"He brought you to me after he beat you. He boasted he'd done a good job of disciplining you. He said it hurt him to do it, but it was a father's job to teach his daughter. Then he put you between his legs and…

"I was weak from the beating, Nata, and afraid. He would

have killed me had I tried to stop him. He was a strong man, and he had no scruples."

Bile rose in Nata's throat and she choked it back. The words were echoing again. She could see him and she wanted to wrap her hands about his throat and strangle the brute. She was glad her mother killed him.

"He'd been asking me to agree to let Joe and Hetty take you in exchange for the loan. He promised it would only be for a little while. After that day, I was happy to let you go. I wanted it to be for as long as he lived. I'd made up me mind, watching you with him, that his days was numbered. I planned his murder that day. The judge was right. It was premeditated. I killed him intentionally, in cold blood, and... God help me... I can't say I'm sorry. I know it was a mortal sin, and I'll go to hell for not repenting, but he deserved it and I can't ask forgiveness."

They sat in silence for a moment. Thoughts and images raced about in Natalie's head: court rooms; trials; pleadings for mercy; pleas of self-defence. It was self-defence... premeditated or no. A good lawyer could have gotten Lidiya off, but of course she had no money to pay a lawyer. State defenders had little experience... and even less incentive.

"I always planned to go back for you after I killed him. I don't know what I was thinking. I thought I'd get off the charges... temporary insanity, self-defence... I don't know. I guess I wasn't quite sane.

"I planned the murder," Lidiya confessed, "and I'm not sorry I did it. I only marvel, sometimes, that I had the strength. But he'd made me give my baby away. He traded my child for money to pay gambling debts... to save his miserable skin from evil men who would've killed him to collect their dues. I wish I'd let them, but I hadn't any choice in the matter. He made the arrangements, and he'd 've killed me if I'd resisted."

FOURTEEN

Nata had been gone for well over a year when Lidiya finally summoned the courage. She'd been waiting and planning, but killing a man more than twice her size wasn't easy. He was strong, and she was weak from all the bashings and from overwork.

Sergei had come home drunk. There was some building work on down the road a bit, and he'd had a few days' work labouring for the bricklayers. Fetching and carrying. He was tired and sore. When he worked hard, he drank harder. He favoured the heavy liquor: rum and vodka. He drank it straight, mostly.

That night, he had come home very late. He'd been drinking for hours. He brought a small bottle of rum with him, and he settled with it in the kitchen. She had cooked him a meal, but he said he wasn't hungry. She planned to put the poison in his dinner, but that plan was foiled.

He had swallowed almost a quarter of a bottle before staggering to the outhouse to relieve himself, and then she'd seen her chance. She moved quickly. She poured most of the bottle down the sink. Knowing he was too drunk to remember how much grog he'd left, she poured the poison into the near empty bottle, then held a towel around the bottle as she handled it. The poison bottle had her fingerprints on it, but she'd used rat poison often, so there was no reason to hide the fact that she'd handled it.

He had finished off the bottle, then fell asleep—collapsed across the table. He was snoring loudly. Lidiya had stowed a part-full rum bottle he'd drunk from earlier in the week. She used part of what remained to wash out the poison, making sure to leave a tiny residue of rum in the bottom. Then she put the empty in the rubbish bin and took the second bottle and pressed it hard against Sergei's lips. She put it on the table in front of him and waited. When nothing happened for a time, she had gone to bed and slept fitfully. When she rose in the morning, he was collapsed over the table. His face had turned a deathly grey. There was no movement of his chest... no sound of air being sucked in or expelled. She didn't touch him. She went to the neighbour."

"Sergei is very ill," she had told them. She had asked them to call an ambulance. They wanted to go back with her to the house to wait, but she told them not to bother. She went back and waited.

They came. They checked his pulse. They pronounced him dead.

"They asked if there was someone they could call to be with me," Lidiya told Nata. "I suppose they thought I was a grieving widow. I told them I'd go next door. The neighbour was kind. They put Sergei on a stretcher and carried him away."

"The wonder, apparently, is that the poison killed him so quickly. The forensic examiner said that symptoms usually appear gradually, and death—if it happens—can take days or even weeks. But Sergei's organs would have been damaged from years of drinking, and he was very drunk that night."

Lidiya paused for a moment to study her daughter's expression. The child had hated her father, but hearing her mother confess to murdering her father in cold blood, and to know that she felt no remorse... How could any girl bear such horror and shame? And yet, now that she had come this far, she had to finish her story. She had to tell all.

"I played the part as I knew would be expected. I pretended

sorrow. I arranged his funeral and went in black with a veil over my face. Then I arranged the sale of the house. I said I couldn't go on living there alone. I found a tiny flat and moved my few possessions. And then I wrote to Hetty.

"The thought of having you back with me gave me such courage… such unaccustomed strength. Whenever my resolve weakened, I imagined hugging my baby. There are no words to describe the depth of my desire to hold you… the depth of my love for you. Hetty and Joe… they condemned me. I saw it in their eyes. I heard it in their voices. They thought me uncaring… unnatural.

"Oh, they knew what Sergei was. Hetty saw it at first glance, and Joe… well, Joe had worked with him. Sergei had done a few casual shifts at the factory when they were busy, but he wasn't skilled, so they wouldn't hire him regular like. He cleaned up and fetched and carried. He could act the part… Sergei… when he tried. He might've fooled some, but Joe would've seen through him. Anyway, he must've confided in Joe. Must've told him enough for Joe to want to take you and give him the loan.

"It broke my heart to leave my baby there. I knew you would be cared for. I could see, in an instant, that they were good people… gentle and kind. They had a cosy little home… well kept. You would like it there, I was sure. But it was hard to part with my baby."

Lidiya paused to blow her nose and wipe tears from her eyes.

"I also saw how they judged me, but what did they know? Hetty found herself a good man. It's easy to be a good woman when you're treated right. Put her in the situation I ended up in and see how she manages. Oh, sure, I brought it on myself. I made choices. I didn't have to work in a bar. I didn't have to become a whore. There were probably other jobs out there."

She shook her head and her bony hands swiped at her cheeks.

"I guess I should've just given my boys away when they was babies. If I'd known what lay ahead, I might have. But I loved my babies. I did... I do. Hetty would never understand. I gave them up because I loved them. And every night, I thought of them. I prayed for them. I wept because they were gone."

"With Sergei dead, all I could think about was bringing you home... being a Mama again... loving my baby. The thought consumed me. I thought about the possibility of getting caught. Deep down, I knew it was only a matter of time, but I'd seen cases on television...

"I thought... it was justifiable; self-defence. Surely they'd have to see it that way. And they would see it was to protect you, too, so that I could have you back and care for you like a Mama should. They'd understand. Surely they would? I'd serve probation, maybe, but that would be okay.

"Then Hetty came, and she wouldn't give you back. I told her Sergei was dead. I didn't tell her how... didn't confess. But she judged me anyway... because I'd given up four children, failed as a mother; because I'd married a beast. She told me how happy my little girl was in her new home. I was glad. In the end, she persuaded me to let it be... to leave you where you were safe and loved and happy... where you could enjoy a life filled with opportunities I could never give you.

"Hetty left gloating. She didn't know my pain. She'll never know. She was barren, and I'm sure it hurt her. But to lose a child... lose it while it still lives... that's the worst pain for a woman. That's a pain that few women can bear. I bore it, because I had no choice. But it broke me.

"They came for me, eventually. I always knew they would."

As a lawyer, Nata knew all too well the procedure that followed. They would have taken her away in handcuffs and pressed her fingers onto inked pads and then on papers. They would take her photograph from various angles, with a sign held under her chin. They would have given her a number and made her memorize it. She would no longer have a name.

"They took my possessions, and they warned me not to say too much without a lawyer present. Then they took me into a little room and two policemen asked a lot of questions. They weren't unkind. They offered me coffee or tea. They gave me water. They asked if I was hungry.

"There was a tape recorder running. I was happy enough to answer their questions, but after the first few, they didn't seem to want me to any more. They asked me if I could afford a lawyer. The money from the house sale had run out by then. There was never much. It had been mortgaged, you see.

"They took me to a cell. There were some other women in cells next to it. They were rough looking types. I was more afraid of them than of the police, but there were walls and bars separating us, so I was all right.

"It was a horrid place: bare concrete floor; one small, very high window, with bars over it; a sort of platform with a thin mattress and pillow on it, and a rough grey blanket folded and placed at the bottom. There was a toilet and wash basin in one corner. No privacy at all. And the heavy bars and locked gate … they were terrifying. Of course they were meant to be. It was a lock-up. I guess I thought that was what a jail would be like. I was relieved to find a regular prison wasn't nearly as dreadful."

Lidiya told Nata they had sent the public defender to talk to her. They took her to a small room and locked them in there and she told him her story. He said she'd best plead guilty. It would be over quickly then; no long drawn out trial; no months of wondering about her fate; minimal publicity. Her daughter need not know.

"And I'll be let off on probation?"

" 'I wish I could say that was likely, Lidiya,' he said. 'But not a chance. You'll go to prison… for quite a long time I should think.' "

She had protested that it was self-defence, but he rejected

her plea. She said it was to protect herself and her child, but he had replied that the child was in no danger, and he wasn't attacking her at the time. He explained that it wasn't self-defence if he was sitting at a table drinking and doing her no harm... if there was no immediate danger to her.

"I protested that he bashed me often. He might've that night, if he'd been hungry and the meal I'd cooked didn't please. Or if he'd been less drunk and wanted... you know... and I didn't please him. That's how it was. I was never safe. If he was so drunk he couldn't... you know... get it up... he'd blame me and he'd beat me. Or if I had my monthlies — he never liked to do it when I was in that condition — he'd bash me."

" 'You could've gone to the police, Lil,' he said."

"I told him I did. They cautioned him, and he beat me for telling. I was too scared to go to them again."

"He said I could've left him. And gone where? He'd have come after me. He'd have found me wherever I went. I had no money, no job, no skills. I used to be a whore, you know? But I was too old and unattractive to go back to that. Besides, I found the thought of a man repulsive. After what he'd done to me, I don't think I could ever let anyone touch me that way again."

" 'There are always solutions, Lidiya,' he said. There was no pity in his tone. It had turned harsh and judgemental. He said 'I'll plead provocation. In some states that would help you, but unfortunately provocation is no longer a defence in Victoria. I'll do my best for you. I'll plead for mercy. But you'll serve time. Maximum security, and it won't be a short holiday.'

"When it finally sank in, I was relieved. I didn't think much about how it might be in prison. All I could think of was that the nightmare was over. I didn't have to worry about how to support myself... how to feed and clothe my child. I'd put an end to the beatings. I didn't have to suffer a man doing *that* again. Sergei had finally got his just desserts. I'd punished the wrongs he did, and I was glad."

It had taken some time for them to get around to a trial. There were a few formalities first. They had taken her to another place—one that wasn't quite so awful. They made her wear a green uniform, and every day they made her strip off to be searched. It was embarrassing, but she'd grown accustomed to humiliation. She'd suffered plenty of that.

"There were so many rules—rigid timetables, guards shouting orders and threatening. But I just did what they told me, and after a while, I found it wasn't so bad."

Eventually, the day had come for the trial to begin. It was short. She told Nata how, each day, they had put handcuffs on her and locked her in the back of a van and drove to the courthouse. Then they took the cuffs off and took her into a big, elegant hall. Lots of polished wood carvings, and fancy plaster work. There were lots of empty seats.

Nata almost wept aloud when her mother whispered, "I guess there's a big audience for some trials, but there was nobody much to care about me."

"They sat me beside my lawyer," she said, "and the judge came in wearing a big black gown and long wig. I'll never forget that wrinkle-crowded face and the worried brow, buried in creases. There were tired lines pulling at the corners of his mouth and eyes too. He looked so old and weary, as if the stress of deciding people's fate had clean wore him out. Well, I guess it would, wouldn't it? Deciding every day who should give up their freedom and for how long. Being responsible for broken lives and broken families, and never knowing for absolute certain if you'd done right, or maybe sent someone down for a crime they never did.

"I made it easy for him. I pled guilty.

"The prosecutor told what I'd done, and how I'd planned to do it and I'd said I wasn't sorry. He made me sound evil... like Sergei was a good husband and I'd had no cause. He made a big thing about how long we'd been married, and about how Sergei took me and my sons in when I was pregnant... took me off the streets... away from a life of prostitution. He told how Sergei bought a house for us to live in, and how I loved him enough to have a child with him, but I'd given that child away to strangers. Just like I'd given my other three kids away."

Her lawyer had told the judge how she'd suffered brutality for years. He showed pictures of her, bruised and bleeding. He told how Sergei had abused her girls, and how she'd had to send them away for their protection. He had told about her boys, too. Then they put her on the stand and made her swear on the Bible to tell the truth, the whole truth, and nothing but the truth.

"I'd been telling the whole truth all along. I told it again. I said how I'd been terrified of Sergei for years... how he made me give up my children... how he drank and gambled and beat me and my children and did dirty stuff with my daughters.

"The judge said he had some sympathy for me. Said it was clear I'd had a hard life and I'd suffered a great deal. Sergei might well have been a nasty man. I thought that was an understatement, but it seemed like the judge had some feeling.

"And then he declared that, no matter what the reason, I'd done cold-blooded murder. There was no immediate danger when I did it. I was not defending myself. And however evil the victim might have been, the law was clear. He said like my lawyer had said: provocation was not a defence under law. He said I'd confessed to murder, and I'd admitted that I planned it. I took the law into my own hands, and I must suffer the penalty prescribed by law.

"Twenty-five years. No parole."

#

The defender had said he was shocked by the harshness of the sentence. He'd expected less. It didn't matter much to Lidiya. A few years... or a lifetime. She would probably die behind bars regardless. All the fight had gone out of her by then. She was resigned to whatever fate dealt her. It couldn't possibly be any worse than what she had already endured.

All but blinded by her tears, Nata reached across and clasped her mother's bony hand and squeezed it tightly. "A good lawyer would… We could appeal, even now. I have colleagues who…"

Lidiya's lips turned up in a grateful smile, but there was no hope in it. The eyes spoke of resignation.

"It's too late, Natalya. All too late…

"I went back for you, but Hetty showed me photos of you wearing lovely dresses she had made for you. She showed me pictures of your room. It was so pretty. You had toys and books. She showed me your school reports too. Your teachers loved you. Hetty loved you. She talked of all the plans they had for you… music lessons, dancing classes, university. What did I have to offer you? Poverty. Homelessness. Waiting in agony for a jury to decide whether I should be locked up… or even put to death… for murdering your father. As my child, you would have suffered such torment and shame. I killed him to protect you… to save your life. But a life with me? It wouldn't have been a life worth saving.

"I know it's not much, Natalya. Maybe it's hard to believe, but I do love you. I love you so much it hurts. I wake thinking of you every day and I go to sleep praying for your happiness. It's all that ever mattered to me… that you were safe and happy."

"And what about you?"

"I'm safe here. As long as I obey the rules… which I am happy to do… I am treated with respect. I have plenty to eat."

"But, Mama…"

Lidiya raised her hand to silence her daughter. "I have friends in here. I have my time to read, play cards or board games with the other women, watch television. Your sister made contact a few months ago. She visits now and then."

Nata lurched forward and began to tremble. "Elena visits

you? Where is she? What—"

"Lives in Albury. She's a social worker. Spends her days helping abused women and kids break free and build new lives. And in her spare time, she works with a group that helps adults who were abused as children heal and rebuild their lives."

Nata paused to take the news of her sister in. She wanted to see her... hug her... renew those unbreakable bonds that bind siblings no matter what may come between them or how long they may be parted. But she must focus on Mama for now. She must set Mama free.

"It's not so bad here," Lidiya was protesting. There is nothing for me on the outside anyway. It's a far better place than the prison I lived in before I came here. I was free then, but I lived in a prison of fear."

A female guard came across to them. Lidiya rose. The guard summoned Nata to follow. They walked through the rear door, through a gate and out into a garden courtyard surrounded, at some distance, by a high chain-wire fence. The guard opened a door and urged Lidiya and Nata in.

The cell was clean and bright: one of five opening from a central kitchen, dining and living area. The furnishings were basic, but comfortable: a neatly made bed, a desk and chair, and a small bank of shelves. The walls were covered: newspaper clippings, photos of Nata, a copy of her graduation certificate and the certificate confirming her entry on the Dean's honours list. There were wedding photos, photos of her with her hands on a rounded belly, pictures of her dancing with Karl... dancing with Joe... hugging Hetty. There were pictures of Nata as a little girl, playing the violin on stage, receiving awards in her dancing dress; Natalie in Europe, standing before the Eiffel Tower... in front of a Swiss chalet; Natalie, shaking hands with the senior partner of the law firm. Underneath, "My little girl, an associate in Melbourne's best law firm. Fancy!" was scrawled in Lidiya's shaky hand.

There were photos of Elena, too. Nata recognized her immediately. So like her! She ached to hear her voice… to hug her… to cry and smile with her and introduce her to Hetty and Joe and Karl and Sean. To know her and love her again.

Lidiya reached into a shelf and brought out two albums. More photos. Letters from Hetty. One every month from the day Hetty had gone to visit her.

"I promised her I'd never intrude on your life… never try to make contact… if only she would write to me every month and tell me how you were and what was happening in your life. Send me photos. She kept her part of the bargain admirably. She never failed me."

The silence stretched out between them as Nata struggled to process all these revelations. At last, her Mama touched her gently and spoke with deep loving concern, her eyes filled with benevolent wisdom.

"You said you came to me for advice," she said gently. "Now I offer it. There is someone you need to meet. He visits here often. I don't have answers about Sean, Natalya. But he will. Let him introduce you to people who have been where you are travelling, and come through it. Let him show you what children with afflictions can become."

She handed her a card with an address and phone number. The name Zac Kenney was printed in neat black capital letters.

"Call him, please," she urged softly. "Go with God, my daughter."

#

The guard summoned Nata to follow her. She kissed her mother's cheek and whimpered goodbye. Struggling to see through a prism of tears, she followed the guard down the long hall and through the visitor's room to a little office. The guard gestured her to sit.

"We have great admiration for your mother, Natalie. She is a courageous and wise lady… an inspiration. She's done great work with some of the younger women here... taught them skills, given them self-respect. There are some, in here or now released, who I suspect would say she saved their lives and those of their families. Gave them something to live for."

"She ought not to be here. I could get her out. Lodge an appeal...."

The guard nodded. "Perhaps. But she is content here. She is safe. For women like her, this is not such a terrible place. It's far less dreadful than the prison their crime released them from. And she hasn't much time left, Nata. She has cancer. It's terminal, and she knows it. She tells us, often, she is looking forward to meeting her Maker, and finally finding peace."

Nata's tears flowed freely then. The sobs racked her body. The guard came around the table to place her arm about her shoulder and hug her.

"This has been painful for you, you poor girl," she whispered.

"Poor girl?" Nata replied. "Her sacrifice gave me the perfect life, while she rotted in this place... desperately alone, with nobody to care."

She stood then and forced a smile for the guard. "But thank you. It's obvious you've done your best for her, and I appreciate that, more than I could ever tell you."

#

Natalie had showered and changed, made her face up and brushed her hair until it shone like burnished copper in the fading sunlight. She lay back on her satin-covered king bed, staring at the ornate ceiling. The panels were outlined in contrasting colours. The carpet was thick and soft. Expensive oil paintings adorned the walls.

"I was mortgaged goods," she whispered to herself. "And look at me now... because she had the courage to give me away. If she had kept me..."

She sat upright and hugged her knees against her chest.

But it's not the same, is it? She mortgaged me to save me from hell. If you give Sean away, you may be condemning him to live in hell.

She closed her eyes and let her mind drift. She was at the hospital. She tiptoed into the nursery. Sean was sleeping. He looked like an angel. She reached down to stroke his cheek. She saw another hospital then… a home for the disabled. She saw a nurse… heard her squeaking across the rubber floor, starched skirt rustling. Sean sat in a wheel chair. He was a big boy now. He dribbled and he spilled his food. He wet himself. The nurse wiped his chin. She lifted him up to change his wet pants. He muttered incomprehensible words. She shrugged at him and did not answer. Her brow was creased with irritation. She stomped away to tend another patient. There was no hug… no kiss… no gentle, "I love you, son," in reply to his gibberish. The room was heated, but it was so cold. He sat alone, staring out the window, wondering if his mother might come today. But she had a big case. She was much too busy to visit her son.

His mother ought to tend him. She brought him into the world. She should love him enough to care for him. But he is such an inconvenience… a burden.

She heard Karl's key in the door. Footsteps. The bedroom door opened and he stood there, eyes demanding answers.

"I went to visit my birth mother yesterday."

"And?"

"She always loved me, Karl. She mortgaged me to save me." She went to the lounge and poured him brandy, then she sat across from him and told him her mother's story.

"She sacrificed herself to buy my freedom and my future. It was the ultimate gift of maternal love."

"That's admirable. But about Sean—?"

"Don't pressure me, Karl, please. I need to be certain. I need to know I'm doing the right thing… for him. This is not about you and me. We do not have the right to be selfish."

"It's a lovely place, Nata. He'll have the best of care. I'll spare no expense. He'll have everything."

"Everything, Karl?" The hot tears flowed again.

"Yes, everything."

"Except his mother's love."

FIFTEEN

Karl had written and asked her to add him to her visitor list. Lidiya had consented readily, and he had entered the Dame Phyllis Frost Centre and was greeted with the usual requests that he register and submit to a search. And then he was shown into a long room furnished with square white tables, at which women in blue prison-tracksuits sat—some in animated conversation, others looking bored or aggravated, or alone and staring expectantly at the doorway.

He recognized her immediately. Nata's deep-green cat-eyes shone in those sunken sockets, and it was clear from which parent Nata had inherited her finely sculptured face and regal posture. Lidiya had been beautiful once. He hesitated for a moment, then marched toward her and extended his hand in greeting.

Her handshake was surprisingly firm and sincere, but the words she spoke were unsettling.

"Reinhard Albrecht's grandson, yes?" she said. "So, you know all about my daughter's sordid past. How much does she know of yours, Mr. Albrecht? Have you told her about your family's business?"

He stared at her, puzzle lines pleating his brow and mouth slightly agape.

"Your grandfather was an evil man, " she said. There was

a moment of silence before she responded to his surprised stare. "But he commands respect, while I suffer condemnation. What I am… what I did… Reinhard Albrecht must carry the blame."

Unsettling seconds ticked by. Karl's eyes begged explanation, but he was struck dumb. He met her accusing glare with such confusion that eventually she softened a little.

"Have your father or grandfather ever spoken of me?" she asked.

"Never," he said honestly. "Do they know you?"

"Perhaps, then, I should start at the beginning," she said. "What has Natalya told you of me?"

She studied him silently for a moment, a little indulgent smile playing at the corners of her mouth.

"Karl… may I call you that?"

"Of course."

"And you must call me Lidiya. Not Liddy. Reinhard called me that… and Sergei. I shall never answer to that name again."

He nodded his understanding. "Lidiya," he said. "It's a lovely name. The Germanic variant means 'noble', I believe."

She huffed and shook her head. "I'm hardly that, but thank you."

She glanced at one of the guards, then up at the clock, and then she began her story.

"Karl, I was orphaned at age four. My parents were both killed in an accident. As new immigrants, there were no relatives to take me in. I was sent to an orphanage run by Catholic nuns. They were harsh… sometimes quite cruel. Life there was regimented. There was no affection.

"I was trained to know my place… equipped for a job as housemaid or laundry maid. And at 15, I was sent to live-in and work for a wealthy family.

"They were kind. I worked hard, but I was treated well— until their teenage son decided he might enjoy my company in his bed. I knew what we were doing was wrong, but I enjoyed his affection. He took it too far. Oh, he told me he loved me, and I was gullible enough to believe it possible. But he also made it very clear—with the gentlest possible explanation— that to refuse him would be to invite instant dismissal without a reference. I'd be cast out in the streets. I'm not sure if it was fear, or the desperate hope that he might feel genuine affection for me, that led me to indulge him so freely and carelessly. But making love with him was surprisingly pleasurable, and he assured me he was taking adequate precautions. I was too naive to consider how unlikely that was.

"I had just turned 17 when my pregnancy was confirmed. I hid it from the family for a few months, but when I could no longer hide it, the boy told his furious father I had led him on. He called me a temptress and a hussy. They sent him away to a military academy, and they branded me a filthy trollop and cast me out.

"I had expected my lover to stand by me, but they had threatened him with the loss of his inheritance, you see. He was terribly afraid of his father's wrath. I didn't stop to think, at the time, that he might never have cared for me… that I wasn't the kind someone like him could ever considering marrying."

Karl shifted uneasily in his chair. Her sad story was really none of his concern. It was ancient history. He was here to… well, he wasn't really sure why he was here. It was just that he had this vague thought that perhaps meeting her might help him understand Natalie better… help him find a way to help her through the darkness and out into the light. She had been so overjoyed at meeting her mother, and at the revelation that her mother had wanted her. But the knowledge that Joe and Hetty lied had shattered her. And there was something more… something she had kept a deep, dark secret, but that had always haunted her and made her fear intimacy.

"And my grandfather's role in this was?" he asked, his tone impatient.

"He advised them how to deal with any attempt I might make to claim their son was the father. Then he arranged alternate employment for me."

"Hardly an act that justifies branding him evil."

"Unless you knew his intent."

She fiddled with her fingers. All traces of a smile had faded; her eyes had clouded and her thin lips twisted in distaste.

"He found me work in a hotel. The proprietor gave me a job cleaning and doing laundry. I lived in. The pay was meagre, but I was well fed. When the babies came—twin boys—the boss let me stay on through my confinement and until I could return to work. He gave me a room with cribs for the boys, and I went back to work. But I owed for my lodgings while not working, and he'd loaned me money for medical expenses and to buy things for the babies. After paying out for daytime child care, there was precious little left to pay off a debt."

"The hotelier said I was too pretty to waste my life scrubbing. Some of the bar girls were moonlighting. The money was good, and I could work nights and care for the babies myself during the day. The job was far more appealing than cleaning and laundering sheets. I already wore a label. No decent man was going to want me for a wife. I knew how to please a man, and there were plenty who found me attractive. Why not be paid for it? It seemed a practical solution, and my employer encouraged me. So I became a whore."

Karl leaned forward and placed an elbow on the table, resting his chin in his palm. "Mrs. Popovich… Lidiya…" he said, his tone sharp with impatience, "I am deeply sorry for the hardship you suffered as a girl, but I'm perplexed as to why it should matter to me, and what it has to do with my grandfather… apart from the fact that he introduced you to someone who showed you kindness."

"He owned the brothel, Mr. Albrecht. He had planned my future right from the day he was called to his friend's home to advise how to dodge a paternity suit. There was obviously no room in his business for a heavily pregnant woman, but he saw the opportunity to recruit me when my body had mended."

Karl jerked forward and his eyebrows shot up. She took no notice, but ploughed on.

"It was a lucrative business: up-market premises, and his girls were hand-picked with the greatest of care. He attracted a variety of clients... many very well-to-do... upper class, some even titled. He ran a tight ship too. The madam was strict, and your grandfather hired henchmen to dispense cruel punishments for any perceived wrongdoing. We were well paid, but we were all well aware of the awful penalties imposed on any girl who dared to speak out of turn, or seek her freedom. We lived in terror, Karl. Mortal terror."

"But you did get away from there. He set you free and you married."

"He didn't set me free. Reinhard Albrecht never set any girl free. I was careless. I got pregnant again. He needed to be rid of me, but he needed to ensure my silence, so he sold me to a client. Sergei made me claim to be a widow, and the lie was appealing. I didn't want my kids to know their mother was a whore. Reinhardt warned me that if he ever learned that Sergei and I were no longer together, he would send his henchmen after me. He knew Sergei would control me. But with Sergei gone, I was at the mercy of Reinhard Albrecht, and I feared him far more than I had ever feared my husband.

"Why do you think I didn't appeal my prison sentence, Karl? I've helped scores of women appeal, and many of them won. I studied law in here. I knew my sentence was excessive, and I knew an appeal judge would agree. But in here, I'm safe."

"Surely you are not afraid still, after all this time? My grandfather is dead, Lidiya."

"And your father would have taken over the family business. I knew him too. He came to the brothel often. And they were two of a kind… men who had no scruples, and neither empathy nor respect for the women they abused.

"I am sorry, Karl, but I could feel only great relief when I learned you and my daughter had parted. And I could never urge her to seek reconciliation. Not with an Albrecht. Not with the grandson of Reinhard."

The colour had drained from Karl's face. He fought the urge to leave, but his tongue locked and his mind somersaulted. The world was turning upside down, and he was struggling to hang on.

"Would you have me believe you knew nothing of the family's involvement in the sex business?" she asked, her tone disbelieving.

"I didn't know, but perhaps I should have. I knew my father and grandfather went out at night often, on business. I knew it disturbed my mother greatly, but I always just assumed it was legal business and her distress was that they paid so little attention to her… that she had no company when I was in bed."

He paused a moment, recollecting, and it came again: that awful memory he had tried so hard to erase. He had believed he'd lived it down… got past the awful guilt and the shock of seeing how his father had reacted... got past the pain of his mother's disfavour and past suffering stinging shame. But it consumed him now. He was burning in the fires of hell. When he spoke again, it was with a slowness that told of his deep pain and guilt.

"I knew how my father and grandfather regarded women," he said. "When I was 17, I took our housemaid to my bed. She was pretty, charming, and available. And I was a randy young buck with a penis that hardened every time she drew near. I got her pregnant. I went to my father for help, and he paid for an abortion. He dismissed her without a reference, but he didn't send me away to the military, Mrs. Popovich. No! He laughed and praised me. It was one of very few times I ever felt my father's approval. He called her a tramp. He said her kind were put on earth to entertain men like me, and asked if I had chained her and whipped her… if I had made her paint my balls with chocolate and lick them clean. My grandfather asked if I had made her suck my penis.

"'A gentleman never asks his wife to indulge his sexual fantasies, son,' my father said. 'Ladies lie on their backs with their eyes closed and pray for conception when they permit their husbands to penetrate. And when conception is no longer desirable or practical, they take a separate bed. Happily, there are plenty of lower class maidens available to indulge the virile man. And if you keep them in their place, and discipline them firmly when they fail to please, they will give you all that a respectable wife cannot.'"

"I can still hear that lecture… the horrifying coarseness in his tone… the raucous laughter. I can feel the thumping on my back, and I can see my mother's strained expression, and the mist in her eyes. Afterward, she came to me and told me I had made her feel deeply ashamed… that she had prayed that I would be different from my father… that I would grow up gentle, and respecting women. But she added 'How could you? How could I expect it, when I let him draw me away from you and left you to be reared by a vile, vulgar beast.'"

"My mother died a few months later. She went to her grave without forgiving me. I wallowed in the deepest and most profound grief, but I made a vow to myself to never use or abuse a woman again. When I graduated university, I left my father's home and declined the offer of employment in the family legal practice. He called me a fool and predicted failure. I set out to prove I could succeed… not for money; I had a generous trust fund. I had to prove my worth to my father.

"I struggle, Mrs. Popovich. Natalie thinks me selfish and self-serving, and perhaps I am. I had a strong example to follow, and intense coaching. I was reared by a tyrant and taught to be every bit as beastly as he was. But you must believe me when I say that I genuinely want to do better. And until Nat gave birth, I honestly believed that, with her help, I could."

She was studying him now. Her cat eyes boring into his, demanding truth. At his last words, the colour drained and her mouth twisted in rage.

"But you cannot accept a flawed child, Karl? And no doubt you now see Nata as an unsuitable partner. What happens when the world learns of her mother's shame, eh?"

He flushed, but his words had dried up.

"What of your family's shame? Ah, but no expense is spared to keep that secret. Those who know are clients… married men whose reputations might be ruined by revelations. They will stay silent. Employees live in fear. Anyone else who might know is paid hush money… and plenty of it. It's in everyone's best interests to avoid exposure. Titled men… politicians… judges…"

"The Fourth Floor," Karl mumbled, and Lidiya's eyes questioned him.

"I was investigating a similar business. Maybe worse… using under-age foreign girls and boys and showing pornographic movies of men with little boys. Nat thinks I was a client. I didn't report it. I took a bribe, of sorts, to stay silent. She said I'd sold my integrity and she couldn't live with a man who would do that. But it wasn't quite like that, Lidiya. I was threatened. I was afraid. You know how far these men will go to protect their interests. I feared for Nat and for my son. And I never used the girls. I was strictly an observer… investigating for a client. I would never—"

"Do you love my daughter, Mr. Albrecht?"

"I wish I could answer 'yes', but I'm not sure I ever really learned what love is. I think I tried to love my father. I know I wanted to love my mother, but she withdrew from me. When she died, my world shifted in a way I never understood. My father was the touchstone of my life. I felt an obligation to respect him… and I did admire him for his career success.

"I thought what I felt for Natalie must be love. I have

always desired her, and I do care, but is that love?"

She smiled and reached for his hand and she stroked it.

"Love is caring so much for another that you will sacrifice your own deepest desires... caring so much that nothing matters except their well-being and happiness, and you will give your all, if asked. Love is being willing to lie down and die so that your loved one can live."

"Then no, I do not love your daughter. I admire her greatly. I care for her... a great deal. But she was a means to an end... an aid to my quest for position and wealth. Her refusal to institutionalize our son threatens my future, and I can't let her stand in the way of success. It means too much, Lidiya. I desire it too strongly."

"Success. So many people aspire to it, Karl. But what is it? A title? Money? Your father's approval?"

"How do you define it, Mrs. Popovich?"

"Becoming rich... and I am."

His head jerked upward and his eyebrows lifted, but she merely smiled a serene smile.

"Wealth and riches, Karl... they are different I think.

"I am not a person anyone much admires or respects. I am a whore and a criminal... the lowest kind of woman. Few will grieve my passing. But I enjoy a kind of freedom I suspect you have never known. And I am rich in the assurance that I will go to my maker knowing that those who care for me love me for what I am, not for what I might give them. No man ever loved me for what I am, but for my daughter... for Nata... that is the love I wish for her.

"She told me she could not live with the shame of divorce. A good Catholic girl... raised to believe marriage is a commitment for life. Joe and Hetty tell her divorce is a mortal sin, and their disapproval... Joe's especially... would destroy her. But she should not love you. You are not good for her. If you care for her even a little, you must let her go."

He nodded sadly.

"But your son, Karl— " she added, swiping at a tear that had begun a slow journey down her left cheek.

"He will be well provided for," Karl interjected hastily.

"He needs more than that. You can divorce Nata, but you can't change the fact that your son needs you, Karl."

"But the way he is... I don't think..."

"Would you come again next week? There is someone I'd like you to meet... Indulge an old lady. Please?"

He stared at her for a time, curious but reluctant. At last, he nodded. Then he extended his hand. She squeezed it and smiled up at him.

"Thank you for coming, Karl."

"Until next week, then," he said, and he nodded to the guards as he made his exit.

#

Karl struggled to focus in the week that followed, and his work performance suffered. Twice, Gil asked him if he needed some time, and when he shook his head, Gil patted his shoulder and told him he appreciated how hard things must be right now, but a partner must keep his personal and professional lives very separate. Clients needed, and deserved, his full attention.

He came to the office later than usual, and he left earlier. He postponed appointments. He lay awake at night reliving nightmares from his childhood and mulling over memories of once seemingly trivial events that had suddenly taken on momentous importance. In his dreams, his father and grandfather visited, and they were ugly and vile and they mocked him with coarse laughter and cruel jibes.

In his dreams, he begged Nat for forgiveness and he tried to make love to her. She was never unkind, but she withdrew from his advances and stood weeping beside their child's crib, staring down at a disfigured infant whose face was a replica of Karl's father's… even to the age lines and the cruel, mocking expression. And the child spoke in his father's voice and condemned Karl as a failure in both work and life. And then he said he would take the Dreyer name, for it was a name he could wear with pride. He could never be an Albrecht. He could never be a descendant of men who used and abused women. He would not be the son of a man who could not love his beautiful mother.

Haunted, Karl crawled from his bed in the wee small hours and stumbled to the mini-bar to choose the strongest spirits. In the morning, his head pounded and his belly churned and he had to taxi to the office, but he could not see clients with his breath stinking, his nose ruddy and his eyelids sagging. The office girls remarked on his dishevelled appearance and his seemingly insatiable thirst for strong black coffee. Renee quietly attended to making necessary excuses to clients, reorganizing his schedule, and submitting requests for court stays. Phillip asked him how long this would continue and told him he understood that life was hard right now, but he really must pull himself together.

#

The following Tuesday night, Karl compelled himself to abstain from drinking for a night and replaced coffee with chamomile tea in the hope of sleeping just a little. In the morning, he took a long, leisurely shower. He dressed casually, but neatly. He drank several cups of coffee and read the newspaper. Then he freshened up for the drive to Ravenhall.

He entered the prison car park, locked his vehicle and strode into the reception area to sign in. Having come as a visitor, rather than in his professional capacity, he submitted to the usual search procedures and questioning. After what seemed an interminable wait, he was escorted into the visitors' room.

She was perched on a stool at the table. A young man sat across from her, callipers on his legs and a stick beside him. Karl approached, and she greeted him with a smile and gestured him to sit.

"Zac Kenney," she said, indicating the young man, "meet my son-in-law, Karl Albrecht."

Karl shook hands, and sat down. "I've heard the name somewhere," he said, his forehead creasing. "Should it be familiar?"

Lidiya smiled.

"A few months ago... Law Society function... Zac was given honourable mention for his contribution to—"

"Ah, yes! A paralegal, I believe, but giving hundreds of hours voluntarily to working with the Justice Program to aid prisoner appeals."

Zac shot him a beaming smile and nodded. "My passion... And Lidiya works with me on cases for the women in here, as well as working with the administration on programs to help women adjust to prison life and on education and rehabilitation programs."

"I'm impressed."

"Some of the women who come here have potential," Lidiya said. "Society sees us as bad, but I see women whose life challenges have led them down a wrong path. With a little guidance, and a lot of love, they can find their way back... But I wanted you to hear Zac's story."

Karl glanced down at the callipers, then up at an arm that hung awkwardly and a face that somehow didn't seem quite proportional. The forehead was too high and the head seemed flattened on one side. It sat slightly askew and he seemed to have difficulty turning it.

"I have Cerebral Palsy, Mr. Albrecht," he said. "Diagnosed just before my second birthday. My parents were devastated, of course. I have three healthy, intelligent older sisters. There was no genetic history of disability... no illness. Mum did all the right things through pregnancy. What do you know about CP?"

"Very little," Karl admitted. "I've made donations to the

Society on occasions… as I have to most worthwhile charities, but—"

"CP is a general term for a set of movement disorders. It's caused by damage to the motor control centres of the brain… during pregnancy, birth, or in early childhood. It can affect cognitive functions, co-ordination, sensory perception, depth perception... It can cause speech and language problems, developmental delay… In some cases, it results in paralysis or partial paralysis. It's not contagious and it's not progressive. But neither is it curable… at least scientists haven't yet found a cure."

"I'm sorry," Karl mumbled, somewhat lost for a more appropriate response.

"I wanted you to meet Zac because I wanted you to hear about the challenges he and his family faced and about what he's been able to achieve. He's a Paralympian, you know?"

"Swimming," Zac interjected. "I love it. I started because a doctor thought hydrotherapy might be helpful. It was… in more ways than one. I've been all over the world competing."

"Amazing," Karl said, still feeling decidedly uncomfortable and questioning the relevance to his dilemma over his son. Zac Kenney may have achieved impressively, but he was a long way from achieving at the level Karl Albrecht expected of his son and heir. "I don't believe my son has CP though," he said. "At least, no doctor has diagnosed cerebral palsy."

"Does it matter what label you put on a condition?" Zac asked.

"It might," Karl replied. "Both prognosis and treatment are usually directly related to the specific condition, and often to its cause."

Zac nodded and grinned. "Sure," he agreed, "but leave prognosis and treatment to the doctors. My parents never accepted that having CP necessarily imposed any limits on what I could achieve. They dismissed the label. To them, I was a bundle of unknown possibilities, and their job was to help me realize my potential; to ensure I had the courage to live with any limits my body or mental capacity imposed. Everyone has limits. Everyone occasionally falls down. They saw it as their responsibility to help me up after falls and keep me focused on moving forward at my own pace... achieving whatever I might be capable of achieving and feeling good about what I could do... not dwelling on what I can't."

Karl shifted uncomfortably in his seat, disturbed by an uneasy sense that Zac and Lidiya were expressing strong disapproval of him as a parent... that they were accusing him of letting his child down.

"My grandmother wrote a little verse when I was diagnosed," Zac continued, seemingly unaware of Karl's discomfort. "Here. I brought you a copy."

As Zac passed Karl a folded sheet of paper, Lidiya began a recitation:

> *Today they stamped a label on me*
> *And sadly predicted what my future might be*
> *They made loved ones cry and nurses sigh*
> *And mum cancelled orders for things to buy.*
> *But they didn't ask me what I plan to become*
> *What I might achieve as a deeply loved son*
> *There's no label that tells what I may be*
> *If only they'll give me the right to be me.*
>
> *Please love me though I'm imperfect*
> *Please love me just as I am*
> *Please take my hand and guide me*
> *To be the best man that I can*
> *You reached into the lucky dip*
> *And drew a little prize*
> *You must surely have expected*

That what you drew might surprise
Every child has flaws and weakness
But surely every child brings joy?
I'm not a sad little label.
I'm your beautiful baby boy.

"It's a doctor's job to prepare you for the worst, Mr. Albrecht. There are so many lawsuits against medical professionals. You would know all about that. To protect themselves, they have to give you all the available data… no matter how depressing. They can't afford to encourage parents to be optimistic. They can't risk encouraging expectations that might not be fulfilled.

"My parents were told I would likely be in a wheelchair for life, possibly incontinent, unable to experience normal sexual function. They were told I would likely prove quite seriously mentally retarded. Many CP sufferers are. They were told I might not ever speak coherently."

He paused to shift in his seat and readjust the position of his legs.

"The legs cramp up a bit. Sitting can be painful, and pretty much anyone would be uncomfortable on these seats."

"And yet you choose to spend a great deal of time in places like this?" Karl said, thinking there was little logic to a disabled person imposing unnecessary suffering on himself.

"If I let a little pain or discomfort deter me, I'd spend my time in an easy chair staring at walls. I can't tolerate boredom... or a sense of being unproductive. I've learned that it's worth the effort to work through the pain. I want to live the fullest life possible, and I do."

Lidiya interjected then. "What Zac has achieved… few able-bodied, healthy men have done even close to as much good in the world."

"Your son might surprise you," Zac said. "If you give him a chance, he might prove the doctors' gloomy prognosis very inaccurate. Or science may find a cure soon. But he needs his father to believe in him, Mr. Albrecht. He needs you to teach him to believe in himself. There are quite enough detractors in the world ready to tell him he has to accept limits to his capacity. There's an abundance of pessimists ready to slap labels on him. He'll be the target, daily, of misguided sympathy, misguided offers of help to do things he ought to do for himself, and grim predictions of repeated falls and failure. The public will shake their heads in dismay and turn away, afraid that their expressions will reveal their fear and their revulsion.

"Who will help him build the courage to strive if his own father can't believe in him?"

Karl stared at the man in sullen silence. Zac reached across and laid his hand on Karl's.

"I don't mean to be judgemental. It's not my place to criticize you... nor to instruct. You're a man of impressive intelligence and ability, Mr. Albrecht. You've achieved a great deal, and no doubt you'll continue to impress with your achievements. And your life choices are your own to make. Nobody has the right to interfere, nor to criticize. We all walk our own path. It's not really possible to walk a mile in another's shoes. But if you'd rather hold hope for your child's future... if you want to believe in him.... then perhaps I can help. At least I can put the suggestion to you that what you've conditioned yourself to expect may not come to pass.

"It's incredibly hard for parents. Harder, in some ways, than for the affected child. And I can't promise that it ever gets easier, no matter which road you choose. It's likely that the journey is very much harder for parents like mine. Abandoning your child is painful, and I'm sure the pain and guilt and doubt never ends. But I'm equally sure it's an easier road than constantly urging a child to embrace mammoth challenges, and putting them back together whenever they fail, then pushing them to try again."

He paused a moment to adjust his position again.

"What my parents would tell you, should you meet them, is that the rewards of parenting a disabled child can be many. They have three lovely, healthy daughters who achieved all the usual milestones... graduated university and pursued careers and produced grandchildren for my mother and father to spoil. But my mother would tell you that a parent experiences a minor momentary thrill when a healthy child learns to walk, or speaks their first sentence, or swims the length of the pool. These are things parents know will happen at some point. They are part of normal growth. But when a child the doctors said would never walk manages to stand and take a step forward.... when a child doctors said would likely never speak a coherent sentence says 'I love you, Mum,' ... when a child doctors predicted would be retarded matriculates...

"I'm sure parents experience indescribable relief and joy at such times," Karl said, ''but—"

"But long months of pain and frustration and fear precede every achievement," Zac nodded. "And that makes the victory so much sweeter. The harder the climb, the greater the triumph. That, I think, is why wealthy people are often so discontent... especially those whose wealth is inherited. My apologies, sir, I don't mean to offend. But it's my experience of life that what is hardest to acquire is most sought after and longed for, and gives greatest pleasure when attained."

"I could have been a partner in my father's law firm," Karl agreed, "but the title held no attraction. I wanted to earn my partnership on merit alone. And I did."

"Good for you! So you see my point? Your son might never achieve as you have. He might not achieve as I have. But surely he must be allowed to achieve according to his abilities? Surely he has a right to experience the satisfaction of jumping his own personal hurdles?

"Sean has a future, Mr. Albrecht. He may not be the child you hoped for, but he can grow to be a person of worth in the world."

"If he were my son," Lidiya chimed in, "I'd want him to be the best person he can be. I'd want him to be happy, and happiness is only possible if one stretches and strives. You don't have to win. You only have to be better than your previous personal best... better than you thought you could be..."

"And if he were my son," Zac added, "I would want him to know that I love him and I am proud of him, regardless of his limitations."

Karl leaned back in his chair and sunk his hands into his pockets. He was back there again... in his father's study, listening to the chiding and the recriminations. That sense of inadequacy flooded over him again. He remembered chafing under his father's disapproving glare. He recalled the sense that no matter how he tried, he would never please his father. His mother loved him. His father, it seemed, could not.

"Sean is a huge question mark right now," Lidiya said. "He's a little mystery box, waiting to be slowly unwrapped. Surely you want to know what's inside? He might prove a huge disappointment, but then again... he might just surprise you. Can you bear the suspense of leaving that box unopened? And what if you abandon him and someone else opens the box and finds great treasure inside?"

"I think it's time I left," Karl said tonelessly. "Thank you for introducing me to Mr. Kenney, Lidiya. It was a pleasure meeting you, Zac. Thank you for your time and your advice. I will think on what you have told me." He extended his shaking hand, nodded to Lidiya, and made a hasty retreat. On Monday, he would ask Renee to arrange a generous donation to the Cerebral Palsy League. He stopped at the liquor store on the way home and purchased a large bottle of brandy. Then he pulled in to the Pizza Hut and bought a large Meatlovers.

"God, what am I doing to myself?" he mumbled as he passed the gym. But his running shoes remained in the hotel closet. He woke next morning on the couch, a half-empty bottle of brandy and a nearly empty pizza box on the floor beside him, his head pounding, and the guilt demon shouting recriminations in his ear. The only change to the pattern of his life was that the guilt demon had taken on Lidiya Popovich's accent. And sometimes it took on Zac Kenney's features.

#

The following Monday, Karl Albrecht was back in form. Renee looked up with relieved surprise when he strode into his office neatly attired, and on time. There was no smell of alcohol on his breath, and he reported that his run that morning had been a challenge. He had spent Sunday fighting demons… wallowing in the depths of despair. But his visit with Zac had forced him to face his situation. If a cripple could overcome the challenges life threw at him daily…

He had to work. Work might prove his only salvation.

…Except his mother's love.

Nata's words echoed, again and again. Everywhere he went… whatever task he turned to… the relentless echo refused to be silenced. Karl had so desperately wanted his mother's love. He could see her now… feel her delicate touch… smell her sweet scent. His heart bled with longing for the comfort of her embrace.

You must learn to stand tall and proud and face the world with courage. There is no place for whimpering sissies in a man's world, and I will not have her pampering you and making you weak.

His father had sent him away to that school. "A school where they make boys into men," he had proclaimed. In the cold dormitories at night, he wept silently, longing for the warmth of his mother's hug. Through long, tiring days of tortuous physical training and dull lectures, he had yearned to hear her reassuring sing-song voice. During interminable hours in the monstrous study hall, teachers' forbidding frowns enforced a reign of silence and ensured writing hands laboured until he thought the finger cramps harder to bear than the harsh punishment that always followed even momentary lapses in concentration. He thrust his shoulders back and held his head high, set his lips firm and took his punishments as his father had taught him, but his heart cried for his mother's soothing touch; for the feel of her silken hair brushing his cheek, and her wet lips on his forehead, and for reassurance that she loved him still.

The training had achieved its ends. It had hardened him. It had taught him to pursue that which was readily attainable: material comfort and professional success. It had made him strong and ambitious and confident. He had withdrawn from his parents. He had grown past needing the approval he could never win; past mourning that he felt unloved and unlovable; past struggling endlessly for the acceptance that never came. He had set his cap to emulate his father's success, and to create a world worthy of his—and his father's—admiration.

He had come to despise his mother for her weak and ineffectual manner and her lack of interest in anything beyond catering to her husband's unreasonable demands. For his father, he felt a mixture of reluctant admiration and glowering contempt. In professional circles, the man was well respected and an admirable achiever, and the lessons he taught his son had served Karl well. But in the privacy of his home, he was rude and arrogant and cruel. He abused the wife he had effectively enslaved. The harsh discipline to which he subjected his son was never balanced with praise or reassurance. Karl lived in a wealthy home, well fed and housed and educated, but there were no frivolous pleasures. He enjoyed none of the playthings or entertainments that were lavished on his peers. His freedom was so curtailed that his memories of childhood were consistently of seething with bitter resentment, and fighting a burning urge to rebel. And yet he never mustered the courage, and for that he despised himself, and he suspected his father despised him even more.

The day was done at last, and he was about to call it a day and seek comfort in Henry's Bar, when Renee announced that a Detective Sergeant Mark Tripp wanted a word with him. He instructed her to show the man in, and bring them coffee.

Mark Tripp was a large, square-looking man with an intelligent face that radiated an aura of controlled energy and dependability. A smattering of silver through his short mouse-coloured hair declared him old enough to be well experienced and most likely considerably senior in years to Karl. He wore plain clothes, but presented semi-formally in tie and sports jacket; and his grooming was immaculate. He introduced himself with a strong handshake and thanked Karl for seeing him on short notice.

"Is this a client-related matter?" Karl asked.

"No." Tripp hesitated for a moment. "You were involved in a motor vehicle accident a few months ago?"

"Yes. But surely that's a traffic police matter?" Tripp was from Forensics.

"Normally, yes. But there were some questions surrounding the incident that led to a request for more detailed investigation."

"What sort of questions?" Karl asked, his brow knitting. "I had thought the matter closed."

Renee tapped just then and Karl called to her to enter. She served Tripp coffee. He took it black and without sugar. She prepared Karl's just the way she knew he liked it, and she took her leave as quietly as she had entered. Tripp waited until she was gone to reply.

"Questions have arisen as to whether it might not have been an accident. Have you any enemies, Mr. Albrecht? Anyone who might have cause to want to harm you or your wife? Anyone who might have threatened you?"

Tension feathered along Karl's spine. The silence stretched out between them as Karl debated with himself how to answer.

Vance? Surely not!

His threat had been mild. Gil knew him and seemed unconcerned by his visit. But Gil had told him to drop the case. He had bought his silence. And then there was that photo. He had asked Phillip Sharpley to look into it, and thus far, Phillip had stalled his reporting. Perhaps now he would learn why?

"I dare say all lawyers have enemies, Detective," he replied. "Especially the good ones."

"Can you give me names?"

Karl shrugged, trying to appear nonchalant, but the hairs on the back of his neck had lifted and he nursed an uneasy suspicion that all was not as it seemed. "I am sure there's nobody who would... What are you saying? That the other driver rammed us on purpose?"

"I'm not saying anything for certain, Mr. Albrecht. But you said your brakes didn't respond. Yet you say you are meticulous about ensuring your cars are always in immaculate condition, and particularly attentive to safety. And you told police they appeared fine earlier in the evening?"

"It was very wet that evening. And brakes do, occasionally, fail, Detective. Even the best made and maintained cars aren't perfect."

He studied the detective's expression before continuing. "There's nobody I could think of who would be likely to tamper with my brakes while my wife and I dined. Absolutely not! The very idea seems preposterous. And the other driver was a total stranger with no connection, as far as I can tell, to anyone who knows me.

"No," he continued with certainty. "I'm quite sure it must have been entirely accidental. And regardless, there is nothing I can offer to assist your investigation, I'm afraid."

Tripp finished his coffee, rose and proffered a business card.

"Thank you for your time, sir." he said. His tone was professional and his expression gave nothing away. "If you should think of anything, please call me."

As Karl showed him out, he turned and asked, almost under his breath, "Do you, by chance, frequent the gentleman's club known as 'The Fourth Floor', Mr. Albrecht?"

Karl struggled to hide his alarm. "Certainly not," he replied, praying his tone was sufficiently even. Tripp gave a little shrug and departed.

Karl called to Renee to ensure he wasn't disturbed, locked his office door, and collapsed into his office chair.

Could it be? Was it possible? Gil had warned him that he was playing a dangerous game. But what could anyone hope to gain by tampering with his brakes? There had been no further threats; only that photo. Surely if someone had caused deliberate harm, they would have made certain he knew it and understood precisely why?

The nagging voice had a great deal more to say now. Karl's head was hammering and his gut was churning and he had a sudden terrible urge to throw and smash things… to up-end furniture and scream profanities. Karl Albrecht had always been so controlled… so proper. In fits of rage, his tone was often overbearing. His jaw tensed and his eyes blazed and he used harsh words and spoke abruptly. Occasionally, he drank far too much, but he never lost control. He regarded anyone who did with great contempt. And yet, this evening, he was consumed by a raging fire that incited him to violence and destruction. He pulled at his tie and thrust it aside and tugged at the top button of his shirt until it popped and flew across the room. He thrust his jacket over his shoulder and stormed out, slammed the door behind him, and barked at Renee that he was unavailable, should anyone want him. Her eyes jerked skyward and she gave a little cry of alarm. She was accustomed to his abrupt and overbearing manner. She was familiar with the tension that radiated from him when he was annoyed. But the madness in his eyes, now, set her to trembling.

He punched the lift button and cursed the slowness of the

response. He charged into the lift and simmered as it descended, and when it opened, he thundered through to the parking lot, slammed into his Ferrari, revved the engine mercilessly, and screamed into the street, leaving dark black tyre tracks in his wake.

Karl stormed into Henry's and snapped his drink order, and tapped impatiently on the bar—remaining standing—until his brandy was served. It burned his throat as he threw it down, but he slammed the glass on the bar and demanded an immediate refill, and he threw down the second and the third, and it wasn't until he held the fourth glass that he recovered some sense of decorum. He spent the next four hours at the bar, and by the time he staggered into the street, Karl Albrecht was blind drunk and thoroughly legless.

The doorman hailed a cab and bundled him into it, and the concierge at his hotel assisted him out and up to his room, where he slept fully dressed and woke, pooled in sweat, to a room filled with swimming furniture. His stomach burned and his mouth tasted vile and his eyes were too tight in his head. He had searing pains that started as an agonizing thundering in the head—from which he was certain his brains had been removed and replaced with nails—and travelled down his spine and into his chest and belly and down his trembling limbs to the very tips of his fingers and toes. And the worst of it was that he had not succeeded in silencing the voice. It screamed accusations and recriminations and blame. It repeated his father's condemnations of him and warnings to his mother to leave him be and not indulge the brat. It echoed Vance's warning and Tripp's questioning. It replayed the awful wailing of the little native boys on the movie screen on The Fourth Floor, bent over or pushed to lay on their bellies and spread their legs to indulge the sick cravings of vile and loathsome old men. And it sang Nat's plaintive question and answer: "Everything, Karl?.... except his mother's love."

Had he grown into his father? But surely this was different?

Sean was not whole. Karl had been a healthy, intelligent child—a child to plume over; one who could be moulded and shaped to replicate his father's success and be worthy of the Albrecht name and the family wealth and status. Karl was a child a mother should love. Sean was a child who would weigh his mother down and bring her heartache.

And how had that come to be? Was it his burning ambition—his ravenous hunger for position and renown? Had he brought this awful fate on them?

Bought your precious promotion? Condoned and excused crime... the most vile kind of crime.

Whether or not his ambition had caused their tragedy, he had sacrificed his integrity for it. He had sold his honour for a title and for the false admiration of those who did not know his secret. But the voice knew, and the voice would allow him no peace.

He fought the temptation to return to Henry's next morning. He staggered to the bathroom and splashed his face with cold water. He stripped off his stinking shirt and vomit-stained trousers and stepped into the shower and let icy water pound his back and chest and hammer onto his face. And then he dressed and called room service to bring breakfast and he forced himself to swallow tomato juice. He downed several cups of strong black coffee. And then he shaved, polished his teeth, combed his hair and fixed his tie, and he stepped out to face the day.

The sunshine burned his eyes and blinded him, and he cursed his indiscretion. Then the voice started again. His veins flooded with burning guilt and remorse. His head hung and his shoulders slumped and as he entered the office lift from the car park. He flushed red with embarrassment and shame. When he stumbled from the lift to enter the Adams Bryant marble-floored reception hall, the girls tittered and whispered, and Renee paled in alarm. He pushed rudely past her and shut himself in his office and collapsed into his chair to gaze at the walls and ask himself why what he did here mattered. Might it have been the cause of such a life shattering tragedy? What was success worth if it came at such intolerable cost?

The answer came, and he recovered his composure. He plucked Tripp's card from his wallet and picked up the phone, and then he set it down again.

"Do you, by chance, frequent the gentleman's club known as 'The Fourth Floor', Mr. Albrecht?"

Why would he ask that? Had he perhaps seen him there? Was he a patron?

There had been something disconcerting in his demeanour— something untoward in the manner of his claimed investigation. Karl's crap detector was buzzing again, and this time he listened. He put the card back in his wallet and pushed back in his chair, chewing the end of a pencil in worried contemplation. Suddenly, he lurched forward. He thumbed through a Rolodex and extracted a card. He picked up the phone again and pressed for a line, then changed his mind again and set it down. He straightened his tie, tucked his shirt, shrugged on his jacket, put the card in his jacket pocket, and stepped out, crisply informing Renee he would be out for an hour or two and asking her not to forward his calls. He noted the palpable relief as she appraised him and saw that he had recovered his aplomb.

SIXTEEN

Levi Wyman called Karl's mobile early on Friday morning. Karl had heard nothing from him or Max since he'd politely advised them that the firm had decided he should not continue to represent them, and recommended an alternate counsellor they might consult. He hadn't asked questions about how the matter proceeded. He had ceased his visits to The Fourth Floor, and his interest in Wanderers, though if he were honest with himself, he had to confess to sparks of idle curiosity at times.

"Levi," he said, reading the name on the screen. "It's been a while. How are you?"

"Fine, thank you," Levi said curtly, then proceeded hastily to advise that Wanderers had been raided two nights earlier.

"You said 'Wanderers'," Karl replied, a nervous ripple bubbling down his spine. "I presume you mean The Fourth Floor?"

"Not exactly," Levi said. "Well, they ostensibly went over all floors, but there was no specific focus on any one of them. And they found nothing. Patrons had been tipped off. Rush was well prepared for them. It's reported Rush was seen entertaining senior vice squad detectives in the coffee shop the following morning, and they all appeared to be having a merry time."

For an instant, the blood froze in Karl's veins. A fine bead of perspiration sprang out on his lips. But he chastised himself, reminding himself that corruption was rife everywhere, and he should have had no expectations.

"It's as we told you it would be, Karl." Wyman was saying. "It goes to the top. I'm glad you're out of it, mate. With a new baby to think of, it's best you're not involved in dirty business like this."

He debated whether or not to tell Levi he had involved himself after all. He decided against it. No good could come of anyone knowing about his visit, earlier in the week, with the Attorney General, and he was smart enough to know that it was best to leave this affair here. He had done what his conscience had directed. He had restored his honour. He could not be held accountable for the moral deficiency of others. It was a dirty world.

"By the way," Levi added, "Congratulations on becoming a father. I hope the little one brings you and Natalie great happiness."

So the grapevine had hummed, but how much did Levi know? Probably not a great deal, and Karl saw no reason to tell him. He thanked him for calling and wished him well, asking him to give Max his regards.

The raid had failed. It was business as usual. Now the question was whether anyone had told Gil about Karl's little visit with the Attorney General.

Karl ate a leisurely breakfast, took his time over preparations for the day, then braced himself for a confrontation and eased his Ferrari out of the hotel parking lot and onto the freeway. But as he drove, the words of a little verse kept echoing in his head.

Work could wait. Gil could wait. He was going to the hospital to visit his son.

#

"Your wife is in the tea room," the sister told him. "She's doing better, I think."

Karl nodded, but kept his eyes on his child.

"He's beautiful," she gushed. "You are lucky, you know. Special children are so deeply rewarding for a parent. They challenge you. They test you in ways other parents could never imagine, but their wins are such rich victories. They teach you so much about life and love—things that other parents will never learn. You see their determination and drive and tolerance. I'm in awe of their courage and strength to accept their lot and to make the best of things… to achieve their fullest potential."

"Perhaps that's true for some," Karl mumbled. "The lucky ones whose children do achieve. But—"

"If you talk to parents—parents whose children have achieved little and who still labour daily to provide the kind of care an infant needs—they'll talk of indescribable fear and pain. They'll tell you they are bone weary and sometimes the task is just too much, and they feel as though they can't face another day of this endless soul-destroying toil. But then they'll tell you of the joy of some tiny win… some achievement that sent their spirits soaring and made it all worthwhile. And they'll tell you of the selfless love and devotion of friends and helpers, who seem to have a sixth sense about just when you need them most, and who come with a hanky and a broad shoulder and an offer to take over for a day or two and give you welcome respite. They'll tell you of the love and appreciation these children show for their carers."

Karl's fingers drummed softly on a trolley next to his son's crib. He understood that the woman meant well, but he wished she would stop her irritating buzz and leave him to his thoughts.

"Kids like Sean are a burden, Karl. Never let anyone tell you they are not, though none who've ever cared for one would let anyone who didn't share our journey hear us use that word. But some burdens are a pleasure to bear. You've heard the song, 'He ain't heavy, he's my brother'? Well, all burdens are heavy, and there's no escaping the fact that you'll sometimes struggle under the weight, but you would never want it to be lifted for more than a brief moment. And if you lost your child, it would be every bit as painful to go on without him as if you lost any child, or the love of your life. You want to be free of the pain, but the pain of loss doesn't set you free. It only transforms a bearable pain into endless, unbearable agony."

Karl had stopped drumming and was listening intently, his hands folded before him. She touched his arm.

"I know what you are going through, Karl," she said, and her voice was rich with empathy and caring. "And I understand the apparent logic in what you want to do. But wait a while. Get to know your son. Experience the indescribable delight of feeling him grip your finger and seeing his first smile. His condition doesn't define him. He is a person, with thoughts and feelings and the capacity to love and want, strive and achieve. His abilities might be far greater than you dare to hope, or they may be far less than you—in your most frightening imaginings—perceive. But he is your child, and no-one in this world can give him what you have to give. Nor can anyone give you the gifts he has to offer you, if you'll just accept him for what he is and help him be the best man he is able to become. I guarantee you, if you choose to love and care for him, there will never be a moment when you will regret his coming into your life. I promise you he will bring you joy that will make all the pain and struggle more than worthwhile. I know. I've travelled your journey."

Karl put his hand into the crib and touched the child's hand, and Sean reached out and gripped his finger. He turned his head to the sound of his father's voice. Karl thought perhaps there was a hint of a smile, though it might only have been wind. It didn't matter. His muscle tone had improved a little, and without the tubes, he looked almost like a normal baby boy. He had a fair complexion, blue eyes, and Natalie's dark red hair. But he had Karl's finely chiselled cheeks and symmetrical nose and that high

Albrecht forehead that Nat had termed "noble." He was, without any doubt, Karl Albrecht's son.

#

Phillip Sharpley was waiting to see Karl when he returned to the office. A criminal lawyer with the firm, Phillip had, for many years now, been Karl's best male friend. He was short and stocky with an extra full-handlebar moustache, and he had a conspicuous, perfectly round bald spot in the back of his head that the office girls often tried to use as a mirror. Equipped with a delicious sense of humour, he would always indulge them with a broad grin, inviting them to place their hands on his head and guide it to just the right angle.

Karl and Phillip exchanged pleasantries and shook hands, and Karl asked Renee to bring coffee and sweet rolls. He never ate at this time of day, and he never asked for sweet rolls, but he was suddenly ravenously hungry.

"So," he asked Phillip when they were settled with their refreshments, "what have you found?"

"Absolutely nothing," Phillip replied coolly. "As far as I can tell, there is no basis for Tripp's suspicion, and I think he knows it. I'm not sure what his game is, but there's no cause to believe it was anything more than a tragic accident, Karl. I can find no connection whatsoever between the driver and Vance or Rush, or anyone else in that arena. And certainly nothing to link him to Gil, who I don't believe had anything to do with that photo. I'm certain he couldn't stoop to such tactics, however strongly he wanted a particular outcome.

"It was wet, Karl. Drivers go crazy in the rain. I can find no evidence of tampering with your brakes—or his—and I'm thoroughly convinced the other driver is suffering hideous remorse and guilt over what was nothing more than a momentary lapse of concentration on his part."

"But the photo," Karl protested.

Phillip shook his head. "Who knows? A nasty prank by someone seeking to take advantage of a situation to shake you up, probably."

"It did that," Karl said, his voice sharp with bitter resentment.

"Will you let it go now?" Phillip asked.

"How can I, Phil? It's not just the accident, is it? It's—"

"Karl, my friend," Phillip cut him off, adopting a commanding tone, tinged with caring, "it's over. You can't go back, and life is too short for regrets. It's time to move on, mate."

"I don't think I can. It's all of it. Everything I've done in—"

"Stop!" Phillip commanded, and the warmth was gone now. His tone was uncompromising, yet his gaze was filled with wisdom and deep understanding. "I work with criminals. I've learnt a thing or two about the difference between good people and evil. The evil among us accept no blame. They expect the world to condone. The good are always the last to forgive their own transgressions. The world has forgotten long before a good man can grant himself absolution. But it's time for you to forgive yourself, my friend."

#

After his meeting with Phillip, the thought of facing Gil no longer bothered Karl a jot. His clients' troubles—what he did for them—suddenly seemed inconsequential. He could no longer puff out his chest and compliment himself on his success, because he'd been forced to adopt a different standard of measure. Gil's standards—and his father's—had lost their importance.

Gil asked him had he thought about what he was doing. "Yes," he'd replied, more confidently than he had ever spoken before. "I have not quite yet granted myself absolution, but hopefully a little bit of tomorrow might make up for a whole lot of yesterdays. At least I've stopped chasing my father's shadow, and I know, now, who I want to be."

Their meeting was brief and his declaration was made with neither hesitation nor compunction. When he left the office, mid-afternoon, he felt as though a great weight had been lifted. The sky looked as though someone had swept the clouds aside to make room for the sun. Its glittering rays danced across the side-walk and reflected off the windows of skyscrapers and made the surface of the river, when he drove across it, glisten rich silver. There were boats on the water and picnickers on the grassed banks. Flowers were blooming.

Karl had discarded his jacket and tie and messed his hair, and his shirt was untucked. He had a sudden insane urge to sing. Natalie sang often, but except under sufferance, in the school or church choir before his voice broke, Karl couldn't recall ever singing. He flicked on the car radio and pressed buttons until he heard a deep male voice pounding out a love song, and he hummed along. Without thinking, he passed right by his hotel, and he didn't turn back. He was heading for Black Rock. She may prefer a life without him, but there were things he must say to her.

SEVENTEEN

She heard the car in the driveway, but the garage door didn't open. She peered down from the upstairs lounge window and she saw him unfold himself from the driver seat and stride to the front door, and then there was that hesitant knock.

Why? He still has a key... and the garage remote.

She descended the stairs and opened the door.

"Sorry," he said. "I should have called, but the car just sort of knew its way here and... Can I come in, please? Maybe order us a pizza?"

"What do you want, Karl?" she asked.

"Just to talk, Nata. Just to sit a while and talk. Please?"

She stood silent for a moment, deeply confused. He had a deep-seated attachment to schedules and never went anywhere without appointment. And he never ate take-away pizza. But she noted that his hair was dishevelled and his shirt-tail hung out, and he had lost that cool, formal countenance. She stepped aside and let him enter and he went to the phone and dialled. He ordered Meatlovers and Hawaiian, with sodas and two of those sugary sundae concoctions Dominos made with fake ice cream. She loved them. He had always claimed to detest them, and he'd absolutely forbidden the consumption of anything so "common" and so detrimental to good health.

When the food arrived, he tipped the boy generously, and he brought it to the lounge; no plates or cutlery. He ate straight from the boxes, pulling slices apart and holding them in his fingers, and when he passed her a slice, he laughingly offered her his sticky fingers to lick, but she wiped them with the paper serviette.

They ate on the couch with the television on, watching silly soapies and those awful reality shows that Karl so detested. He dropped pizza boxes on the carpet, kicked off his shoes, and put his feet up.

"I visited Lidiya, Nata," he said. "I don't know why, but I felt an urge to meet her."

She shivered, painfully aware of his standards of judgement.

"You have her eyes," he said. "Deep and expressive. I could see where your beauty came from. She would have been a stunner in her youth. And now, what she lacks in looks she makes up for in wisdom, I think."

His words startled Nata, but she acknowledged them with just a slight nod.

"She talked of being free."

"That's odd," Nata said. "She told me she was happy there. When I said we could appeal her sentence, she seemed quite disinclined."

"Yes," he agreed. "But she spoke of another kind of freedom—one she astutely guessed I'd never known."

He turned to face her then, and his face was painted with wistful regret.

"I visited my father too," he said. "I told him I'd been made a partner. He replied that he had expected I would have achieved that status much earlier in my career."

He imitated his father's stentorian tone. "Two failed marriages, forty before including your name in the firm's title, and incapable—apparently—of producing an heir who can carry on the proud family tradition."

"I'm a terrible disappointment to the old man," he added, with a nervous chuckle.

"Oh Karl, I'm so sorry," she said, but he shook his head.

"I'm not," he replied. "He helped me remember who I was before he told me who I must be. I remembered the dreams I once longed to chase."

He took her hand in his and twisted her wedding ring.

"You haven't removed it," he said, more in the form of state ment than question.

"Should I have?" she asked.

"Not if you don't want to, only… " He stumbled over the words, "Your Mama said she would ask you why you would want to love when it hurts you so much."

"Maybe hurting love is the only kind I know," she replied. "Joe is good and kind, but life in the Dreyer household was work and prayer and unquestioning conformance to Joe's rules. He permitted very little leisure."

"Yet you adore him?"

"Because of what he saved me from. Because he was not cruel and depraved like Papa."

She told him then. She confessed it all. She opened all the still festering sores and let the pus flow. He took her in his arms and let her cry on his broad shoulder, and he stroked her hair and kissed the top of her head and said, "Dear God… my poor darling!" And he did not condemn her.

"And now there is Sean," she mumbled. "And loving him hurts so much. But I do love him, Karl. And I know what love can do. I have great faith in its power."

"I talked to Zac," he said.

"And?" she asked, without daring to hope. But he just shook his head and looked sad. Then his face flushed and his eyes filled with guilt and pain. He turned away from her and spoke hesitantly.

"I had a visit from a detective, Nata," he said, "from Forensics. The accident... he thought maybe it wasn't. It seems I might have caused it. There was a threat—mild, but from a nasty character. Gil said to ignore it, but there was something else… a photograph… a message suggesting—

"Oh God!" he cried, lowering his head into his hands. "My ambition… my blind determination to make my mark on the world—"

Cold rage began to course through her. The trickle became a stream and then a torrent so fierce she struggled to steady herself, but the depth of his mortification aroused her sympathy and she fought for a way to rationalise his sin.

"To stand up for what is right and moral," she said. "To defend young people against depravity and vile crime." But he hung his head and brooded and heat flooded his neck and cheeks. He clenched his fists and his shoulders slumped in defeat.

"No," he said, at last. "I only wish my motives were that noble. I risked our safety for profit and prestige. And I abandoned all my principles and turned my back on crime when offered payment to do so."

"Perhaps you should instigate an investigation," she suggested. "If you genuinely believe it might not have been an accident—"

"I did, Nata. Phil said he left no stone unturned to uncover the truth."

"And?"

"He found nothing. He is absolutely convinced it was a pure accident. Both the mechanic and the police said there was no evidence of tampering with our car, and the police could find no connection whatsoever between the driver and anyone involved with The Fourth Floor. The detective's visit was, in itself, suspicious. I couldn't help suspecting him of involvement in a conspiracy to silence me."

"So you are not to blame," she said, but he shook his head

and his eyes watered.

"Yes, I am," he said. "And others may someday forgive me, but I will live with the shame forever, and every glance at Sean will remind me of who I am and of the awful cost of my pride and ambition."

"Whatever caused the accident, Karl, the accident didn't cause Sean's condition. The doctors have assured me of that, and I believe them." She reached out and squeezed his hand. "And Zac has convinced me that Sean has a future, if only we can both believe in him and love him. We owe him that, Karl. Every child deserves that from their parents."

He bent down, then, and picked up the rubbish. When he came back from clearing it away, he asked her if she'd like to walk on the beach.

The tide was out. Green waters—softly risen peaks dusted lightly with white foam— lapped over the sands and against the great grey stone wall. The sky was a dull grey. Behind them, dense foliage climbed the cliffs—tall strong trees that reminded her of Joe. Joe was a tree: tall, solid and unbending, but with arms that reached to give safety and shade from the hurts of daily life. Yet he could not help her hurt.

They strolled along the foreshore. She walked barefoot on the grubby yellow sand, carrying her sandals. She always urged her mother to shed her shoes and stockings when they walked here together, but Hetty declined. She would retire to the bathroom, after, to shake the sand from her clothing and wash her feet. She claimed to enjoy beach walks, but she would never expose her heavily veined legs to public view.

Nata found the feel of sand between her toes strangely liberating. Sometimes she hitched her skirt and waded knee deep in the cool water. It was unbecoming, Joe would say. Poor Joe. His industriousness and devotion to religion had denied her so many of the simple pleasures of childhood, but how could he know what it was to be a child? Hetty told her that he'd had no childhood at all. All he would say of his past was that his memories—from his earliest days until the day that he arrived in Footscray—were of pain and terror.

And Hetty? She never spoke of family, or of the days when she was known as Henriëtte Elke de Hass. Nata had asked her once, but she replied that she had no past. She was born with calloused hands and blue-black markings on her legs—already old and tired and knowing far more than she should. All those years of bending over other people's laundry had erased all memories of being young and carefree.

"Marriage set me free," she had said once, smiling warmly. It released her from the steamy prison she toiled in five days a week. It released her to cook and scrub and wash for Joe—a man whose world was black and white and whose belief system was never open to question. But he was loyal and protective and a good provider, and his rigidity had kept her safe.

Hetty and Joe had set Nata free, and then Nata had moved from Joe's disciplined protection to the protection of an autocratic husband—equally industrious and committed to his belief system, and equally demanding and unbending. Like Hetty, she had buried her past. For her, life began the day Joe lectured her about responsibility and set out his "house rules". And now the door to her past had opened and she had been forced to confront the little girl she had once been. She had been compelled to relive the pain. She had swallowed her pride and admitted what she was and where she came from and what was buried deep inside her that made it so hard for her to love Karl. Karl, in turn, had opened up and let his heart speak.

She shared Karl's guilt. She'd encouraged his quest for status. They were both guilty of cupidity and excessive ambition. But somehow, between pizza and sundaes and all the painful confessions, the clouds had lifted and her choice became clear. She knew precisely what lay ahead for Sean and what it was she must do.

"Mama told me she believes the only disability in life is a bad attitude," she said.

He replied, "Then, with our help, Sean will do just fine. But do you think there's hope for me?"

He didn't wait for her reply, but took her arm and guided her up the slope and back to the house. With a faint, mysterious smile he said, "Today was a rare treat. Thank you." And then he slung his jacket carelessly over his shoulder and left. As he drove off, he turned the window down, and she heard the car radio playing. She was certain he was singing along.

\#

Nata guided her mama through wide double doors and out into the prison courtyard. The high fence was topped with rows of barbed wire. Security cameras were mounted at the corners. The only seating was a stone bench. But the skies had begun to clear. A tiny ray of sunlight danced over the asphalt. Nata found the brightest corner, so that Lidiya could feel a little warmth.

"So, did you decide?" Lidiya asked in a trembling voice.

"Yes," said Nata. She reached across and rested her hand on her mother's. "The firm will have to do without me. I don't know if it will work out, but I'm going to try to care for Sean at home."

"It will be hard, Nata."

"Motherhood is. You should know. But love can work miracles, Mama… and new medical discoveries are made every day."

For a minute, there was silence between them. Nata studied her mother thoughtfully.

She's so old. Old and broken, at only 67. And with nothing to look forward to. Never had anything to look forward to... only darkness, pain and regret. But it will be different now. She has a family, and we will find a way to get her out of here. I will bring her home. She will spend her last days free and loved.

"How should I know?" Lidiya was mumbling. "I wasn't a mother. I let you down… let all my children down."

"You saved my life," Nata said, squeezing a frail hand. "And you may have given Sean a life worth living."

"Will you bring him to visit?"

"Of course I will. I want him to know his Grandmama."

"But this place… when he's older…"

"He'll understand. I'll make sure of it."

Lidiya lifted her head to gaze up at the sky.

"Look, Natalya. There's a rainbow."

Nata looked up at the ribbon of colour.

"I love you, Mama," she said softly.

A faint smile trembled at the corners of the dying woman's lips. Her head drooped, her body sagged, and she was gone.

EIGHTEEN

Hetty went with Nata to Albury to visit Elena. She had asked her to go.

They were alike, but not so. There was always a fragility in Nata, despite her strength. Elena had none of Nata's delicacy and refinement. She was loud and rough and commanding.

The girls' embrace was long and warm. Despite Elena's toughness, she cried when Nata wept with joy.

Hetty went for coffee and left them to their reminiscing, for they had a great deal to catch up on. When she returned, an hour later, she had an odd sense that Nata had undergone a transformation. She seemed more at peace than she had been in a long time.

"Elena tells me there is huge demand for lawyers to help abused women enforce their rights. They need representation in custody battles and to demand maintenance and child support. They need lawyers to help them plead for protection orders and to seek appropriate punishment for their abusers. There's so much work to be done."

Hetty nodded, smiling.

"It's not good for me to have nothing outside housework and Sean." She gasped then, and her hand shot to her mouth. "I'm so sorry, Mum. I know that was your life. But it can't be mine. I need to use what I have learned. And others need my knowledge and skill."

Hetty touched her arm lightly. "I agree, my love."

"Elena says I can volunteer my services for a few hours each week. I might save women from the fate Mama suffered. I might save children. Not all foster parents are as kind and loving as you and Joe. I was lucky. But if I can keep a child with its mama… Oh Hetty, there's so much to do. Elena works sixty hours each week and more, and it's not enough. So many women and children end up in refuges, or running. So many women and infants need her help."

"Your mama would have been very proud of you," Hetty said, turning to Elena. "What you have made of your life… it does you great credit. It must have been hard to rebuild your life after the abuse you suffered."

"It was the suffering that drove me," Elena said. "I resolved that I'd never let it destroy me, and I'd save as many children as I could from suffering what I did. And I swore that one day, Nata and I would be reunited. And Mama. Our little family would be together again. I swore it when I heard Sergei was dead. I swore I would avenge his cruelty and we would all mend.

"I would have sought Nata out sooner," she said "I thought to many times. But I heard she had a good home and loving foster parents. And then I heard she had gone to university and… oh my! My little sister, Summa Cum Laude! A lawyer. Married into one of Melbourne's wealthiest families! And here was I, with neither education nor style. Just a peasant girl. I feared I might embarrass her, and so I left her alone."

Nata gave a nervous giggle. "Embarrass me? Never! Oh, Elena, I've missed you so much. How many nights I lay in my bed wondering where you were… praying one day we'd be together again. And now? I'm so proud of you. What you've made of yourself. What you do… It is so much more honourable than… How come people who do most good in this evil world are so poorly rewarded and so little acknowledged? And we who only fight for people who have no need of anyone to fight for them… we are showered with accolades and paid a king's ransom. For what? We do nothing of real worth.

"But I will. I'll make you proud of me, Elena. And together, we'll make the world better."

Elena's smile was indulgent…. maternal, almost. They hugged again, and Hetty feared she would never break them apart. But she was filled with joy. Another broken part of Nata had been made whole.

#

Nata came to tell Hetty of her mother's passing. She brought the child. They had taken him home from the hospital and settled him in the little nursery she had so lovingly prepared for him, and she had eased herself into that exhausting routine that must surely be familiar to every mother who has cared for a newborn. But she had no hesitation in also signing up to offer twenty hours each week to give legal advice at the local women's refuge.

"It's my vocation, Mum," she said. "And my passion. I need to work, and this is the kind of work I can truly put my heart into."

Hetty hid a smile. Caring was her vocation, and the thought of having Sean to herself for four mornings each week delighted her.

Hetty asked after Karl. Nata said he was plagued by guilt, but regardless of what might have caused the accident, Sean's condition was not a result of the crash. She had forgiven Karl, but he needed to find a way to forgive himself.

Nata wore a little sling. Sean slept there, warm and content. Hetty studied her daughter. There was something different in her demeanour. The tired, haunted look was gone. The face paint was removed. Her cheeks and eyelids were scrubbed clean. She wore a radiant glow. Her hair was coiled and knotted at the nape of her neck, devoid of decoration. She wore no jewels.

She had filled out and her skirt hugged her hips as it had a year before, but her blouse hung loosely over swollen breasts, and there were faint yellow stains on the shoulders that seemed not to embarrass her at all. When the child hungered, she unself-consciously unbuttoned her front, draped a towel over her shoulder, and pressed him to her naked breast. She smiled serenely at Joe, and he merely nodded and sat across from her with eyes tactfully averted.

Hetty watched her with her child. She was gentle and protective, but self-assured and unwavering in her response to his vocal demands. The sophistication that had masked her insecurity was gone. There was a quiet confidence about her now.

When Joe asked of her intentions for her marriage and her child's future, she didn't quail. She squared her shoulders and faced him, head high, announcing that she would provide for her child, and she would be grateful for their help to see to his care, but her marital relationship was none of his affair.

"That's for Karl and I to resolve, Dad," she answered with resolve. "With the help of lawyers if required."

"Will you bring Sean up as a child of the Father?" Joe asked. "Teach him God's ways." His tone was strident. Hers, in response, was soft but firm.

"I will raise him to be honest, kind and fair, and to treat others with respect. But he will not be taught to fear a devil or Hell, nor to bow always to mine or a priest's will. He can choose whether or not he bows to a deity and in what form, but I want him to believe in himself, and to know the happiness that comes from setting his own path; chasing his own dreams; living and loving on his own terms."

Listening to her, Hetty had a sudden overwhelming sense of loss, as though her use-by date had expired. But her sorrow was mixed with relief and deep pride. Nata had defeated her demons. Her little girl had grown up.

#

Lidiya was buried in consecrated ground. The priest said her sins had been forgiven.

Karl came. He walked with Natalie, behind the coffin. Later, he went to Hetty and they faced each other, holding black umbrellas against the grey Melbourne mist.

"I quit my job, Hetty," he said. "Gave up the partnership I wanted so desperately. Threw away all I've worked for. Crazy, huh?"

She stared at him in confusion. There was something odd about his demeanour. He had lost that urbane, confident look. His tie knot was loose, and he'd run his fingers through his hair, dishevelling the ordered waves. His voice no longer had that ring of certainty and command.

"I'm taking a job as a public defender," he said. "The pay isn't much, and there isn't a great deal of prestige attached."

"It always seemed to matter greatly to you…. the position, the image?"

He nodded.

They walked a little way in silence, and then he turned to her and she saw, in his eyes, deep pools of pain and regret.

"It's easy to adore that which is perfect, Hetty," he answered, "and I was always confident I could make everything in my world worthy of my adoration. But despite all my talent and hard work, and all my wealth…" He shrugged dispirited shoulders. "People like Lidiya… they need someone to fight for them." he said.

"Nata and Sean?" Hetty asked.

"Nata is strong," he said. "I'll support them, of course. Nata says I may visit. Maybe…someday…. if I can find peace with myself…"

He glanced up, then, to see Natalie carefully strapping their tiny son into his car seat. The child turned his head, smiled, raised a hand, and waved to Hetty and his father. As Natalie's face flooded with surprise and joy, Karl felt his heart swell with hope. His voice dropped to a whisper.

"Someday, Hetty, I might learn how to love."

#

They buried Lidiya this morning–and with her, a thousand fears and nightmares. Hetty and Joe are finally unburdened. Their lies no longer haunt them.

Karl has forsaken his ambitions and found his soul.

Nata's demons are banished. Her cup, and little Sean's, overflow with hope and promise.

Trauma, a birth and a revelation have transformed them all.

###

THANK YOU FOR READING...

Self-published authors rely heavily on readers who enjoy their work passing on recommendations to friends and associates and posting their comments online. If you enjoyed reading *Mortgaged Goods*, please consider posting your review on Goodreads, Amazon, your Facebook page, and anywhere else readers might look for recommendations for their next read.

You can connect with the author by emailing *writer@ rainbowriter.com*, or visiting *https://www.facebook.com/Rainbow-Works-307269883240*. I would love to hear from you.

I have always had a strong interest in what makes people who they are and what drives behaviour. In particular, I'm interested in the effects of childhood trauma, neglect, or deprivation, and how people overcome challenges. I created Nata and Karl to explore how two very different upbringings shaped individuals and how they responded to the challenges their vastly different character and goals presented in their relationship.

In my earlier work, *The Pencil Case*, I sought to examine the effect on a child of cruel separation from family, and of institutional deprivation and abuse.

I am currently working on a novel that explores the effect of an extraordinary crisis on the parenting style of a mother, and the consequences for her two daughters.

In all of these works, I hope to convey a message of hope, and a belief in the extraordinary power of the human spirit to overcome any obstacle. Above all, I believe in the power of love to mend broken souls—the love of family, the love of friends, and the kindness of caring strangers. I enjoy great love and have benefited from extraordinary kindness from strangers and friends alike. May you also enjoy an abundance of love, a strong spirit, and a life filled with joy.

THANK YOU FOR READING.

ABOUT THE AUTHOR

Born in Armidale, in the New England region of New South Wales, Australia, Lorraine Cobcroft has lived in four countries and worked at dozens of different jobs in a vast range of industries. She finally found her niche in her forties, writing instructional material to accompany computer software. After achieving success with courseware that sold  around the globe, Lorraine turned to writing fiction and creative non-fiction. She has published several short stories and articles and a children's picture book, *Melanie's Easter Gift*. In 2010, she completed *The Pencil Case*, a minimally fictionalized biography of a stolen white child that shines a light on a shameful chapter of Australia's social history.

After supporting her daughter through the traumatic birth and challenging first months of her grandson's life, Lorraine wrote a short story that exposed the challenges faced by mothers who give birth to special children. That story was later expanded to create the novel, *Mortgaged Goods*, a story, based heavily on personal experience, that challenges popular social values and questions common perceptions about womanhood and mothering.

Lorraine also operates Rainbow Works Pty Ltd, a web-based business (*www.chasearainbow.com*) offering mentoring, publishing and support services to writers. Her business log line, "nudge the world a little", reflects her passion for producing works that question, challenge, motivate, and inspire, hopefully assisting positive social change.

Other Writings by Lorraine Cobcroft

The Pencil Case: They Stole Us White Kids Too
A minimally fictionalized biography that sheds a light on one of the grave wrongs of Australia's past. A Noveltunity award winner. ISBN 978-0-9805714-1-7

Melanie's Easter Gift
A picture book with a Christian message, for children up to 12 years of age ISBN 978-0-9805714-0-0

"After the Flood" and "Generations"
Short stories published in *Life's a Roller Coaster,* by Fairfield Writers Group. ISBN 978-0-9805714-3-1

"Wanda's Chimney", "Spiders in Fairy Lane", "Over the Back Fence", and "What the Gypsy Knew".
Short stories published in *Changing Seasons*, by Fairfield Writers Group. ISBN 978-0-9805714-6-2

"Guilt by Association"
A short story published in *Crime Stories*, by Fairfield Writers Group. ISBN 978-0-9942792-0-0.

"Losing Tony", "Meeting Fred" and "The Empty Chair"
A short story published in *Christmas Stories: A Collection for Adults*, by Fairfield Writers Group. ISBN 978-0-9942792-4-8

For more information, or to purchase Lorraine's books, visit www.rainbowriter.com/My_books.php or search Amazon. To purchase short story collections by Fairfield Writers Group, please visit www.fairfieldwritersgroupqld.org/Books.php.
You can read short stories, poetry and article by Lorraine Cobcroft at www.rainbowriter.com/My_Other_Writings.php.

FIND MORE GREAT READS...

Find more great reading published by Rainbow Works Pty Ltd at *www.chasearainbow.com*, or search online bookstores for:

The Bond, by Giuseppe Sorbello
Fly Francesca Fly by Venera Concetta
Iron Rice Bowl by Tom Kwok
The Brighter Side of a Death Threat by Lance C. Smith
Deeds of Salvation by Lance Colbert Smith

and coming soon...
Ese to Master Jefe by Raul R. Ramos

Also check out the book reviews page for books the author of *Mortgaged Goods* has particularly enjoyed reading.

Thank you.